Flesh a

Andrew Shanahan

Copyright © 2021 Andrew Shanahan

All rights reserved. The moral rights of the author have been asserted. No part of this book may be reproduced or used in any manner without written permission of the copyright owner except for the use of quotations in a book review.

This is a work of fiction. Names, characters, places, and incidents are either the product of the author's imagination or are used fictitiously. Any resemblance to actual persons, living or dead, events, or locales is entirely coincidental.

First paperback edition December 2021.

Cover design by Yolander Yeo

"Dark Days" written and performed by PUP. Published by Rough Trade Publishing

For more information about this book and Andrew Shanahan visit www.helloshan.co.uk.

CONTENTS

Chapter 1 - 26th March 2021

Chapter 2 - 14th July 2019

Chapter 3 - 1st April 2021

Chapter 4 - January 3rd 2020

Chapter 5 - 7th April 2021

Chapter 6 - 14th July 2020

Chapter 7 - 10th April 2021

Chapter 8 - 28th July 2020

Chapter 9 - 10th April 2021

Chapter 10 - 4th August 2020

Chapter 11 - 12th April 2021

Chapter 12 - 4th August 2020

Chapter 13 - 12th April 2021

Chapter 14 - 12th April 2021

Chapter 15 - 13th April 2021

Chapter 16 - 15th April 2021

Chapter 17 - 17th April 2021

Chapter 18 - 26th April 2021

Chapter 19 - 3rd May 2021

Chapter 20 - 4th May 2021

Chapter 21 - 4th May 2021

Chapter 22 - 4th May 2021

Chapter 23 - 5th May 2021

Chapter 24 - 17th June 2021

For mothers

"Man plans, God laughs."

Traditional

"The ice is closing in and nothing will remain."

PUP – Dark Days

Chapter 1

26th March 2021
7 Months and 22 Days After

There is a three second pause and then the Vengaboys' *We Like To Party!* resets and honks out once more across the broken streets of Salford below me.

"Shut that fucking song up! Shut it up! Shut it fucking up!" a cracked voice screams into the air.

"Eurotrash shite!" another agrees.

A knot of ten dishevelled wraths smash bins and bikes aside and reach long-nailed fingers towards the drone and speaker hovering just over their heads. Their hatred, the noises of destruction and the hum of the drone's blades are all obliterated by the volume of the song.

There's a particularly loud smash as a grey-haired wrath in a brown hooded jacket and cargo shorts stumbles and falls headfirst through a café window. Other wraths from the pack get distracted by the carnage and turn to stamp on the old man. I have to lower the drone so that it's nearly within reach of the crowd to regain their attention. As it always does, *We Like To Party!* works its magic and the group are once more mesmerised in their fury - desperate to pull the disturbance to the ground and destroy it.

I don't let that happen. Instead, I pull the control sticks to one side and fly the drone down a side street I've used before. I think it's behind what used to be one of the BBC buildings, but it's a charred shell these days. The drone is only at head height now and the wraths sense that the chase is nearing its end. There's another moment of silence as the song resets, then the beat kicks in again.

HONNNNNK.

HONNNNNK-HONNNNNK.

The wraths sprint with their endless reserves of energy down the cobbled street, and the narrow alley funnels them into rows of threes and fours. Then, they see the drone just ahead and with shrieks of dark satisfaction they launch themselves at it, but find the ground beneath them vanish as they stand not upon solid ground, but on the black waters of Salford Quays. The drone's camera relays the expressions on their faces into my headset as one after another they plunge beneath the surface. They sink into the frigid depths, hating and frenzied, their lungs filling as they continue to shout at the drone even as they descend.

I leave the drone hovering in place and watch the display as the last straggling wrath limps down the road. It's the old guy who fell into the shop window - his jacket has ripped, and it now hangs only by the hood over his head. He looks like a kid playing Batman. Underneath his long, straggly hair I can see blood on his face from a deep wound. He drags his left leg as he focuses on the music coming from the drone.

"Stop! Stop! Stop! Stop! Stop!" he shouts.

He's oblivious to the fate of the rest of the group as the song's siren call lures him into the waters. As he sinks, his coat comes off and I can see the back of the Manchester United top underneath. There's a name printed across the top: "CARTER".

It's hard to think of this person as once having had a name, a job, a house, or a family. Carter *was* a person, but nearly eight months ago, like most of the people in the world, Carter became a wrath – a monster, consumed with rage. Now Carter, or whatever he became, is dead.

I scan the cameras around but there are no more wraths to be harvested, so I hit the button to autopilot the drone home and it rises into the sky with a speed that makes my stomach lurch. As the camera beneath the drone parses the expanse of Trafford below, I try not to look at the bodies floating in the quays. As many as I can see on the surface, I know there are more under the waters. Those floating on the surface jostle for space. Most are face down, but a few are staring at the sky with waterlogged eyes motionless in their bloated faces. They bob in the waters like croutons in soup. I don't want to look at what I've done, but I do.

"I NEED A HUG!" declares a slurred, robotic voice and I nearly shit myself. I tear the headset off my face and see Brown emerging from the ship's bridge with a chewed and gnarled teddy bear clutched between her teeth. The teddy is wearing a grimy, once-white shirt that displays the barely-legible words "BEAR HUG!" inside a pink heart. It's Bear that needs the hug.

I assume that Bear's voice would once have been as perky as a chipmunk, but weeks of relentless love from an overly-maternal Manchester Terrier has done something to the electronics and now when the pressure sensor in its paw is activated, it sounds like a rugby prop who has suffered a stroke. Brown stands close and nudges her bloated stomach into my shins. I reach down and stroke her silky ears flat against her skull and fantasise for the millionth time about punting Bear into the Manchester Ship Canal.

The drone appears high above the *Our Kid* – the cargo ship that has been our home for the last few weeks. I take manual control and bring it in to land on the wide deck next to the bridge. Brown re-positions herself between my legs, drawing the warmth from my body as she gives the drone space to touch down. She looks up at me hopefully, a ghost of her training somehow connecting drones with memories of chicken and sausages. But our lives are different now, and Brown doesn't need to fly away with a drone to reach food anymore. The accommodation block of the *Our Kid* is stocked with more food than the three of us could eat in a year. As the drone's rotors power down and the draft from the blades dies, I walk to the machine and power down the speaker taped underneath. The

Vengaboys are cut off just in the middle of explaining that they have things to tell me.

"And might you also have news for me?" I ask, and the ringing silence that follows is blissful.

As I speak, I notice the cloud billowing from my mouth. The thermometer on the deck read 3 Celsius earlier in the day and it looks as if it might have dropped further. The cold air dries my mouth as I pull a tarpaulin over the drone. Brown sniffs at the corners. I look over the rail that runs around the bridge, across the immediate skyline and my eyes are drawn to the copper-green dome of the Trafford Centre looming above the surrounding warehouses and industrial units. The white early evening light makes it hard to see much further, but I can still make out the right side of the dome, which is the only bit intact. The rest has caved in, leaving only a dark hole behind.

The height of the *Our Kid's* bridge usually gives a much broader view. It towers like a capital L over the cargo ship's deck, but tonight it feels like looking into static. From my vantage point I can see the Barton Swing Aqueduct upstream from us. To the left I can see the wedge-shaped silhouette of the vast indoor ski centre, and beyond that to the south, there is the ruined stretch of the M60 motorway that crosses the canal. Most of the bridge has crumbled into the streets and canal below and there's only a single, fragile strand of the road joining the two ends. The stench of old sewage hangs in the air. The streets are empty and frosty, the wraths are either trapped somewhere or they're already clogging up the locks further down the canal.

Brown breaks my reverie by chewing at the trouser of my right leg, and again I reach down and smooth her ears back to make her look like she's just had some shocking news. Quite rightly she nips at my fingers and I gently pat her cold flanks in apology. She's so much bigger than she was.

"You'll be a great mum," I tell her and she tilts her head, trying to unlock the mystery of human speech. "Just trust me. One day all of this will be yours. I'll make sure it's free of wraths and it will just be you and your puppies. And Bear if you insist."

That's my plan, anyway.

***

I notice the snow for the first time when I let Brown out for a wee an hour later. She's claimed the right side of the deck that runs around the bridge as her toilet. I think that's the port side, but I'm not 100% sure. I try to resist referring to it as the poop deck, but what's the point? In an apocalypse you have to take your fun where you can. The night is clouded and moonless, but the bright spotlights from the bridge illuminate a thick flurry of snowflakes, which Brown half-heartedly chases.

Apart from some miserly overnight flourishes that were mostly melted from the balcony by morning, I don't think she's ever actually seen snow before. March seems late to have snow, but then my capacity to be surprised has been somewhat diminished lately. I make a snowball and lob it up for Brown to catch, which results in a mouthful of ice. She instantly drops the residual clump and barks at it, which produces only a breathy whisper of noise, since she and the rest of her litter were debarked when they were born. The scar on her neck has long faded now, but the consequences of the breeder's choice live on in her silence. I wish I could have heard her bark, even once. The world is as quiet as Brown tonight, as the falling snow pulls sounds into it and leaves the world as a hushed library. Even the occasional metallic groan of the ship beneath me is reverentially muted.

I don't know whether it's Brown's anger with the snowball, the naughtiness of laughing out loud in this stillness, or it's the first Custard Cream edible kicking in that gives me the giggles. Before long the laughter multiplies and then, tears are running down my face. Abruptly, my stomach churns and I lean over the railing and streak the ship's white paint with meagre, yellowish vomit. Brown backs off a few feet at the sound, which has become her habit since the retching has become a regular thing. I don't blame her. I hate being sick. I grab a handful of the clean white snow from the rail and put it in my mouth until it dissolves. The cold sends chills through my teeth, but it dilutes the bile and I spit overboard. I press the flesh of my numb, pink fingers against my head and my forehead feels hot and tight, so I rub more snow into the skin and imagine I can hear a hissing noise. I giggle again. I whistle Brown, we head back inside and slide the heavy door shut, which seals with a satisfying *schlup*.

The bridge is toasty warm and I immediately shrug off the thick wool cardigan I borrowed from the captain's wardrobe. I don't know if it's the marijuana in the biscuits, or just the relief of the warmth after the cold outside but going into the bridge of the *Our Kid* feels like coming home. Perhaps because it's one of the few places left in the world with power and heating. That certainly helps. The main area of the bridge is given over to banks of instruments, radar screens and monitoring equipment that a smarter person than me was once able to deduce precise information from: locations, speed, weather. I now use them to prop up books. At the back of the bridge is a large table about five metres wide for charts and communication equipment. As far as I can tell, all the equipment works, there's just no one to talk to. All frequencies return static or silence, no one answers a mayday or an emergency broadcast. I've fired flares into the sky and hung a banner that reads "ALIVE" out of the window, but I don't think there is anyone else.

At the rear of the bridge is a small lounge area, which is where Brown, Bear and I have made our bedroom. When we first came aboard and claimed the ship, I pulled all the mattresses, duvets and pillows I could find up the stairs to create a mega-bed. I could have used the ship's small lift that runs from deck to bridge to shift it all, but I'm not going to have my epitaph be that the last man on earth died stuck in a lift. The mega-bed is within easy reach of the bridge's mini-kitchen and is conveniently located for the small bathroom. It's weird how much the room reminds me of my old flat. It's even four flights of stairs up, like the flat was. It does have more steering wheels than the flat though. Although disappointingly, the ship's steering isn't a big wheel like I'd imagined it would have, but a simple, underwhelming joystick that seemingly does nothing when you flick it from side to side. Not that there's anywhere I could take the ship, with the remnants of the motorway blocking the canal.

Through a combination of the ship's manual and trial-and-error, I've slowly learned what twenty or so of the buttons on the many consoles do. Fortunately, the thermostat is straightforward and consequently, the bridge sits at a toasty 23 degrees. Since I lost weight, it's amazing how much I feel the cold. There is a set of scales in the main crew bathroom downstairs which tell me I'm now 68kg. That brings the total I've lost since last August to 204kg. A lot of that is from the initial six months of being trapped in the flat with only vitamins to eat and exercise to amuse myself. Some of it will also be because I'm one leg down on where I was back then. And then a portion of that weight loss is also to do with the cancer that sits somewhere in my colon like an unwelcome turd.

On a whim, I slip off my t-shirt and look at myself in the reflection of the window. Swoops of excess skin from my depleted belly are tucked into my underwear and I pull at the tissue of my once glorious man-breasts and marvel anew at the burst balloons now hanging in their place. If you can look past the layers of drooping flesh, my thinness has become more prominent. It's noticeable mostly in the lines of my ribs and the sharp jut of my hip bones. I let the gathered skin down and walk closer to the window to see more clearly. My face is starting to look gaunt and dark pools now lie under my eyes. A full black beard and messy hair make me appear even more pallid. I don't look 26-years-old, I look 126. I bare my teeth and chatter them together imagining the skull lurking beneath. I watch the skull grow bigger and brighter, it swells until it's a pulsing beacon shining out for the rest of the world.

Fuck, I'm stoned.

I switch the bridge spotlights off and lower myself onto the mega-bed. The room spins slightly and I try and breathe in some calm to my churning stomach. I wish that I had a cool cloth to put on my head. I could get one from the bathroom, but when I'm having one of these moments when everything gets a bit cancery, the toilet may as well be in a different postcode. I feel Brown flop down on the bed next to me. She rolls over so I can rub her belly. As her body has swollen, her teats have become more pronounced, until it feels slightly odd to be rubbing her belly at all. Sometimes they leak a bit of milk and I don't know why, but the whole thing looks faintly ridiculous.

"Hussy," I say with a croaky voice and laugh to myself.

I focus my stroking on the downy hair under her chin and fight against a new wave of nausea that is rising inside me. Although it's the last thing I want to do, I reach over to the table next to the bed and pull out another Custard Cream from the Tupperware box. I've moved on from Bourbons. That's a biscuit for a different time. It was always hard to find a vegan version of a Custard Cream, but times change. On the minus side, the entire world's population has either changed into vicious, murder-frenzied wraths, or been killed by them. On the plus side, supermarkets now have an abundance of vegan Custard Creams. Very much a swings-and-roundabouts thing.

I push the Custard Cream into my mouth and force myself to chew it. The solid biscuit gives way to the sweet cream filling with its signature herbal tinge, that I've introduced by mixing the icing with stinky green weed. That came from the kitchen table of an empty house near Denton. I've never had weed before – Mum wouldn't even keep Lemsip in the house in case it proved to be a gateway drug – so my first attempts to roll and smoke a joint ended with burnt fingers and a coughing fit that dislodged my prosthetic leg. Eventually, I put the weed in a blender and mixed the powdered remnant with buttercream icing to try and overpower the hedgerow taste. Provided I can keep the biscuits down, I've found that the weed stops me from feeling so nauseous. I also get some relief from the dull ache that sits permanently in my stomach these days. Plus, as I get the munchies, I can contemplate getting more food into me.

I breathe in through my nose and stroke the point between Brown's eyes and try to focus on one of the ceiling tiles. After ten minutes I feel well enough to get to my feet and adjust the temperature. Somewhere near one of the warehouses a sodium streetlamp, powered by some unseen renewable energy source, still blasts out a little cone of light. Its illumination shows how hard and fast the snow is coming down. I rub my stomach and sit in the captain's chair to examine the board of switches and dials again. I push the ship's joystick forward and backwards. *Poot. Poot.* Perhaps I could leap the debris in the canal and sail to America. Maybe in the land of opportunity, they're all safe and well and I could get treatment and be healed. Brown and I could live in a house by the sea and get old together watching the waves on the beach. We could go to Disneyland.

I look over at Brown, sleeping with Bear tucked tightly against her stomach. I remember when she came back from some undergrowth near the edges of a housing estate we were working our way around. I thought she'd just gone to sniff after a rat, but she returned with this small brown teddy bear clamped in her mouth. She was looking as pleased with herself as I'd ever seen her. We both nearly died of shock when later that day she held its paw in her mouth and it loudly declared, "I NEED A HUG!" It just made Brown more smitten though, and now Bear is treated with a reverence given only to the most precious things. I guess her hormones are preparing her for when she has the puppies. Sometimes it's hard not to think about who owned Bear before.

I slide off the captain's chair, lie on the floor and do 50 press-ups. It sometimes still surprises me that I can do even a single press up. I love the feeling of heat that builds in my arms and the way that it temporarily overcomes any other form of pain or nausea. It's better than cannabis. As I stand up, I do thirty ass-to-grass squats. Once more I give thanks for the prosthetic clinic near Gatley we came across. As much as I loved my Lego leg, the extra stability I get from having a genuine prosthetic that fits perfectly is too valuable to pass up. This leg hugs to my stump so tightly that I'm no longer worried about can-canning it off into the distance and my movement is close to normal as long as I take care to fit it properly. As the lactic acid from the squats builds in my thighs I shake my legs, walk across to the biscuit tin and take another few Custard Creams. I wonder if I'll be happy-high or scared high-tonight.

I drink a glass of rum. If you've got one leg and live on a ship you may as well lean into the pirate cliches. I read another few pages of *The Strange Last Voyage of Donald Crowhurst*. I've now read it three times. I don't know why I find it so compelling, perhaps because it's a true story. Ultimately, I think it's the idea that Donald's finale will become my own. When I've seen Brown through her pregnancy, I will walk her and her puppies down the gangplank and onto the dock. We'll take a walk and I'll show her the place I've been preparing for her, a place that is as safe as somewhere can be these days, a place where she can raise her family. I will kiss her head and smell her warm sleek coat for the last time, and then I will leave her.

I'll sail down the Manchester Ship Canal to Liverpool, and then out to sea. And when I can no longer see land behind me, I will step off the back of the ship. As Donald did, I will watch my boat continue on its journey as I tread water until I no longer can. I don't have control over much, but I am determined to die in the way that *I* choose, not sprawled on the floor eaten by cancer. I raise my glass of rum to Brown and toast her.

"To your future, my beautiful dog. And to the future of all the dogs that you contain."

I shudder as I drain the glass. Is that my second or third? I switch the ship's radio on and hit record on the tape player. It's been a few nights since I've recorded a podcast episode. I say podcast, but really it's just me getting wasted and venting into the microphone. It's very Joe Rogan. Maybe one day it will be a vital document for a future civilisation that stumble across whatever this planet is becoming.

"Hello and good evening. It's the somethingth of March 2021 and today we have snow. That's a nice twist: snow. Newsflash: snow is very cold. Took the drone out and did a bit of clearing the Quays today. Did some good murdering today. Well done, Ben. Big tick for the murdering. It's getting harder and harder to find any wraths around here now, which is good for Brown. Not good for my soul really. Doesn't feel good. Not very happy. No. Going to finish the work on Brown's house tomorrow. So much to do, so little time. On that note, I have a question for you, God, so let me direct this to you directly, heh – that's very direct. What exactly were you thinking? You let the entire world turn into wraths or get killed by them – everyone in Middleton. Everyone in Manchester. London I can understand. Fine. Let it go. But what bugs me is that you decide that there will be just one cockroach that scuttles out from under the kitchen cupboard: me! What was your thinking, God? Care to share? As always on the podcast, we're happy to take callers. Fancy calling in God? Have a chat? Explaining maybe what the plan is? Squeeze all the fat from me and spit me into this new world? Seems a bit odd. You keep me going, but not indefinitely! Oh no! You don't make me healthy, or make this easy for me – *noooooo,* you give me fucking cancer! Why do you have to move mysteriously? What is the point? Why not just move in a simple and easily-understandable way? Can't you do that? Do you not have the eggs? Heh, heh! Sorry. I think I mean stones. Or is it eggs? Are eggs testicles? Someone call in if you know. Do we have any callers Brown?"

Brown looks up from the bed. I feel like I'm going to be sick again. I've had too much to drink and eat. I drop the radio on the console and slither across the floor into bed and roll myself in a duvet. I stop moving but the world goes on rolling. Brown adjusts her position and circles around Bear. Her belly strains to contain her offspring. She looks at me with her quizzical brown-black eyes and we drift into tonight's nausea. Goodnight room. Goodnight moon.

***

My mum isn't happy because I'm stoned.

"Did I raise you to do *drugs* Benjamin Stone?"

"Do I not get a tiny little break for *having cancer*, Mum?"

"Oh, and when I was dying of cancer, did you see me rolling marijuana joints?"

"Not that I'm aware of," I reply.

"Aware of nothing – I did not take marijuana."

"Stop saying marijuana, Mum, you sound like a narc."

"I'll stop if you open your eyes and look at me," she says.

I don't want to open my eyes because I can sense it's morning and the brightness will offendeth mine rum-and-dope-stained eyes. You have to do what your mum tells you to do though, even in dreams, so I open my eyes.

To my surprise it's night and we're on the deck at the far end of the ship. The high white tower of the accommodation block and the bridge is a distant blurry monolith in the snow. I'm stood up and Mum's lying on her back. She's still wearing that shit purple cagoule. Couldn't the afterlife have equipped her with glowing white robes? She's lifting and lowering her arms and gently brushing the settled powder aside. I realise she's making a snow angel.

"That's nice," I say. "I've not seen an angel in a cagoule before. Is this the new season's look?"

She doesn't laugh and I wonder if I've upset her, so I shut up. She sits up and I notice how bright she seems. Clumps of snow cling to the back of her hair. I wonder if she's cold. She smiles at me and some of the fear in my stomach dissipates.

"Ben, be not afeared."

"But Mum, it's all falling apart! I can't help being scared!" I sob out loud – open and raw. "It's all falling apart. The world's gone. I'm going. I'm so scared. I don't want to leave Brown! She's having puppies - why is he doing this?"

"*Shhhh*, love, *shhh*! Don't cry. Be not afeared. Ok? Remember in the Bible? For I know the plans I have-"

There's a loud crack and I sit up in bed, disorientated, my hand automatically searching for the shotgun. Brown is going crazy, she's on her feet and she's turned her body side-on to protect Bear and me. She's facing the door and I get unsteadily to my feet and creep to the door with the gun in my hand. I slide the door open and there on the deck, twitching slightly, is a large seagull. Its neck is broken.

Chapter 2

14th July 2019
1 year and 21 days before

It's too early and too damp. Of course, Manchester is seeing me off with rain. Despite the conditions, I'm so excited that even the mizzle that coats everything doesn't phase me. I heft my bag into the boot of the Golf and struggle to get everything in, because there's boxes and boxes of Dinky toy cars taking up most of the space. I'd ask Dad what that's all about, but he'd only tell me.

I turn to look at the house. The mid-terraced house where I've lived since I was born. There are photos of me wearing my school uniform at the beginning of every school year by that green front door. Then as I get older there are photos of me in various nurse uniforms. In the pictures, I get taller as the paint on the door gets flakier. There's a movement in the house and I see my brother's curtains flick aside and I look up at his big round face gazing blearily through the window. I hold up my hand and wonder when I'll see him again. He gives me the Vs and disappears. It's one of those moments when it's hard not to burst into song or commemorate it with a photo. I wonder if Dad would take a photo of me by the front door.

"Shut the bleeding door, you daft mare!" he shouts from inside the car where he's got the heater blowing on full. I yank the boot closed and it slams. "Jesus, Mary, Joseph and the bastard donkey, Nat!"

"Sorry!" I shout and get into the passenger side.

"Just check the boot's shut for me, will you?"

"I said I'm sorry!"

"You'll smash that window one day. You're weak as a kitten most of the time, but when it comes to shutting a boot, you're bloody She-Ra!"

"Dad, I said I'm sorry! Don't get narky."

He grumbles something under his breath and looks out of the window and pulls out into the street, taking care to navigate between the narrow rows of parked cars that line either side.

"You'll not miss this, will you? In America, you'll get residential roads like motorways. Not little pissy things like this."

"I'll miss it," I say and start to tear up. I can't do this so early in the journey. Dad's always said that his one weakness is seeing me get emotional. If I cry, he bursts into tears. He always has. At mum's funeral, we were like a black hole of misery. The more I cried, the more he cried and the more I wanted to cry. In the end, it was funny, I think mum would have laughed. Daft buggers, she'd have said.

As a distraction, I check the little rucksack that will be my hand luggage for the journey. Besides my tickets and a few books, there's enough boiled sweets to choke an Oompa Loompa. Auntie Pam bought them round on Sunday and made me promise to take them all with me. She said her Alan hadn't had one on a flight and had got an ear infection when they went to one of the Costas back in the day and his ear leaked pus the whole time they were there. She said the best thing was he couldn't hear her so she could say what she wanted about him, so she sat on the sunbed next to him and slagged him off for seven days. It sounded like she'd had a good time.

There's also a money belt with $300 in it. $100 from dad and $200 for picking up shifts at the care home. I try not to convert the money into 'arses wiped' because the exchange rate isn't good. I take my ticket out and check it. Ms Natalie Cross. Seat 15B. Premium Economy. That sounds good. I don't care that all it means is that I'll get my peanuts before the rest of cattle class. I do not care. I'm going to New York.

"Got tickets? Cash? Passport?"

"Check."

"Spectacles? Testicles? Wallet and watch?"

I cross myself as is tradition and say "Amen."

"Right, well the rest is pisswater, but for God's sake, Nat just keep that wallet close to you. If someone mugs you then let them have the big bag but just keep that on you. You'll put the money belt under your shirt, right?"

"Dad, stop it, we've gone through this a hundred times, I will put the money belt under my shirt. I will keep the rape whistle clenched in my teeth the entire time I'm in the States."

"Don't get het up, I'm just giving you the benefit of my wisdom."

I bite my tongue and don't say what I want to say, which is that the furthest he's ever been is Morecambe, which he said was "shit" and came back two days early. The majority of his worldly experience comes from his mates at The Prince Charles who have mostly been around Europe following City. Never to the States though. Auntie Pam said none of us have ever been to the States, quite a few went Down Under but they were exported direct from Ireland and they mostly only saw the inside of a cell.

The roads are dead and Dad weaves the Golf in and out of the lanes for fun as we head into town. It's so quiet. When I was doing my training, we always hated the shift that covered 3 to 5am. It always felt the earliest, and the eeriest. Midnight to 3am would be busy with the blood and barf people, but if you got anyone after that then they were usually mental health cases. People who the night hadn't quite collected. They would look about uncertainly as if they weren't quite sure where they belonged, they'd look at you, hoping that you might tell them. There was never much we could do for them, you could refer the worst ones to social services but that never felt enough. A cup of tea and a hug when the ward sister wasn't looking was about the best you could do for them. You're not supposed to hug patients, but it's a bit daft because it's about the most effective thing you can do for any patient. We drive past the Manchester Royal Infirmary. It looks quiet too, there's just one bloke sat on the kerb with his knees hunched up and his head leaning down, trailing a long string of spit into the gutter.

"Charming," Dad says.

I reach over and turn the heating down. Unusually, Dad doesn't complain. I think he doesn't want an argument before I go. I take a deep breath and look out of the window. We're climbing onto the Mancunian Way, the raised motorway that allows you to see over the buildings and peer down Oxford Road towards work.

"Why are you coming this way?"

"I thought you might like to say goodbye to the place."

"I'll be back you know Dad."

"I know, Henny,"

We're both breathing hard and I definitely should have got a bloody taxi. I want a cigarette - and I haven't smoked since my best friend Martin went through his cheroot phase. I want something other than this unbearable tension. Neither of us can talk about anything because everything is so loaded with emotion, but underneath it all my stomach is churning with adrenaline.

The buildings on either side of the road are mostly empty, some of the offices are illuminated by default and in one of them I see a matronly woman wrestling with a hoover. I'll miss Manchester so much. It's home. The people are mine. It's made me everything I am. My fun, my education, my work. It's me. I don't know why I'm leaving really, other than there's always been this thing in me that I knew Manchester was home and I was curious about what wasn't home. Mum dying made it easier.

"Dad!" I shout as a rusty smell fills the car and I slap his leg. "You dirty article!"

"I'm sorry! Emotions always come out of my arse for some reason."

He reaches over and flicks on the air conditioning. I open my window and feel the spray of the rain covering me. The smell of the city, it's like a promise of secret things down the end of an alley. A memory comes to mind of Martin scoring speed from this ratty bloke round the back of the club we were going to. He got a wrap and turned around and bumped into Mr Monroe, our geography teacher, who was next in the queue. "So, can I get an extension on my coursework?" Martin asked and Mr Monroe looked guilty and nodded. Jesus, that lad was quick.

"Do your window up now, Hen," Dad says and I obey; the handle is slick with spray and the smell has gone.

"I'm not joking Dad, don't do another one, it's rotten."

We're on the Parkway now. The lights of the big Asda shine out into the early morning. The stacks of the brewery are smoking. The lights are on in some of the homes in Moss Side, early shifts starting soon. I know all about yawning over breakfast, strong cups of tea and trying not to wake anyone as you close the door behind you.

"I want you to have a lovely time, you know," Dad says quietly as if he's just admitting something to himself. "I want you to do it all and see it all. I just want you to come back safe," he gulps a bit. "You're so precious to me Nat. Even Rick will miss you. The bloody dog is going to whine like hell for a week. Send her a postcard, won't you?"

"I'll send you all a postcard." The last words only just come out. It's like my lungs have switched off and the words just rattle around my mouth, bouncing off my teeth.

"I'll miss you all too."

"Oh Nat, I love you so much, I could not be prouder to be your dad. You're my whole entire world you know. More than anything. Don't tell Rick, but you're worth a hundred of him. He knows you are too, you can tell him if you like."

And then I'm crying, just tears at first, no sobs. I turn to look out of the window and the road rises and we're passing the hotel in Northenden where the hospital had the staff do one year and Vicky shagged the porter with the bent knob. I try and think about that. I really picture the kink of his dick to stop myself from crying, but it doesn't work and the tears are now streaming down my face.

"I love you too Dad!" It just comes out. The words. The tears. The emotion. Then the sobbing.

"Don't Henny! Don't bloody cry, I can't take it!" You never see my Dad cry and he looks at me pained as if he's frozen in mid-sneeze and then his voice catches up and he bellows out a sob. He dashes his sleeve at his eyes. The car veers from the fast lane to the hard shoulder and he puts the hazards on as we stop abruptly. Despite his large size, he seems so delicate.

"Dad! What are you doing? You can't pull up here!"

"Well, I can't drive down the M56 blarting can I? Stop it, Nat, I'm serious, it's not good for me."

I take some deep breaths and try and get my emotions under control.

"Ok, I'm all right. Just don't say anything else until we get to the airport, all right?"

"Right," he says and sniffs noisily. He peers into the rear-view, indicates and pulls us back onto the nearly deserted motorway. There's a flash: intense white light, close to the rear of the car and the shock of sudden motion. There's noise too, but it's the movement that's clearest. My arm whips up and my thumb strikes me somewhere above my eye. My head shoots toward the dashboard and I swear I see the airbag deploy, billowing out beneath my face. There's wicked pain followed by a crunch. My head is thrown back against the headrest and I notice that the windscreen has gone.

We're still moving. There's a grinding noise and sparks across the tarmac as the car slides its way down the slow lane. I look up and barely comprehend that we're upside down. I can see through the gap in the front window and I'm looking at the road, which is bobbled and wet. There's a pressure – hot and hard – on my shoulder and I realise that it's the weight of my body being held against the seatbelt. My brain goes over the basics: you are upside down and you are being held in place by your seatbelt. If I could unclick my seatbelt I could get out, but I'd fall and crumple into a heap. I don't want to fall on my bag because it's got my passport in. My arm hangs limply up by my face and when I see my hand, I think it looks like a swastika with fingers firing off unnaturally every which way.

"Dad, we've been in an accident," I try and say but it comes out burbled. There's a cut on my face somewhere and the blood is running downwards towards the earth and coating my mouth and my nose and my eyes. When I talk it runs into my mouth and it tastes like when Rick dared me to lick a battery. My other hand pushes the blood from my eyes. I will drown in my own blood. I will kill me.

"Dad?"

"Just hold still love, you're okay, we're going to get you out."

"I'm a nurse. I work at Saint James's hospital," I shout back.

"What's she saying?"

I lick around my lips with my tongue to get some clear space to talk properly. Something falls out of my mouth and bounces off my nose.

"I can't turn my head."

"Don't worry love, just keep talking to me, what's your name?"

"Natalie Cross, 15B."

"That's great, I'm Karl and you've got a whole team here with you, all right? Just keep talking to me, yeah?"

"I love you Nat, I love you."

The road ahead looks black.

Chapter 3

1st *April 2021*
7 months 28 days after

April Fools' day. Maybe today is the day that everyone bursts out and says that the last year has been a huge practical joke. Karl was an actor! That wasn't blood – it was make-up! This isn't even a boat – it's a TV set! Okay, world, you've got until midday, or the joke's on you.

I have been sleeping badly since the seagull smashed into the window a few days ago, so I pace around the outside of the bridge, trying to tire myself out and push some fresh air into my reluctant lungs. One thing I've noticed when you have cancer is that it's very hard not to take every twinge and minor pain as a sign that the cancer has multiplied. It's like your body has started a secret members' club inside of you and you're the only one not invited. The deep paranoia of another rum-and-weed hangover isn't helping and before long I've diagnosed myself with fifteen different cancers and botulism from when I had to pull the dead seagull from Brown's teeth.

As I try and stay warm I think about the coat I'm wearing. I took it from a dead body on a sodden country lane near Bredbury, to the southeast of Manchester. After we left the farmhouse, I had no real idea about where we should go, or what we should do. It just seemed more important that we should go somewhere and do something. Staying even one more day felt like it would stretch into a year or more of indecision. Let's face it, I've got form for digging in and I didn't want that again.

Of course, it was a huge mistake. I'm not sure what the alternative would have been, but for two hellish weeks, we skulked along back lanes, trying to cycle inconspicuously and keep watch for the endless wraths who were kept alert and angry by the driving rain. We kept moving day and night and I slept in ten-minute bursts, often slumped over the handlebars of the bike. Adrenaline fuelled me and I learned to watch Brown's ears for twitches that warned of approaching wraths. When we couldn't avoid or outrun them, we hid in sodden ditches, or shivered in manky toilets at the back of petrol stations. When we couldn't hide, we fought.

Everywhere we went I hoped for signs of life. I wanted to see lights and fires. I listened for voices and searched for other humans who had not been affected. All I found was wraths and senseless, ceaseless death. Burned houses. Looted shops. Crashed cars. Dead bodies. Sadness. Then I found the coat. It was a black waterproof parka with a thick fleece lining. It was unusual to see coats on any of the wraths. The change had fallen in the middle of a heatwave, on such a muggy day that most of the male wraths that you saw were in shorts, flip flops and t-shirts. The female wraths were in skimpy clothing or loose, billowy fabrics that rain now slicked to their bodies.

The man with the coat was lying near the high verge of the lane, about ten feet away from a spilled mountain bike with a yellow chariot hooked on the back. So not only could I steal his coat, but the trailer and bike would be a great upgrade on our current ladies' bike with basket. The man was clearly dead. His bones were showing, but in places patches of weathered skin hung to his frame like jerky. A clump of black hair hung over the front of his skull. I imagined that in a different time he was a rocker with an amazing quiff.

As I lifted his body to take the coat from him, I found that he was lying on the inert body of a shorter man wearing a white t-shirt, with an ancient yellow stain across it. The pair had their hands around each other's necks. Looking at the bodies and reading the scene, it looked strangely intimate, as if they'd been overcome with desire rather than bloodlust. Last August they had been out in the fresh summer air and then they had changed and seen out their life with their hands around the neck of a stranger, entwined together until their bodies rotted to dust and the winds freed them. I shook the coat to rid it of ghosts and biological detritus, shrugged it on, and zipped it up. A bit small, but waterproof and warm. I turned to examine the bike and there, in the back of the chariot, were the bones of a small skeleton – about two feet high, clothed in plain shorts and a t-shirt. The skeleton was intact, held in place by the straps of the chariot and this body, unlike the man with the coat, had lost all its flesh. I couldn't even tell if it had been a boy or a girl.

I stood frozen in the lane, the rain bouncing off my hood. Somehow, among all the death that I had witnessed, this one broke me. The cruelty of his or her death was monstrous. How could a loving God allow such a thing to happen? The child had sat there unable to undo the straps and presumably starved, but what good would it have done them if they could have got out? They could only have escaped into a world that had become a hell, a world where strangers strangled each other as they passed in country lanes. I sat on the muddy verge of the road, leaning back into the hedge's brambles trying to understand what was happening, trying to guess *why* it was happening. I had no answers; I felt dwarfed by the enormity of my loneliness.

My breathing became faster and I fanned my face, trying to push oxygen into my mouth. I became acutely aware of every heartbeat as my chest pounded and adrenaline coursed through me. Panic ripped my senses from me and I was stuck in a moment of abject horror. Brown approached me and stood close to my legs. The touch of her sodden fur and the prod of her nose into my knee recentred my thoughts, enough that I could begin to pace. The movement gradually restored my breathing and I picked a wriggling Brown up and squashed her against my face until all my senses returned.

I couldn't leave the child's skeleton there. It was too much for me. I felt compelled to honour and restore this one to some kind of dignity. At this point I didn't care if wraths descended and eviscerated me, I needed to bury this child. I walked up the lane a few hundred feet, to a gate leading into a farmer's field. The field was a mess of oats, grown too long and since decayed to slime, but the tireless plants had thrown up new shoots and a patchy new crop was growing that no one would ever harvest. I returned to the body of the man and pulled a blue cotton shirt from his bones, sending his skull skittering across the concrete as I disrobed him. I approached the chariot, carefully unclipped the straps and let the bones and clothes fall into the shirt, which I bundled up as carefully as I could.

I took the shirt into the field and walked to the headland. A long furrow had been ploughed many months before, creating a perfect trench where I could place the body. The rain had softened the exposed mud and let it run to a slurry, punctuated by puddles. I lay the child on the ground as gently as I could and pulled clods of brown soil over it. I worked until the ground was made good and my hands were caked with mud. The nails on my hand were black and I could see the lines of my palms like a network of roads. I wiped them on my trousers and stood by the side of the makeshift grave and tried to think of what to say. God's name wouldn't come to my lips. The rain continued to fall from a dark grey sky as I tried to put the experience into words, to capture it and give it meaning. I felt so angry and hurt that a child had suffered such a callous end that coherent thought drained away. After a minute, I managed to croak out a hope that wherever this child had gone that it had found justice. I asked the soil to hold the child, safe and warm. I asked the birds to sing a song over this place if they felt they could stomach it. I wept as if this had been my own child.

My mind kept returning to the injustice of why I'd survived. I knew my mum would have said that it was because I was destined to save the world, but that seemed as stupidly optimistic as the plants trying to grow. The world was gone. Mum would have said that God knows the plans he has for us and that they are good. I looked at my mud-caked hands and my mud-shod feet and I could not agree. I was no hero. I was a vessel for a cancer that would kill me and make my death as futile as all the others. When mum was ill, they'd suggested that she could give her cancer a name. The idea was that it helped you to see that this was an interloper, something "other" that existed in your body and that it was, therefore, right and proper to seek to eject it. Mum said she couldn't think of a name that she hated enough.

"How about Ronald?" I asked.

"I could never hate a clown," she said.

I wondered if I should name my cancer and what I could call it. The only thing that occurred to me was that it should be called Ben.

When I returned to the lane and walked back to the bike, Brown was nowhere to be seen, which was unusual. Sometimes as we travelled, she liked to range either side of the road, her nose pressed to the ground as she registered and decoded the scents. But she would always lift her head and check where I was and keep within a few metres, able to sprint back if she felt I was getting too far away, or if I whistled for her to come to heel.

I whistled for her. While I waited, I started to transfer our belongings – some tins of corned beef for Brown and several tins of beans for me, the shotgun and boxes of ammunition, a rucksack of spare clothes, several knives and a baseball bat. By the time I finished she still wasn't back. I looked around for wraths and put my fingers in my mouth and whistled louder. She still didn't return. I looked up and down the deserted lane and saw nothing. Panic surged in my veins once more and I tried to whistle again. My voice became shrill and desperate as I forgot caution and called her name over and over.

As I waited for a response, or for a wrath to burst through the hedge and attack me, I thought I heard something in the hedges to the right of the road. I heard a yelping noise and a whine and I realised there must be another dog there. Brown's debarking meant that the only noise she could omit was a tiny *peep,* like a broken squeaky toy, if she really tried to bark loudly. We had seen surprisingly few animals at large in the world, and at some point, I'd had the grim realisation that the majority of animals would have been trapped inside with their owners when the change happened. The ones that had managed to escape were wary of humans now they had ceased to be a benign presence.

I reached for the shotgun in case this dog was dangerous. I slowly mounted the slippery bank, using the shotgun as balance and tried to look through the hedge. I pushed aside the branches and felt the thorns scratching my hands and there I saw Brown. Beyond her, a larger black dog – a pitbull or Staffy - was skulking away, keeping to the hedgeline of the field. When she turned, Brown regarded me with a curious expression which I couldn't place, but the longer I held her gaze, the more I realised the caption underneath her face would have read: Busted.

We were both marked that day. For Brown, the dalliance has left her pregnant. For me, the memory of the child is only ever a thought away. I feel exposed to a depth of anger that I've never felt before. I've lost the ability to pray. Even when I pulled us into a ditch somewhere near Timperley and smothered Brown with my body while a group of four wraths searched for us, I couldn't ask God for protection. Even as I scouted the *Our Kid* and hoped that it would be a sanctuary, I couldn't ask God to bless us. Even after I shot the captain of the ship in the face and plastered his wrath-ruined brains over the stairway, I couldn't ask God for forgiveness.

***

It's been a few days now since it started to snow and something about the weight of the white sky suggests that it isn't going to turn nice again anytime soon. The canal is the one strip of darkness in an otherwise blindingly white world. I don't know how long it will be until Brown gives birth but given her size and the fact that she is lactating, I don't think it will be long. My weight loss means that I feel as if every breath of wind blows through me. When I'm in bed I look at the long angular line of my arm with its excess skin and see it dotted with goose flesh. If I stand in the cold for more than a minute, it leaves my teeth rattling. I have all the plans ready for Brown's new home, but I still have physical work to do and that means venturing out into the cold, so I need a new coat.

It is only a ten-minute walk to the indoor ski centre, but nothing can convince Brown and Bear to leave the bridge today. She has only left her nest of towels and t-shirts that she's been constructing in order to eat. At night she's restless and keeps pacing and piling up blankets. I cook her some strips of liver and bacon from the freezer and pep it up with instant gravy. I can't summon any appetite for myself, but I make a milkshake with some long-life coconut milk and protein powder. The smell of the liver fills the bridge and makes me feel queasy. I put it in front of Brown and she carefully lays Bear to the side of her bowl and eats. I notice that she's started leaving a little portion of her food in the bowl and my guess is that it is her way of feeding Bear. To complete the illusion, I distract her with milk and empty the food bowl. She sniffs at the food bowl and then carefully grasps Bear in her jaws again and returns to bed.

I settle Brown into her nest and fold a blanket over her haunches, and as I clumsily tuck it in, she whips her head around and nips at my hand. She is getting very fussy about how she is petted lately. I look at her belly and wonder how many puppies it is holding. I feel an urge to stay in bed and cuddle her, to savour this time when it is just the two of us, before the puppies arrive and before I leave them. I reach out to scratch at a spot on her neck she is trying to reach with her hind leg, but her newfound girth means that instead she is scratching about four inches into the air. Her teeth latch onto my finger and I pull it back as she drags her lip back to show me that this is serious. A bead of blood blooms on my knuckle. Time to go.

My breath clouds the air as I walk down the four flights of external stairs, which lead to the deck of the *Our Kid*. I press the button to lower the metal gangway on the side of the ship and crunch down the steps into the snow on the dockside. I heave on a rope and the pulley lifts the gangplank into the air. I tie it off and know that at least Brown is safe now. *Unless something happens to you*, an unwelcome voice of paranoia whispers in my ear. I stand frozen about ten metres from the ship and contemplate returning. Fuck that, I'm too cold for paranoia.

The snow is thick on the ground, reaching up to the middle of my shin. I'll need waterproof trousers if I'm not going to die of pneumonia before I complete Brown's hideaway. I try sipping on the shake I've made, but I only manage a few mouthfuls before it makes me want to be sick. I detour from the path to put the cup in the bin. As I do so I remember that no one is ever coming to empty that bin. I could throw it on the floor and it would make no difference whatsoever. I dare myself to throw it on the floor, but I can't do it, so I put it in the bin. I keep alert and edge cautiously around the corners of the buildings, keeping my line of sight as far as possible. The shotgun is unslung and hangs down by my side while I've got a one-metre crowbar from the engine room slung over me like a bag. I've drone-swept this area extensively so I'm not expecting any wraths on the loose, but it never hurts to be prepared.

As I reach the large car park that surrounds the ski centre, I keep low and skirt around the outer edge. Sure enough, I spot several wraths in their cars. Near to the entrance, there's an entire coachful, with most of the wraths slumped over and packed in by the front door. The others seem to be in that weird standby state they go into when they're not disturbed. The ones in the vehicles don't worry me, experience shows that even if they are woken up then they lack the technical ability to open the door. If they've got a seatbelt on then they're doubly stuck. You can stand on the other side of a wrath shut in a car and they just get madder and madder until they pulp their face on the window trying to get at you.

I skulk around the car park as the deep snow works its way through my boots. Finally, I come to the back of the building where the slanted roofline falls to meet the floor. A large pen of recycling bins gives way to an employee smoking area, as indicated by the wall-mounted ashtrays and warnings from HR about clearing up butts and vape containers. Lying by a set of double doors is a body. It is mostly obscured by snow, so it's only because I am moving so slowly and deliberately that I spot it. The decayed torso of the body is under the cover of a small porch and he or she is wearing a thick yellow waterproof jacket, which I take to be a security coat. I suppose the porch kept the weather off the body which is why it's not as decomposed. The person's head is nowhere to be seen and the neck is a ruined stump. The grainy powder of the protein shake swirls in my stomach and I breathe hard to keep it down.

I walk past the body being careful not to disturb it. I notice the catch on the double door into the building has a numeric keypad, which I won't be able to guess, so I resolve to force the door open with the crowbar, but as I get closer I notice a tiny wooden wedge holding the doors open a fraction. I level the shotgun for whatever lays behind and slide a finger inside the crack of the doors and pull. The doors open to reveal a supply corridor that I calculate must run past the back of the shop units inside the building. To the right the corridor is empty and to the left is a darker section that must lead to the main ski slope section of the building. Apart from a few wire cages that hold folded cardboard boxes and plastic wrappings, there doesn't seem to be anything here, so I step inside. It is dark in the corridor but one security light at the end of the corridor is on, illustrating a fire exit and that throws enough light into the hallway that I can just make out the name plates on the doors that I pass. I pause at a grey one marked Ice Gear and put my ear to it. I can't hear anything so I pull the grey handle down, and grimace when it emits a loud squeak and I carefully pull back the door.

The door opens into the main floor of the shop and I emerge behind the counter at the centre of the room. I take a moment to get my bearings and inspect every corner, ready to fire. Metal grill shutters are down on the front and I nearly fire a shot at one of the mannequins as I round a corner by a short flight of stairs, but the place is empty. The chaos of the change which saw the wraths arrive happened on a Tuesday, so the shop would probably have been open, but something that I've seen at several locations is a gathering of bodies and wraths at the emergency exits of buildings. In the chaos, it seems that many places triggered a fire alarm, which led to the evacuation of the shops and all the people gathering at a mustering point, where the wraths would have killed the non-wraths, until only a few remained.

I put the shotgun and my coat onto the counter and go shopping. Fifteen minutes later and I am kitted out. There's a display in the store with advice on winter clothing that advises a double layer approach for legs – tight leggings and waterproof trousers over the top. The right leg hangs slightly loose over the bottom of the prosthetic leg, but I love the way it hugs the top of the leg even tighter onto my body. I choose a pair of lightweight, waterproof mountaineering boots and make sure that it's a good fit for the prosthetic foot. I'll never be much of a tap dancer, but it's comfortable and stable. For my top half, I start with a synthetic base layer that clings tight to my skin like a swimming costume. This gathers in the loose skin from my stomach and chest and pins it in place. I have a limited range of clothes to choose from as the labels show that most of the coats use duck down, and I'd rather freeze. I end up with a very loud orange pair of Mammut trousers, a fleece, a double-zip Mammut parka, also in orange, and an array of hats and equipment from the rails.

Standing in my new gear, for the first time since the snow arrived, I feel warm. I stuff the accessories and crowbar in a large backpack, and with a final look around I gather up the gun and exit into the back corridor, where I trip on a wraith who is crawling along the floor.

"Fuck!" I shout and fumble the shotgun out of my hands. The wraith grabs feebly at my leg and I shake him off and stagger backwards down the corridor. His legs don't appear to be working, although I can't see an obvious reason. He's grunting loudly and spit is gathering at his lips as he shouts. As he gets closer, I can see a wide band of bruising on his neck and wonder what happened. I feel a degree of sympathy for him. He is only young – late teens, probably, although he has the weathered and unkempt look that all the wraths have. His long hair covers his face and his nails are long and jagged and rip on the floor as he drags himself towards me.

I breathe deeply and back off down the corridor to give myself time to think. I wish I'd brought a knife. I normally carry a long hunting knife everywhere, but for some reason, I'd assumed that the shotgun would be enough. It would do the job, but if I shoot him, I'll summon every wrath for a mile. I grab the shotgun from the floor and make sure the safety is on and flip it over so I'm holding the gun by the barrel.

"Fffffffkyu," the wrath says. He continues to pull himself along the corridor, intent on reaching my legs and pulling me down to his level.

"Sorry," I say, backing away enough to keep his grasping arms at bay. The wrath coughs and dredges something up from his throat, which he spits towards me. A greenish lump of discharge sits on the floor. I step over him and thump him twice in the back of the head with the butt of the gun. His head bounces off the linoleum and he goes still.

I shoulder my bag and gun and walk to the double doors I came in by. I look down to the end of the corridor. My eyes have adjusted to the murk and I see another door marked Main Slope. I look around for other wraths and then walk down to the door. I push it open and it reveals a huge room, nearly half a mile long with a long banking slope leading from about fifteen feet in front of me away into the distance. The slope is no longer covered by artificial snow as it was before the world changed. Instead, there are two long expanses of bare grey material running towards me, with a number of mounds and divots along the length. To the far side of the slopes are the button-operated ski lifts, which would have carried customers to the top. Looking closely, the slope looks as if the material is made up of tiny brushes. I walk towards it, checking for wraths as I go. I sweep the perimeter of the room with the crowbar in my hands, but like the shop, the slope room is sealed with a security shutter and the only thing I can see is a decomposed body on the other side of the shutter, lying in a crusted pool of blood.

At the bottom of the ramp, two containers hold large inflatable red donuts with plastic handles on the side. I dump my bag, sling the shotgun over my shoulder and take one out. I hold it over my head like a novelty hat and head to the walkway at the side of the slope and begin to trudge my way up. I walk next to the wall so that I can reach out a hand to steady myself as I feel a bit dizzy as I climb – probably from a combination of hunger, hangover and cancer.

As I reach the top, I look down the slope and feel a sense of excitement and anticipation. I'm nervous! I place the inflatable ring on the matted flooring and marvel at how easily it glides over the shiny surface. I position myself in front of the ring and fall backwards with a thump. I position the shotgun to the front so I don't accidentally shoot myself in the arse. Then I shuffle my bum forwards, until the combination of the material and the fall of the slope take hold and with a whooshing noise the fabric carries me. The world starts to rush past and I scream. The donut spins and I watch the printed alpine scenes on the wall blur. The viewing gallery windows looking onto the slopes bounce in my vision as my donut gains speed. Just at the bottom I hit a small hillock and feel the lurch as I get a few inches of air. At the bottom, the slope levels out and I slide onwards until I crash into a large red plastic barrier. I sit in my donut, looking at the roof above me and feel stupid. I wonder what it will be like when I'm dead.

Chapter 4

January 3rd 2020
7 months, 1 day before

When I packed to come to France I wasn't concentrating. I just found a big bag and jammed things in. So, although I've got my laptop, I don't have a power cable and the battery is dead. I also only packed two pairs of knickers, but it's been so hot that I've lived in my swimming costume since I arrived. Martin ordered me a power cable – and some knickers – but in the meantime, he's given me one of his laptops. It's some kind of Macbook, so all the buttons are different and I keep forgetting the commands for things. Pressing an apple button just feels weird. I don't know why it's any weirder than pressing a window button though. At least the apple looks like an apple.

As he does every day the chef has prepared a range of fresh juices that he left covered with a little white doily on the long grey marble kitchen counter. I pour a long glass of blood orange juice with ice and carry it with the laptop out onto the terrace area. Martin loves to tell the story about why their three pools are shaped like tears. The locals were outraged when the plans went public, but the mayor intervened personally in the fight when Martin told him why he wanted the pools to be in that precise shape and configuration. The mayor laughed and said "Ahhh, c'est le sperme emoji! D'accord!" The approval went through the next week. The mayor's campaign fund received a sizeable anonymous boost a few months later.

I set the juice and laptop down on the glass-topped rattan table and fight with the parasol to provide some shade for the screen. The sky is a relentless blue and I can feel my shoulders burning, even in this short time. I sit in the little patch of shade I've created and open the laptop to find the email from work. I should probably read it in full but I've skimmed it and I get the gist. It's some HR thing to allow me to bypass normal CPD requirements so I don't get struck off the nursing register in my absence. All I know is that enough higher-ups shouted and they'll probably stop if I fill in the form. The basics like my name and job title are all pre-filled, so I skip through those and add my birth date. The form wants me to tick a box asking if I'm currently on a long-term leave of absence. The rest of the form is greyed out and won't let me add anything until I deal with this box. I try and think. My mind is so flabby these days, and I get confused so easily. But I'm definitely on a long-term leave of absence, so I try and tick into the box that is currently blank, but the little tick box is the same shade of grey as the rest of the form. I try with different jabs, sweeps and pecks to position the arrow above the box and click into it. Nothing.

"Are you on a long-term leave of absence? Yes. Tick. Uh-huh."

The box stays tick free.

"Yes. Yes. Yes. Yes! I am on a long-term leave of absence. YES. TICK, YOU PIECE OF CRAP!"

I double click again and the whole form is shaded in blue as if it's been selected before being copied.

I press delete and the browser window returns to the Google home screen.

"Oh, you stupid fucking thing!"

In a sudden fury that takes me by surprise, I slam the lid of the laptop and then hope that the crunching noise was a product of my imagination. I feel a rush of desperation and I try and focus on my surroundings. I take a deep breath and look at the colour of the juice on the table. It's a deeper, *realer* purple than anything I've ever seen in my life. I stare at it and it becomes venous blood coursing up through the glass in a sinus rhythm. With each beat, it jolts up and spills over the side of the glass in a rhythmic slush. The glass of the table is covered. The red-blue blood drips over the side and splatters on the limestone paving, each drop birthing a splatter of smaller dots. I close my eyes and when I open them the juice is back in the glass and the surge of emotion is gone as quickly as it arrived. I reach out and take a sip of the juice and it's so sharp it's like being whipped with a towel. I close my eyes again and hear the click and buzz of unfamiliar French insects.

My conclusion about the life of rich people like Martin and Noam is that they get to experience sensations in a deeper and more satisfying way than the rest of us. A lot of work goes into making sure that the tastes they get are deeper. The towels are fluffier. The alcohol is more potent. The cascading pools, just beyond the edge of my lounger, are a good example. They are three different shades of blue – an essay of blueness that develops from a light, joyful sky blue to a nearly whale-black navy. That final pool is about thirty feet deep and is buried in the hillside. I have no idea why they wanted a pool that deep. I should ask.

I've been staying with my best friend Martin and his husband Noam for three weeks now. It may even be more. I've been trying not to get too caught up in the days of the week and just to focus on how I'm feeling. I know that Christmas was one of the days, but Martin knew one of the reasons I'd accepted his invitation to be with them was because I didn't want my first Christmas after Dad to be stuck at home in Middleton doing the normal seasonal things in a weird time. So, Martin banned TV, festive decorations and we stayed off our phones and just drank, chatted and read. The chef came and made whatever we asked for. Most days I had a peanut butter sandwich and some Quavers. I don't even know which day was Christmas.

I stretch out on the sunbed and look at my legs. A diagonal line of shadow from the parasol cuts across the upper thigh. My lower legs are brown and start to fry lightly in the heat. I watch them and wonder how long it would take for them to go red, and then black and then grey. Beyond my legs and the pool lies the valley – a lush green expanse that pinches down to a broad, shallow river. You know it's exclusive because there are more castles than houses dotted across the landscape. Neighbours keep a respectful distance around here, and besides, Martin says that Noam bought most of the land. There's a village about 15 kilometres away but the house has everything you could ever need. There are three saferooms and an escape tunnel, two helipads and toilets that sense who has just entered the room and heat the seat according to your preference. Then there are pools shaped like the sperm emoji. It's pretty different to Middleton.

I wake up and find Martin looming over me with his finger extended. It's smeared in some kind of white ointment and he's dabbing it on my face.

"Shhhh, go back to sleep. I just wanted to put some zinc on your scar."

He draws a line with his finger down from my lower lip to the point of my chin. The zinc is cold and smells medicinal. I try and keep my eyes closed.

"Go back to sleep, shhhhh, shhhhh."

"I'm not going to sleep now, am I?"

"Hush-hush, pretend this never happened. It's all a wonderful dream. You've just been visited by the zinc fairy. Shhhhh. Dream on, dreamer. Oh, look there's Matt Damon and he wants to have dinner with you. Naked dinner. Oh, Matt! Hot dog dinner with naked Matt Damon."

I open my eyes and Martin is waving his fingers at me trying to hypnotise me back to sleep.

"I wasn't sleeping, I was just resting my eyes."

"Do you remember Patty O'Doors at school when she used to draw eyes on her eyelids, God she was a freak."

"She'd spend forever on it as well," I say.

"She's got three kids now," Martin says. "Maaaaasssive arse too."

"How do you know that?"

"I hacked her Facebook. I'll send you the pictures."

Martin drags one of the sunbeds over with a scratching noise and he sits down next to me. He's wearing a pair of bright yellow Speedos and a floating silk robe that is undone. He's always been skinny, but he's been working with a personal trainer for a few months and there are lines of discernible muscle appearing.

"You still look like shit," he says.

"Thank you," I reply.

"I was hoping that you'd reanimate while you were out here. Fresh air, good food, all that stuff. Maybe we should just get you some anti-depressants. Our doctor will come out if you want? Or we could just get hammered on ketamine?"

"I don't know," I say.

I pick up the orange juice to give me something to do. All I want to do is say nothing and just stop time, so I don't have to live with this pain. I touch the liquid to my lips and a line of the sweet-sharp juice wets my lips and the taste blooms across my mouth. Martin is not talking. I know him well enough to know that this is killing him. He's trying to actively listen. As I've felt so many times since I came here, running from a weirdly warm December in Manchester, I'm aware of being grateful to Martin and Noam. The feeling somehow doesn't permeate my heart, but I'm aware of it. It's like I'm the computer form. Everything is greyed out and nothing can be clicked into.

"I think I broke your laptop."

"That's ok."

"I closed it too hard and I think it's smashed. I'm sorry. I daren't open it up."

"That's ok, we'll tell Noam he did it and make him get us both new ones."

"Are you going to swim?"

"I'm too terrified of Frönk not too. He'll burpee me to death. He'll make me do battle ropes until I could wank off two elephants simultaneously."

He stands and lets the robe fall onto his sunbed. He flounces to the side of the pool and elegantly raises his hands over his head. He intertwines his arms so that the back of his hands are touching. His body is lithe, tanned and healthy. He flexes the muscle of his left buttock twice and then the right one. He looks over his shoulder to check I'm watching. He does it again. Two on the right, one on the left.

"Sing it," he commands.

"No," I reply.

"You have to. It's one of the foundation stones of our friendship. Come on! Bum-bum-cha! Bum-bum-cha! Sing, girl!"

"Buddy you're a tall man, fat man, living in a bin, going to crawl into a hole and die,"

"Yes! More!" Martin cries, encouraging himself. We switch and I provide the bum-bum-chas.

"Got jizz on your chin, where to begin, looking like a kitten hanging from string. Singing!"

Martin leaps and pikes into the water, producing the merest ripple as he breaches. He surfaces at the other end of the pool twenty metres away. He turns and swims back. He leans on the side of the pool and flicks his long dark hair back away from his face. He smiles at me and I do my best to smile back.

"You'll get there, kid."

"So they say."

Martin drops back down and does another two lengths, completely underwater this time. He gasps as he rises back to the surface and smiles at me again. There's something in his smile that makes me sadder than I've ever been. I think it's because he loves me so much.

"I want to do it, Mart."

"What?"

"The surrogate thing. You and Noam will be great dads."

Martin fixes me with a look that flashes with a mix of emotions. The raw want of having a family. The fear that I'm joking.

"No joke, I want to do this for you and Noam."

"Are you serious? You know we were just chatting, we wouldn't have brought it up if we hadn't been pissed."

"It's ok. I'm glad we talked about it. I'd like to do it."

I think it had been New Year's Eve. Off and away in the valley, I'd seen some fireworks over one of the houses. That was the only tangible sign of the start of 2020, otherwise, we'd been observing our own holiday where conversations took place over days, punctuated only by food and sleep. Noam had read us a poem called Japanese Maple, which made Martin laugh initially because he thought it was pretentious, but then it had expressed such a solemn hope for something, and Noam had asked each of us what we thought the poet had hoped for. I answered time. Martin answered family. The discussion had grown from there.

I was surprised because I'd just never thought of Martin as a dad. Dads were like my dad – farters, ale-drinkers, plug-menders. It wasn't because Martin was gay that I couldn't see him as a dad, it was because he'd never really made mention of it. He talked then about their past and how Noam's diagnosis had changed things for them. Day-to-day, being HIV+ made no difference. He took a pill each morning and it rendered the virus negligible. Apparently, at some point, a doctor had lectured them about the dangers if they wanted to conceive and from then on Martin had decided that he wanted nothing more than to raise babies with Noam. As with most personal things he kept that hope so close to his chest that it was imperceptible to other people. As they talked, I knew that they had the only qualification that any parents needed – that they loved each other enough to survive a child.

Martin had explained that they'd made some enquiries and learned how being HIV+ wasn't an issue with regards to the health of the surrogate – a lab could ensure that the sperm was safe before implanting the fertilised eggs, but potential surrogates usually ran screaming when they found out. Martin also felt that their surrogate had to be someone they felt connected to, someone they loved. Noam said "someone like you" and we left it there.

"But what about work?" Martin asks as he levers himself out of the pool.

"I can still work."

"You know we'd pay you though?"

"I don't want money, Martin, you can pay for all the billowy maternity dresses I'm going to wear, but I don't want money. I love you, but I think I need this as well. Dad always loved you too."

"How do you think he'd feel about you having little gay babies?" Martin asks.

"He'd be fine. I don't think he'd understand that we don't have to have sex."

"He always thought we were having sex anyway."

"Yeah, he never really understood that did he?"

"Are you sure Nat?"

"I'm sure."

Martin's face crumples. In a second he's fourteen again and I'm consoling him after the lad he fancied, Connor Wright called him a poof and broke his young heart for the first time. Martin stumbles over to me like he's dragging himself from a trench in the war, one hand covers his eyes as he weeps openly. He sits on the edge of my sunbed and says over and over, "I love you, Nat. I love you."

I know that it's probably bad timing, but maybe this is a good choice. Maybe this is the chance I have to stop being the box that's greyed out.

Chapter 5

7th April 2021
8 months and 3 days after

I wake up with my stomach roiling and as quickly as I can I slap my leg on and hobble to the toilet while clenching my cheeks. I make it just in time. I know that if I looked in the bowl then I'd see a spritz of bright red blood. I don't want to look at the toilet paper, so I just bundle it all in the bowl and double flush it away as quickly as possible. Even after that though, there's still the faintest hint of pink to the water – it looks like the mouth rinse the dentist makes you swill with. I stare at it and then close the top lid of the toilet and consider the matter resolved. After all, you can't be dying of cancer if you don't acknowledge any of the symptoms, that's basic male health in action. What a mess.

I wash my hands and try to follow the absurd diagram on the toilet wall. Scrub back of palms together. Interlace fingers. Nails to nails. I rinse them off in scalding water and dry them on a towel. I see the scales in the corner of the room. Conditioning makes me get them out and position them on the toilet floor. I neatly align them with the tiles, so I know they're in the same place as before. I step on with my right foot, exhale so that the weight of my breath doesn't interfere with the reading and then step on with my left. 65kg. Another 3kg off. I wish I still had my red exercise book, it just doesn't seem right not to record this data. I pull the skin tight around one of my arms and flex the bicep; it's still there but I just feel so enfeebled. At this rate, I'm going to shit myself down that toilet.

The whole thing just seems so unfair! I know that I've had this thing bubbling away in my gut since at least last July when the doctor first told me. I got a book on cancer from a trip I made to Eccles Library when I was searching for a book on how dogs give birth. I looked at survival rates for colorectal cancer and all I'll say is that I wish I hadn't. The shock has faded somewhat and I'm glad now that I know what I'm playing with in terms of the time available. It gives me a better idea of what I can hope to achieve for Brown before I die. My only other regret is that I could have earned so many green faces and slimmer-of-the-week fruit baskets from the slimming club. Another opportunity robbed from me by the end of the world.

Brown is waiting outside the bathroom door and hassles me for breakfast as soon as I open the door. I'm too queasy to prepare any meat, so I mush up some kibble with butter and hot water and set it down for her. She looks at the dish and gives me a disgusted look that suggests she's thinking of leaving a desultory tip, but she reluctantly tucks in as it's clear I'm not capable of much more this morning. I wander down the warm, carpeted corridors of the ship into the larger crew bathroom and run the showers so hot that steam fills the room. I stand in the bathroom and breathe in the vapour. It makes me sweat and helps me to clear my head, and by the time I've washed and I'm dressed in my new winter gear I feel like I can manage a basic breakfast.

I make a giant mug of tea, take it out onto the bridge and marvel at the rows of icicles forming on the underside of the railings like a jagged line of teeth. The snow is still falling so I loiter under the cover of the bridge's roof. Along with the tea I manage to force down four custard creams, swallowing them with mouthfuls of the rapidly-cooling tea as if they're medicine. Getting stoned before a day out in the world isn't a great idea, but neither is passing out from hunger. It's a choice of which type of light-headedness is best. I look at my hands in the daylight and it's easy to make out the bones flitting under the papery skin.

Brown disrupts my trance and she's energised enough to want some form of exercise. I don't want to take her with me for the day, so I give a little follow-me whistle and we trot down the stairs. She trails me and hops in the divots of snow I leave behind with my footsteps. Once we're at deck level Brown looks at me as if I've sold her a lemon. She wants a walk, not to be buried up to her neck in snow. I ignore her disdain and follow the accommodation block round to the back where there's a white door that accesses the lower level of the ship. For the first steep run of steps, I pick Brown up. She fidgets but keeps still when I tuck her tightly to my chest. I hold the railing firmly and we're brought out onto a narrow stairway which Brown can just about descend.

As the steps drop into the guts of the ship, there are a few cutout sections of the stairway that afford you a view of the hold beyond. Even though the *Our Kid* isn't the biggest container ship, its hold still seems cavernous and when we reach the floor I look up at the containers around us and the cathedral size void. It's a dim, eerie place. Shadows cast by emergency lights play across the walls and dive into the gaps between the stacked containers. Sometimes, seemingly for no reason, metallic clangs sound out, setting Brown to her silent barking. I've got the shotgun, but I also know that I swept this area several times when we first made the *Our Kid* our temporary home. As I explored, I opened as many of the containers as I could reach and found thousands of boxes of golf shoes, stacks of car tyres, boxes of Bluetooth speakers, large wooden crates containing sacks of sawdust, and an Audi Q7. One container was stuffed with consumer electronics including two crates full of drones. They were slightly more basic than the model I had back in the flat, but they flew fast and combined with the speakers they made a ruthlessly efficient tool for wrath hunting.

I pull a book, a tennis ball and a little sachet of silica gel from the pocket of my new coat. "Do Not Eat", the sachet urges, and I have to wonder what harm it could possibly do to me now. Maybe I should eat it. I grind the sachet into the floor before the temptation to swallow it consumes me. I sit on the bottom steps and throw the ball for Brown. She gamely puts aside her fear of ghosts in the hold and chases after the ball, dropping it at my feet each time. While she's waddling around and burning off some energy, I finish reading *My Dog Is Having A Dog!* which is the closest that Eccles Library has to anything approaching veterinary advice for the concerned canine birth partner. If I had been after a large print Catherine Cookson then I would have gone to the right place, but not so much for anything else. The gist of the book is that dogs are programmed to give birth and the best thing you can do is keep out of the way. Finally, something I can do. There's a diagram of a gormless cartoon Labrador which helpfully points out a dog's primary exit routes. Brown drops the ball at my feet again as I commit the information to memory.

"And you're ok with this?" I ask and show her the picture. She looks at me and her tongue lolls out of her mouth.

"You do know that dogs are going to come out of you, don't you? Specifically, from here," I say and point to the relevant part of the diagram. She sits obediently. I laugh and realise that the bubbles of giddiness I've been experiencing are likely just the Custard Creams starting to kick in. Here I am in the hold of a cargo ship, with my pregnant dog, getting messed up on biscuits, at the very end of the world. Totally normal. I throw my head back and howl into the echoing space.

We trudge back up the steps and I carry Brown up the steeper inclines. By the time we get back to the bridge, I'm convulsing with laughter. I don't know what sets me off, but as the bridge door *schlups* into place I'm weeping and pointing at the door to try and explain to Brown what I'm laughing at. Brown just stares at me, hoping to somehow divine the mysteries of human behaviour. I shouldn't have eaten four biscuits. I breathe, trying to force the laughter back down inside of me, but bubbles keep rising to the surface and it takes me nearly an hour of stumbling and cackling to myself to get ready. I eventually settle Brown back into her nest with its warm-dog smell and see that Bear is cocooned in its epicentre. Not for the first time, I'm openly jealous of that teddy.

I grab some thick bin bags and my rucksack and spend twenty minutes packing all the things I think I'll need. I take a saw, screwdrivers, a hammer and tin-snips from the tool cupboard. I pack as much food as I can carry, including the remaining kibble I got from our trip to the nearby supermarket. That means that Brown will have to eat human food back on the ship until it's time for me to go, but I'm sure she won't mind. I wonder about stuffing Bear in the pack, but Brown would be bereft if she thought it had gone missing and that can't be good for a pregnant dog. I put some tennis balls in instead. Then I remember that no one will be there to throw them for her and I feel a pang of hurt so strong that I put my hand to my chest. I console myself with the thought that maybe the puppies will play with them. I fill another two bin bags with duvets and pillows.

I slide the bridge door shut and make my way off the ship. I leave the rucksack and bin bags by the ship's gangway and retrace my steps from the other day. My footsteps have been filled in with snow but it doesn't take me long to get into the ski slope and retrieve one of the big red donuts. I step over the silent body of the wrath in the corridor and take a length of rope from the outdoor shop. I loop the rope around my shoulders and drag the donut across the car park. It would have been better if there was a less conspicuous colour than the bright red donut, but given that I look like a giant Oompa Loompa I don't suppose subtlety matters too much. I pile the bin bags in the donut and shoulder the pack alongside the shotgun, which I realise with dismay I've not brought any spare ammunition for. There's a hunting knife gaffer-taped and zip-tied to the top of the barrel like a bayonet, but that and two shotgun shells are my only weapons. I wonder if I should return to the ship and try again tomorrow, but the snow is lighter today and I don't know how many more days I've got until I'm too weak to get the work done. Plus, the weed is giving me an aura of invincibility, so I plod on through the snow.

I walk along the towpath up to the nearest bridge pulling my cargo behind me. The road is silent and calm now, but the signs that wraths visited here are everywhere. Crashed cars, smashed windows, a bus wedged under a low bridge with the front half of the top deck missing. I pass by a run of terraced houses and one of them is lit up. I sneak up to the window and I can see the static of the television in the front room. Somewhere above a solar panel must be harvesting the meagre sunlight and keeping the deserted property powered up. It's been so long now that I have to remember that at one point, these houses with lights and activity were normal, they were part of a jumble of noises that filled these streets. Voices, music, engines, animals. Now there's just silence.

I pause for a breather and a mouthful of water at a crossroads and skulk behind a billboard advertising a pension plan. It reminds me that I need to sort my pension out, never too early to think of the future. I consult my *Manchester A to Z* and look over the road and see the giant form of George R.R. Martin waving at me. There's a large speech bubble coming out of his mouth that says, "Summer Club Is Coming!" I stole the cut-out when I visited the library at the top of the road and used it as a makeshift sledge. I look at his white beard and the little cap perched on his head. I level the shotgun at the cutout and make a "Pew! Pew!" noise with my mouth. With perfect aim my laser blasts the hat from his head.

"That'll learn you to finish your books before the world ends," I say.

I shuffle the donut out to the middle of the road and grip onto the two handles and sit back. With some shuffling the donut gradually starts to slip over the surface. I manage to sledge nearly a mile with some pit-stops for repositioning. The donut makes a *shhhhh* noise as it travels over the virgin snow and I give over control and let it spin me around and bump me wherever it will take me. I look up at the low white sky and focus on the tumbling flakes of snow as they land on me. After a while, the road levels out and I have to get out and pull again. The earlier high of the edibles has subsided and left me with a sort of hangover that sits like a question mark over my head. I lean into the snow and lick my dry lips until they start to chap as I head towards the motorway.

Between the houses and buildings, I get a glimpse of the *Our Kid* on the other side of the canal and I wave at Brown and Bear. It must be nice to be warm right now, with rum close to hand. By the time I go under the M60, all that lies ahead is an unbroken patch of white after which are the training fields for the nearby rugby club. I'd scoped out the fields as a potential home for Brown using the powerful binoculars from the bridge of the ship. Just one field over I'd spotted a small building next to the canal and that was where I was planning to set up Brown's retreat. The snow is deep across the field and as I push the donut I find myself sweating, despite the constant blizzard stinging my eyes and turning everything around me into a flat blur. By the time I get closer to the shed, I can see that it's a supply shed. There's cover from the nearby trees and the grass is still visible in places. I dump everything at the door and circle around the sides. Close by a small brook feeds into the canal. The top layer of the water is frozen but I stamp on the ice and see that it's running clear underneath. I don't know for certain but it looks clean to me. I scoop my hands in and drink. It's cold enough to set my teeth on edge, but it tastes clean.

I return to the shed and inspect the walls. They're plain concrete slabs that have been painted white. I turn and examine the view. On the other side of the canal there's a mishmash of trees and beyond them the dome of some buildings that look like containers, perhaps for gas. Much closer by is Barton Lock. I can't see another soul. I know that if I wandered over to the lock then I wouldn't have to search too hard to find wrath bodies, but I can't do that to myself right now. Instead, I fetch the crowbar and prise open the doors, which open with a crack to reveal a set of corner flags and a machine for painting the white lines onto pitches. Usefully, there's also a brush, and I begin my home-making by sweeping the floors until there's not a speck of dust to be found. There are sacks of fertiliser in the corner of the room which I start to drag outside and then think better of it and haul back in. With the duvets and pillows from the bin bags arranged on the bags, I create a fort with a few separate entrances. It reminds me of a comfier version of a pillbox by the time I finish. The puppies are going to love it in here. Brown will be safe here, I know it.

I unload the bag of kibble. There's enough dry food here to last at least a month, and with the water from the brook behind the shed, I feel reassured that I'm doing everything I can to give my best friend the best possible start to her new life as a lone parent. I remove the screwdriver and saw from the bag and cut out a square in the door big enough to allow access for Brown, but high up enough that the babies will have to grow a bit before they can independently get through the door. I've seen mother dogs carrying puppies by the scruff of their necks so I think Brown will be able to wrangle her brood. Once more I have to accept that this isn't a precise science and that I can only do my best.

I flash forward and imagine the days ahead. The smell of the room. The noise of the puppies. I wonder if their noises will surprise Brown, or if because of her enforced muteness that they too will communicate more through gesture and touch. I wonder if she'll be too busy with the puppies to look at the door and wonder when I'm coming back. I push the square of plywood out and sweep up the sawdust. The weed has worn off completely now and I'm depleted. I sit on the duvets and look at the wall. It's so tempting to take her with me when I head out to sea. Or just to let the cancer play out while I still have her and the pups around me. But I'd be dooming her. The puppies mean she has something else to live for. There will be new life. Who knows for how long, but it is the only thing I can do right now. "I know the plans I have for you," declares the Lord, "plans to prosper you and not to harm you, plans to give you hope and a future."

Horseshit.

***

It's night by the time I get back to the ship. I forgot to bring a torch and the night feels too close. I nod to the cut-out of George and make my way across the road, incapable of caring anymore if I'm attacked. The wraths are welcome to whatever is left of me. None appear anyway and I trudge back down the towpath to the ship's gantry. I lower the steps and climb wearily upwards. I raise the stairs and start up another flight. Each step feels like climbing a mountain and I pause on each landing to catch my breath and let the ache in my back subside. I slide the bridge door back and Brown leaps out, bouncing excitedly at seeing me after a day inside. She can't wait to play and be stroked but she's also desperate for the toilet, so she's still leaking wee as she's jumping up at my thighs. She's getting quite cumbersome now, and is beginning to resemble a bumblebee. I smile at her oblivious joy.

I sit on the captain's chair and loosen my boots. I pull my prosthetic leg off and throw it onto the mattresses so that it will be nearby if I need to run to the toilet. I strip my coat off and peel the underlayers that are soaked with a musty sweat and melted snow. Even my underwear is wet. There's nothing else I can do but crawl across to the bed. I take a long draw from an old bottle of water by my bedside and sneeze twice. Brown accepts that this is as interesting as I'm going to be and drops Bear on my head. I bat him away and she picks him up and drops him again.

"I NEED A HUG!" Bear announces.

Horseshit.

Chapter 6

14th July 2020
21 days before

Dr Ranjit rolls his sleeves up very deliberately, folding them over turn by turn until they are level with his elbows. He smiles at me as he elaborately washes his hands in that way that doctors and nurses are taught – fingernails together, scrubbing the back of one hand, then the other, rinse, paper, anti-bacterial foam. It feels like a hygiene melodrama given that he's just going to read us a result from a piece of paper, but I suppose this is the sort of treatment that top dollar gets you.

"Now, how are we all?" he asks our strange ensemble.

"I'm good thanks Doctor Ranjit," I reply and wonder if everyone else can hear the nerves in my voice.

"All good here thanks Doc," Martin replies through the laptop I've set up on the table next to me. He's in France.

"Bon merci," Noam says. "Sorry, I mean good. Thank you." He's on the iPad leaning against the wall. He's somewhere classified in Africa.

"Now, we have met before for blood tests and such Ms Cross, but this is the first time I am meeting these two gentlemen, so let's make sure we know who is who here and if you have questions then you can ask them of me too."

"Okay, I'm the surrogate," I reply. "We have my eggs fertilised with sperm from Martin and Noam and both eggs have been implanted."

"Okay, okay," Dr Ranjit says and he uses a heavy gold pen to make a note on the piece of paper.

"Martin, you are the laptop?"

"Correct," the laptop replies.

"And Noam, you are the iPad?"

"Yes," the iPad says.

"And you are the human, Natalie?"

"Exactly," I say.

"Got. It." Dr Ranjit says and proceeds to make copious notes. What's he writing? I try and read it but it's upside down and written in the standard doctor scrawl that they spend the extra time at university learning how to do.

I look at Martin and Noam on their screens. Martin is feigning nonchalance, sipping from a *Finding Nemo* mug, but he's watching every move that the doctor makes with a crocodilian focus. Noam looks nervous and I love him for that. He's working with a militia movement attempting to either promote or subdue democracy, he's never that specific about which side he's on. I suspect it might change depending on the paymaster. Martin is at home in France, swimming and keeping himself busy in ways I hope I never find out about. Given who their parents are, if I am pregnant, this baby, or babies, are going to either end up running the world or destroying it from their supervillain base in a hollowed-out volcano – there's no middle ground.

I'm the only one actually present in the fancy clinic in Heywood, aside from Dr Ranjit. It's the only doctor's surgery I've been to where they have valet parking. You enter through a set of ornate iron gates and there's a big crunchy gravel drive and then you're at the front of this country house. An orderly appears and bids you enter and car elves spirit your vehicle away to who-knows-where. I ruined the effect by Uber-ing here.

I might be here in person, but in spirit, I'm orbiting the earth somewhere in the troposphere. It was less than three weeks ago when I was at the private hospital in India getting the fertilised eggs implanted. After hours of discussion, we decided to implant two eggs and see what happens. Ordinarily, there are stringent controls on becoming a surrogate if you've not had children of your own. As with most things though, money makes those problems irrelevant. I had been to the hospital and back home, three times in a matter of weeks for tests and all manner of prodding. The last time I was there I was hoping to see India from closer than 15,000 feet, but the hospital was on a lush estate away from anywhere. I flew in on a private jet carrying only myself, two pilots and an air stewardess who looked so unnervingly like Scarlett Johansson that when we landed she confided that I was the first person in ages who hadn't asked if she was her. After that, I couldn't ask if she was.

The plane landed at a private airfield about twenty miles from the hospital. Passport control was a broad smile and a handshake from a man in a uniform and a short walk across the tarmac to a classic car with a little green and red flag on the bonnet, which picked me up and took me straight to the hospital. There was no seatbelt in the car and the leather seats were deep enough to sleep a family of four on. The hospital was set in landscaped grounds but the building itself looked incongruously like any hospital in Britain, lots of signs and large glass windows. Inside, the hospital gleamed, and the staff wore uniforms so pressed and starched that it looked like they'd snap if they bent an arm. The only foreign thing about it was that the staff were Indian and they had elaborate gardens at the rear of the hospital with a huge set of ornate fountains. A family of kittens wound around my legs when I went outside to get some fresh air after the procedure, and a smiling nurse never left my side the entire time. One of the kittens looked like the runt of the litter, with matted fur and a wonky eye. I picked it up and did what I could to clean it in the fountain's water.

We'd already done a mock implantation, so the doctors could map out my uterus and make a decision about where to implant the eggs. They were apparently very happy with my uterus because they told me there was much discussion about which implantation site to use. Normally they had scant choice, but apparently my uterus was a generous home. Good to know. There was no sedation for the implantation, but the whole procedure only took about twenty minutes. I remember a cold sensation and a group of doctors, gathered around my fanny, urging me to relax. I felt the tenderness of my overly full bladder and then there was clapping and the doctor's words: "Go go, baby!"

Then I was in France. A long weekend with Martin, swimming and eating. I finally found out that the chef is called Kurt. Then back home to the hottest and stickiest British summer I'd ever known, where shoppers were wrestling each other in Home Bargains over cheap three-speed fans and omnipresent barbecue smells waft over every fence. I wonder if the nausea I've been feeling is a symptom of pregnancy, but I know it is probably too early to tell. While I was with him Martin nagged me endlessly to move out to France for the duration of the pregnancy, but it would just be too weird. I need to work or I'll go mad and I can't leave my patients. I tried to explain that back in the real world if people didn't turn up for work, not only did they not get paid, but it had an impact on other people's lives. Martin nodded politely as if he understood the concept of other people having lives.

He and Noam wanted to get me a driver for the next nine months who would be available at my beck and call, but I'll be buggered if I'm going to live like Middleton's answer to Lady Penelope. We agreed in the end that I'd have access to an Uber Platinum service. It's weird. There's a separate app for it and there's always a car just around the corner and it's invariably the same driver, some shaven-headed lunk, who doesn't talk and watches me in the rear-view mirror. He said he's Polish but I'm not sure if that's true. I wouldn't have put it past Martin to have just hired a driver and car anyway and made the whole Uber Platinum app up. The thing with Martin is that you can only deny him for so long. Eventually, he'll just do what he wants, so it's really about how stubborn you want to be and how long you can thwart him.

***

"So here we are," Dr Ranjit says at last and he takes a single crisp piece of paper from a briefcase on the floor. "Here we are," he says to himself again, as he reads carefully.

"And?" Martin says.

"And...interesting," Dr Ranjit replies, still reading the paper.

"Interesting good or interesting bad?" I ask.

"One second please," he replies.

"Doctor?" Martin says half a second later.

"Qu'est qui se passe?" Noam asks. Martin answers from the laptop "Je ne sais pas, attendre."

"Doctor?"

Dr Ranjit lays all of his fingers on the piece of paper and looks at me first.

"You have some good news," he smiles – a beautiful, warming smile. "You are pregnant with twins."

Martin whoops and Noam, the most taciturn man I've ever known, covers his eyes with his hands and blows out a long breath that seems to be equal parts fear and elation.

"I love you Noam! I love you Nat!" Martin says and I can hear him popping the cork on a bottle of something.

"I am a daddy," Noam says and he looks like a four-year-old boy trapped in the body of a powerlifter. I look at the happiness emanating from the laptop and the iPad and tell myself that I did that. I created that happiness.

"Why did you say it was interesting?" I ask.

"Ahhh, ok." Dr Ranjit says. "You must not panic, but we need to start treating you for something called toxoplasmosis. I also need to take more bloods today and I'd feel better if we could get you a scan. Nothing serious, just routine."

"What!?" Martin screams and I see Noam switch into business mode.

"Say that again. What's this thing?"

"It's okay," Dr Ranjit says. "There is no need to panic. Natalie's blood results show that she has an infection called toxoplasmosis. Have you felt tired, or ill at all? Any fever?"

"Nothing," I say.

"It's very unusual that we would pick it up at this stage, but we're testing you for nearly everything under the sun at the moment."

"Will it hurt the babies?" I ask, a second before Martin does.

"We don't know is the truthful answer, but we have lots of medications that we can direct at this parasite to keep it from doing harm. I'd like to do another blood test and then start you on an antibiotic that will protect you and the babies."

"I don't care about me, protect the babies."

"Parasite! Oh my God! Oh Noam!" Martin starts to get louder and the pitch of his voice is getting higher. "Get me a plane Noam, I'm on my way to the airport. Natalie Cross, do not do *anything,* do not go *anywhere* and I will be with you in two hours." Martin disappears from the screen and briefly reappears to grab his phone and then he's gone again. The laptop stays open filming a blank wall of the house.

"What is this parasite?" Noam asks, his voice is serious and flat.

"Well, it's a very tiny thing, about a thousandth of a centimetre, if you can imagine that. It's also very, very common. Some estimates say that up to 70% of the world's population has this parasite in them already, so it is normal. Our only concern is when pregnant mothers are exposed to it. Sometimes it can cause problems for the children."

"What problems?" Noam asks.

"Babies can be born smaller, or pre-term. Sometimes it has an impact on the eyes of the foetus. But sometimes it has no impact at all and we can give you medicines to keep those risks at bay. Let's not get ahead of ourselves, we need to keep calm and follow good medicine, yes?"

"Doctor Ranjit, I want you to listen to me. We will do anything, *anything*, that our babies need. My husband will be with you soon, but I say this to you now: whatever it takes to make these babies safe, yes? If you have to bring in specialists, I will get them to you this moment. Do you understand?"

"Of course," Dr Ranjit says.

"How do you get it?" I ask.

"Well, it can come from undercooked meats. Or contact with soil."

"She is vegan," Noam replies as if he can rationalise the situation away.

"Have you been in contact with any cats recently?" Dr Ranjit asks.

I think about sitting on the hot marble steps next to the fountain, breathing in the unfamiliar scents of the Indian air and feeling the heat of the sun, two kittens weaving between my legs as I dip the runt in the fountain to wash it clean.

Chapter 7

10th April 2021
8 months, 6 days after

Mum is pumping up a tyre with an old hand pump. I can't remember her ever having a bike, so this bike must have been dredged from another part of my subconscious. Maybe it's figurative and the bike actually represents Vietnam, or the works of Beethoven. If I keep my eyes closed, I can still see her looking at me with a deadpan expression as she pumps the tyre up. I slither open one eye and let the world pull me away from the dream. I pat the bed around me to try and find my leg. I can still hear the psh-psh-psh noises of the pump.

"I have to fix the bike pump," I say out loud and the sound of my words wakes me fully.

The pump noises continue though and I lift my head and look around. In the dim light of the bridge, I can see Brown is out of her nest of clothes and she's lying flat with her belly on the dimpled metal floor. She's staring straight at me with sad eyes and from her breathing she seems to be in pain. I flick the lamp on so I can see her properly. She blinks at the light but continues to stare at me and I finally understand that the noise is her panting.

"Hey girl, what's the matter? Are you ok?"

I'm fully awake now and pulling my leg on. Her only response is to blink at the light and continue panting. I look around and notice that she's dragged a number of items from her nest over to the bank of equipment next to the captain's chair. She's created a smaller version of the nest in the recess under the desk, where the chair fits in.

"Is this it? Is it happening? Oh, man. I thought we had more time!"

Adrenaline pumps through my system. It's too soon. *My Dog Is Having A Dog!* said that it would be around nine weeks until the full labour. As it is, Brown's only been pregnant for just over a month. This is bad. I think it's bad. I don't know, maybe it's not bad. I scoot over to her and see that she's actually smushing her belly against the floor. I wonder if she's too hot and quickly head over to get her water bowl. I should probably put some trousers on. I carefully lay the water next to Brown and she sniffs absently at it and then lays her head on the floor. For the first time since burying the bones of the child I find a prayer on my lips, a fervent hope that Brown will be ok. I can't lose my dog. Don't take my dog from me. Make her pups safe. Amen.

Even though I've read it enough to have memorised it, I go and find *My Dog Is Having A Dog!* and read through the checklist of things that I need to do. Again, it's very clear that the essence of the advice is to do nothing and keep well out of the way. Dogs aren't used to having midwives tell them what position to adopt, or to leap in and take the pain of birth away. They have a deep instinctual knowledge of how to give birth. All the same, it's agonising to think that my friend is in pain and that anything I do would only make things worse. The book doesn't say about what to do if your dog starts to labour prematurely, and yet there are two whole pages on how to name the puppies. I have nothing to do and the energy to do anything.

"Do you want music?" I ask and Brown continues to pant. I take that as a yes.

She seems so small lying on the floor. Just a dot really. Her black and tan coat shines in the low light of the lamp. I see her as a puppy, with her stubbier nose between large triangular ears, one pricked up and one lolling over. In front of my eyes, she morphs into her adult form, her ears folded perfectly, her snout longer and toothier. God, I love this dog. I can't help the sudden rush of tears, the sheer fucking unfairness that I won't get to help her any more than this. The idea that I can't do the one thing I know I can do – keep my dog and her puppies safe. Brown stops panting to look at me and looks worried. I stop crying. The very least I can do is help her now. I'm here now and that's all I can do. I can be a positive voice.

"It's all good Brown, you're doing great. I love you. You're a winner."

I go and find the mini tape player that I rescued from one of the cabins when we first came aboard. Initially, I thought it was weird that tapes still existed but then I realised that out at sea it might not always be possible to get a decent WiFi signal, and that a rough sea could cause a CD to skip. There was something quite lovely about the reassurance of opening one of the cases and removing the bulky tape, formal as a miniature book, and lodging it upside-down in the player. It's a technology from another time, but then that's true of all technology now. I watch the reels of the tape turn and see the thin brown plastic strip move from one side to the other. The gentle sounds of ABBA fill the room. Brown resumes her panting, which I take as a good sign. At least she's breathing. The album is a series of covers and a tender male voice I can't place is singing a soft, heart-breaking version of Knowing Me, Knowing You. Singing along on the "Ah-has" just makes me want to cry all over again so I shut up.

I fast forward the tape and it lands in the middle of a rockier version of Dancing Queen. I turn the volume down and place it on the floor. I head to the bathroom and piss quickly. Then I put some trousers on and go and collect the bag of labour items that I've started to gather. These include several rolls of kitchen towel and a pair of razor-sharp scissors from the kitchen. The book says that Brown will probably chew through her own umbilical cord, but if she doesn't then I need to be ready to cut it. Unhelpfully, it doesn't tell you where or how to do that, but I'm hoping that if I'm called upon to do so then it will be obvious. Maybe it's too much to hope that there will be a dotted line and a tiny picture of scissors imprinted on the cord itself. I also have a bottle of water and some hot dog sausages in case she gets hungry. In a show of understanding I even fetch Bear, who has been discarded on the bed, and bring it over to Brown.

Brown gets to her feet and wobbles over to the breakaway nest she's created next to the captain's chair. I crawl over with her and help her to settle in. She bares her teeth when I run my hand lightly over her side, but she graciously accepts me rubbing my thumb over the crown of her head. She even momentarily closes her eyes and I loop the pattern over and over, stroking her head in a long sweep from her eyes to the top of her head and over her ears, smoothing them down. She feels hot, but I can't tell if that's because she's still panting. Every ten minutes or so she stands up and turns around a few times but then settles back down. After an hour of this pattern repeating, everything starts getting a bit more intense and the next time she stands up she effectively launches herself at the nest, scrabbling around among the various t-shirts and towels. There's lots of exasperated sighs and restless panting followed by a sudden decision that this still isn't the right spot and another readjustment.

After a couple of hours of this I realise that my calf is cramping, so I stand and walk around the bridge trying to stretch it out. The tape has come to an end so I eject it and turn it over. The scrawled writing on the other side says "*Chronic Town – R.E.M*" so I put that on and a jangly, looping guitar and solid bass drum plays out. The windows show the day's first slivers of early light, and the snow is still coming down. I've never known a period of snow like it – it's like a giant duvet is being draped over the world. On sections of the railing across the canal it seems to be about a foot high and I imagine the ship being slowly buried, never to be seen again. I return to my position next to Brown, but drag enough of my own duvets and pillows over so that I can at least make myself comfortable. After the initial panic, the adrenaline caused by Brown's premature labour has worn off and I'm left trying to keep my eyes open. After all, if the book says that the best thing I can do is stay out of the way, maybe my proximity is even holding things back? I'd pay a hundred thousand pounds to speak to a vet right now. I build up a tower of cushions so that I'm supported in a seated position right next to Brown and reach out and touch her snout.

"Good girl, you're doing great. I'm so proud of you."

We pass the remainder of the night in this way. Brown panting and jostling to find comfort. I feed her half a sausage and give her some water, but after a few laps she's not interested. I sip at a bottle of water myself and do what I can to help, which is precisely nothing. To try and keep myself awake I absent-mindedly pull at the drooping bingo wings that sit under my arms like an empty scrotum. I pull the skin around my arm and bicep and think about fajitas. As I'm letting my mind wander, I lay my head back against the cushions. I close my eyes so that I can focus more on the continued panting Brown is doing. I let this narrative play out in my head. She's fine. It's good. I'm here for her and she'll alert me if she needs me. I'm staying out of the way and that's the right thing to do.

"Good girl, you're a very good, good girl. You're the best girl."

I open my eyes and it's so light that it feels like that moment I've heard people talk about on a plane journey, when you ascend through the clouds and the world outside is just whiteness. I realise that I can no longer hear panting. I sit bolt upright and crack the top of my head into the desk above. I cry out and moan, "Fucccccccccckkkkk!" as I rub my head and hiss through gritted teeth. I look around and I can't see Brown. I forget my head and look around. There's a brown and black lump in her previous nest on my bed and I realise she must have relocated while I was sleeping. Did I sleep through it all? They're here! With my heart in my mouth, I scoot excitedly across the floor to her. She is sleeping and her body is curled around something that is attached to her belly, I carefully peep over the top of her body and there, nestled in the heart of comfort, is Bear. Confused, I tap at Brown and she rolls over and I swear she smiles at me.

"Heyyyy, little mother, where are they?"

Brown stretches and flexes her spine, a ripple of muscular relief shuddering along her small body. I notice that already her weight seems to have dropped. I spin around and look under my feet, suddenly terrified that I might be squashing one of the puppies. How the hell could I have slept through their birth!

"Hey girl – where are the puppies?"

Brown settles herself back into the bed and surrounds Bear with all of her maternal warmth. I stand up so, so carefully and start to look around the bridge. All the doors are shut firm, so I know that they're in here somewhere. I walk to the far wall and start a forensic search of the bridge. I lift up chairs. I carefully shake out blankets and duvets. I size up the gap between the side of the fridge and the units to see if they could have lodged themselves in there. After ten minutes of fruitless searching Brown joins me and starts to sniff around.

"Where are they? Find them Brown."

She gets a scent of something and follows her nose which dances across the floor. She heads back over towards the captain's chair and I wonder if I could have missed a puppy in my search of that area. Brown seems excited so I follow her and watch as she noses through the secondary nest before teasing a small thumb of sausage from the blanket and eating it. She turns and heads straight back to the original nest and cleans Bear before coiling herself around it once more.

I'm perplexed. I check the clock to see that it's mid-morning. I slept for nearly four hours. Somehow in that time Brown has birthed and misplaced an entire litter of puppies. Is it possible that she didn't give birth and that she's still in labour? I squat next to her and gingerly smooth the hair on the side of her body, expecting her to bite me. She turns slightly, not bothering about being touched now. As she rolls over, I see her teats are much less pronounced. I even pick up Bear and gently squeeze it to make sure that a puppy hasn't somehow magically been absorbed into it. Brown gives a jump when Bear shouts: "I NEED A HUG!"

I pace around the bridge sipping at a bottle of water, trying to deconstruct what has happened. Crazy thoughts begin to surface: maybe she ate them? Maybe I ate them? Did they eat each other? But then there would be blood? And at least one really fat puppy sitting there, licking its lips. None of it makes any sense! I sit in the captain's chair and spin, watching the vista of Trafford blur past. After 30 minutes I conclude that the only logical answer is that there are no puppies, and that there never were. Brown again nudges me, clearly wanting food, but I ignore her and she goes and fetches a ball from under one of the cabinets. She drops it at my feet and sits staring at me.

I stand, slip my boots on, pull my Mammut jacket around my shoulders and let myself out of the bridge, pulling the door shut behind me before my Velcro dog can follow me out. The unseasonal wintry air is painful on my bare face, so I pull the coat collar up. I feel my stomach flip and know that it signifies yet more diarrhoea is on its way. I wrap my arms around myself and stomp along the bridge. The snow is thick but after a few laps I beat a path down. I follow my own footsteps trying to work out what happened in the night. The freezing air dries my lips and I lick them until they chap and I taste blood. I'm not wearing gloves and the skin on the back of my hands dries out.

Every time I pass the door, I can see Brown waiting patiently, wondering what I'm doing. I start to get irritated with her. The point is that I don't know what I'm doing.

I'm lost. I'm hopelessly lost and alone. My big dumb fucking plan was to equip Brown and her puppies with as much of a head start as I can give her in this fucked-up world and go and die quietly in the manner of my choosing. But now I can't even do that because there are no fucking puppies! What am I supposed to do? I'm going to be dead soon and Brown is going to be entirely alone. I am abandoning the one thing I love to a lifetime of loneliness. I just know from her vacant, loyal face that she's going to Greyfriars Bobby me. She'll sit by my corpse and slowly waste away not wanting to leave my side. I slide open the bridge door and she bounds out, her earlier cumbersome form reduced by half already.

"What the fuck, Brown?" she looks at me and steps back slightly, caught off-guard by my anger.

"What the fuck? What are you doing? You were pregnant and now you're not? How does that happen? What kind of weird joke is that?" Brown mutely barks at me. I turn my attention to the sky.

"Or is this more of your fuckery, you voyeur? Is this some Book of Job shit? Are you testing me to see how much I can take before I break? Well, I fucking break! I'm done! What do you want me to do? What can I give that you haven't already stolen?"

I'm trembling with anger and Brown steps back inside the bridge. I stalk in after her and, overcome with the need to express this fury, I march over to the bed and pick Bear up from the nest. I storm back out onto the bridge, walk to the edge of the platform and draw my arm back. I fling the ratty little shitbag as hard as I can over the side of the ship. It flies far, far away into the snow, and as I turn back, I can just hear a muffled voice emanating from the snowdrift, and I know exactly what it's saying. I need one too.

Chapter 8

28*th* July 2020
7 days before

Martin looks entirely too pleased with himself. He's been in a foul mood ever since I told him that I was moving out of the penthouse in Beetham Tower and back to Middleton, but his demeanour has shifted abruptly and it's making me suspicious.

Martin wanted me to stay with him until I was ready to give birth. The flat here is amazing – if anything it's even more stunning than the compound in the South of France. There's an actual olive grove in the atrium area, there's also a splash pool and entirely too many floor-to-ceiling windows. As a novelty it's fun to get a bird's-eye view of the city, but you really don't need to feel like you're flying above the city while you're eating cornflakes.

I packed my bags a couple of days ago and told Martin it was a done deal, and that he couldn't stop me. I promised to use the Uber Platinum and keep taking my meds, but told him he had to let me make my own decisions. He seems to have come around to the idea, he even sounded happy about something. I've seen his weasel grin at least three times this morning and that's why I'm worrying.

Martin is about 5'4" and weighs about 50kg wet through. Every year when we were younger, Dad would pick him up and pretend to put him on the top of the Christmas tree, until one year in my early teens I challenged him on it and said it wasn't nice to make fairy jokes and I didn't think he should do it anymore. I've never seen Dad so confused. He had no idea that Martin was gay. He really did have the absolute worst gaydar.

"He carried a cane, Dad! Did that not give you a clue?"

"I thought he had polio!"

I told Martin about it, of course, and he thought it was hilarious. In his Fashion and Fabrics class, Martin made Dad a doll version of himself for the Christmas tree, complete with tiny velvet jacket and cane. Dad proudly put him on top of the tree every year from then on. It's just not Christmas until someone makes the first "I can't wait to get Little Martin out..." joke. We didn't do it this year.

"Come on! Leaver's lunch! Ten minutes until exfil!" Martin shouts and disappears to further primp himself. I don't know why he's chivvying me. I already have everything in my small suitcase and I'm the one waiting for him.

Contrary to how puny he looks, Martin is one of the most dangerous people I know and it's mostly because of that weasel grin. That's the smile he does when he's contemplating something that most people would consider clinically insane, but for Martin it's just yet another instance of decency, morality and legality all being concepts for other people to consider. Being with Noam and Noam's money had just moved him to the next level. Martin likes to tell the story that on their first date, Noam gave him a psychiatric evaluation that his company used on their mercenary recruits. It was all just for fun, but Martin went along with it. Noam submitted the evaluation and it came back marked as IMMEDIATELY TERMINATE and even prompted the HR Director to phone Noam to ensure that he never thought about recruiting this person. Noam and Martin had married six months later.

I take one last look around the apartment. The most beautiful thing about the raised view of Manchester is the comfort of the Pennines to the East. It reminds you how small Manchester is in the grand scheme of things. When you are at street level it's easy to feel that the place has sprawled in the last couple of decades, but when you see that the whole thing is just a little soup of buildings and people slopping around at the bottom of a big green bowl, it's calming somehow. I try and spot Middleton off to the northeast and walk around the flat until I can see Saint James to the south of the city. I re-orientate myself between home and hospital – where I'm from and where I belong. I cup my hand under my belly. The babies aren't showing yet but I still feel puffy like I've been eating nothing but pizza and muffins for weeks.

"Look kids, that's Manchester: the best city in the world."

"Lunch! Lunch! Lunch!" Martin calls and flies in grabbing my hand, shocking me. "Oh, my babies! I'm so sorry, did I scare you?"

"Come on, I'm starving."

"Have you taken your meds?"

"*Yes* Martin of course!"

"Sorry! Sorry! I just like to remind you."

"However will I cope without you, Mart?"

We walk hand-in-hand over to the lift door, a double-width gold-embossed monstrosity, and Martin taps the call button and runs his other hand over the door's pattern.

"I love this door. I couldn't care less for the whole flat, but there's something truly sexy about a giant lift door. That's when you know you've made it."

"You should come round to the porter's entrance at the hospital, they've got bigger lift doors than this."

"Natalie Cross, I can't believe you think you're going to tempt me, a happily married man and father-to-be, with an offer to come over the porter's entrance, what kind of homosexual do you take me for? I won't rise to it!" The lift dings its muted tone and the doors open. "Going down?" he asks me with a pantomime wink and wheels my bag into the lift.

In the lift Martin turns to look out over the city, but I shut my eyes and hold onto the handrail and once more mourn the loss of my equilibrium. Since the diagnosis I take three different types of antibiotics to protect the babies from the parasite. Dr Ranjit has been clear that there isn't any real danger to me, but that they have to medicate me for the twins' safety. I'm more than happy to take the drugs if it helps them, but the side effects include wicked vertigo. Frankly, that alone kills the idea of living in a building where I have to go up and down in a glass lift. I didn't tell Martin that was part of the reason, because he'd have just bought me a flat on the first floor and complained when I didn't want to move in.

I couldn't explain, but I just want to go home. I want a cup of tea and to shout at Rick for eating all the KitKats. I want a normal life for as long as I can get it. Pregnancy seems to rewrite your relationship with time. Days go by slowly, but months pass at a sprint. Anyway, I could tell that Martin was pining to be back in France with Noam. Noam had a few outstanding issues with law enforcement in the UK so he can only fly privately into the UK and he doesn't like to stay more than a day – so, by leaving the penthouse it frees both of us to go where we need to be.

"Are you going to vomit?" Martin asks as the lift silently drops towards the street below.

"Not unless you talk about something gross," I reply.

"Hey! I'm being gold star nice to you since you now house my children. I can't vouch for my behaviour after nine months has elapsed though. Would you like a peppermint?"

I open one eye and see that he is holding out a pink and white striped sweet bag.

"No, I'm fine. Thank you." Just two more floors and then the sense of falling and horror will stop.

"They're really nice."

"Martin, I don't want a peppermint, none of those sweets are vegan anyway."

"Ok, we're going to have to stop and get some more because I've run out."

"Fine, I'll even buy them for you, just shut up about peppermints."

The lift doors open and we make our way outside. Walking onto the street is like opening the oven door. My coat is instantly too hot and too tight and I take it off. Martin takes it and folds it over his arm. I just can't get comfortable in my own skin. Seeing my discomfort, Martin hails a taxi and directs it to the Arndale Centre. The driver raises his eyebrows when he hears that we want to go less than a mile and Martin affects a horrified posh military voice and says, "Don't raise your eyebrows at me, cabbie. I'll have you know I'm a lieutenant general in the

Queen's army! This lady is pregnant with mine and my husband's babies and needs protecting!"

Martin throws in a few braying "Baaaaaas!" for good measure. The driver looks at us with contempt and clicks a mysterious button on the meter, which is clearly some sort of arsehole tax as the fare starts jumping up.

I settle back into the seats and feel my bare arms meeting the tacky, black vinyl. Martin fiddles with the air con and a stream of cooler air hits my face. Vertigo and nausea dance in the background.

"How are you about your dad now?" Martin asks. I feel my abdomen tighten as dread squirms inside me.

"I don't know."

"I just noticed you don't talk about him much. I miss your old man. I never got to take him to Heaven. Remember he said he'd come with me when he was 64. I was going to get him laid and everything."

"It's strange, I know I miss him, but I don't feel like I'm able to say it. Not that I don't have permission, more that I just can't shape the words." I remember the greyed-out checkbox on the form. I know it's me.

"Hey, did you ever get that laptop fixed? Remember when I was at yours and I shut it and it broke?"

"I don't know sweetie, I think Noam took it, so maybe?"

"Let me know how much it cost and I'll get it back to you."

"Yes, of course I will. I will absolutely garnish the salary of an NHS hero nurse."

"That's not the point, I don't want to take advantage of you. I'd feel bad."

"Well, how about you give me the gift of carrying my children, keeping them safe always and we'll call it quits?" He holds out his hand and I shake it.

"Sure. I don't think I've asked you yet: how do you feel about being a dad?"

Martin sits back in the seat and looks at me, mock-seriously.

"I'm undecided. Noam has made the role of the Giddy Daddy his own and is signing up for Mumsnet and posting new-dad questions. The man has opinions on nappies, Nat. He video called me from a warzone with questions about whether we should start a nappy library, because there isn't one near us. I'm not sure what role that leaves me. I think I have to be the realist. For someone whose line of work involves bloodshed Noam can be worryingly flighty at times. I guess I'll be the stern disciplinarian, nodding cordially at the children once a year on their birthdays. A firm handshake to console them when Noam steps on a landmine in a decade or so. What sort of mum are you going to be?"

"I don't know. I'm still trying to figure out how this works. I've been reading about it and the surrogate people said that we need to draw clear lines about where the relationships begin and end – it's not just important for us, but for the children too."

"We'll figure it out. We love you. We love each other. We love the children. I'm not sure what else they need."

I let the conversation fade out and look at the bustling streets. The crowds are thick and all I want to do is go home and sit naked next to a fan. We leave the cab and run into the Arndale, hoping that it has air conditioning. It doesn't. An atmosphere of super-heated grumpiness seems to hang about in the corridors and shops. We see two women outside Carphone Warehouse screaming into each other's faces. One of them is gripping the hand of her distraught toddler, but the woman looks more like she is going to use her as a weapon than console her. Martin hums *What The World Needs Now Is Love*.

"Can't we get the sweets later?" I ask.

"Nope! Just round this corner, it's the best pick-n-mix in the city – honestly," Martin replies.

The main thoroughfare of shops and cafés give way to the market and Martin squeezes my hand as we walk past the different foods, including a fishmongers which makes me gag. This is going to be a long eight months.

"There it is!" he squeals in excitement, pointing at a bog-standard pick-n-mix stall, shelves of drawers loaded with various sweets and small plastic scoops to fill your bags. A bored-looking woman sits behind a till scrolling through her phone – Martin weasel grins, picks up a pink and white striped bag and fills it with a few peppermints.

"Do you want owt?" he asks.

"I'm fine, thanks."

"Ok, this should do us then," he says and takes the bag containing barely a handful of mints over to the till and drops it on the scales.

"You're under the minimum weight, add some more," the assistant says without looking up.

"It's ok, I don't mind paying the minimum," Martin says.

"Your choice," the lady says.

"Oh my God! Emily?! Emily Reeves!" Martin squeals with sudden delight. I look at the lady and her face looks faintly familiar. Her hair is bleached blonde, but there sits Emily Reeves – Queen Bitch of our school year. She made our lives hell for years, for no other reason than she could, and we were there.

"Look Natalie, it's Emily Reeves, you remember, Emily from *school*! She was suspended for getting drunk on the ferry to Flanders. You know – *Emily*!"

"Oh yeah, hi Emily," I say and look at Martin, the weasel grin is smeared all over his face. Emily looks taken aback that she's been found here in her apron, striped to match the sweet bags. Martin passes over a fifty-pound note and it is immediately obvious to me that this is all planned and scripted – at least from Martin's side.

"I can't take fifties," Emily says.

"Oh, that's all I've got. Nat, do you have any smaller notes?"

"I've not got my purse – I can pay on my phone if you've got wireless?"

"No wireless, sorry."

"Oh, never mind. I'll pop them back," Martin says and before Emily can object, he upends the bag back into the peppermint drawer. "Wow! So, how've you been Emily? What are you up to these days? It says you're an entrepreneur on Facebook, so do you do this on the side?"

"I'm not on Facebook," Emily answers with suspicion.

"Huh! I'm fairly sure I've been on your profile. I can't remember who sent it to me. I'll have a look through my emails. Yeah, there were some posts about your new business and some pictures of your children and their various fathers. You live close by in those flats. I'm sure it was on Facebook, I can't have got all that from my crystal ball, or from a team of people going through your bins!"

"It's not under my name and it's private. Who sent it to you?"

"Oh! I'll let you know who posted it to me and you can let them know! Anyway, so great to see you - so is the sweetie work on top of your real business?"

"This is my real business."

"Oh! I'm sorry. No. It's great. You've done really great starting this business. Emily Reeves, wow! Look Natalie, stand in here and I'll get a selfie."

Martin pulls me into him and turns away from Emily and holds his phone aloft and takes a photo, Emily is squirming with discomfort in the background.

"How's yer dad Nat?" Emily asks. "I heard he'd been in some sort of crash – is that what did that?" she juts her chin out. I turn and walk off. Martin thrives in this sort of awkward situation, but to my mind, it always ends up with nastiness rather than justice. Horrible people stay horrible.

There is a fistfight going on next to a mobile phone stall in the market and a customer sweeps all the products off the stall onto the floor. I skirt around the commotion, turn left and follow the exit signs out onto the pavement by the bus station. In the shade, I take a few breaths while a whisper of cool air chases down the street. I wait briefly for Martin, who pushes through the heavy bronze and glass door.

"Wow! Emily Reeves – who would have thought we'd find her grubbing around in a pick-n-mix stall. She always seemed to have it so together at school. Remember when she poured paint over your coursework just before you had to hand it in?"

"I take it you knew she was there?"

"Of course I knew. You should have hung around, I've got a load of the sexts she's been sending to Jeremy Todd – remember him? They hooked up at a school reunion and have been having an affair for six months – she's told him she might be pregnant, but she's lying – she had a test at the family health clinic and it came back negative. She does have chlamydia though."

"Jesus Martin, Noam gives you access to all this information and you use it to spy on people you hated from school, couldn't you bring down a corrupt dictator or something?"

"That's Noam's job! Mine is printing out pictures of Jeremy Todd's cock to amaze you!"

He holds up a creased picture which looks like a walnut whip.

"That's not a real picture."

"The realest."

"Why would anyone send that photo to anyone other than a qualified doctor?"

"Men are pigs, they think everyone is amazed with their curly tails."

"That looks more like a snout."

"Or a trotter. Come on, now we've had fun we can go for lunch and shop! Maybe there'll be more surprises on this day of days! There are too many beautiful things I have to buy you, I don't know when I'll see you next, so this is a baby shower. I insist on you having beautiful things. Oh, wait up," Martin pulls his phone out and clicks a button on the side, he taps in a number and dials.

"Police, please. Yes hi, I'd like to report something weird. I've just bought some pick-n-mix from the market stall in the Arndale – it's called "Give Me Something Sweet" – well, I bought some and I've just found a load of pills among the sweets. It looks like drugs of some sort. I don't know, that's not something I do. It's yellow and has a smiley face on it. I didn't know who to report it to. No, I don't want to give my name, I'm no grass."

He hangs up and smiles that weasel grin.

"'Vengeance is in my heart, death in my hand.' Titus Andronicus, darling! Onward to lunch!"

Chapter 9

10th April 2021
8 months, 6 days after

Of course, I go and get the stupid thing.

No sooner has Bear left my hand and started to arc through the air than the wanton, pointless cruelty hits me. For a horrible moment, Brown runs as if she is going to leap straight from the bridge in Bear's direction, but I grab her by the back legs and sweep her into the bridge, slamming the door shut. The fear of what almost happened slaps me and I know I have to put it right. I tramp down the outer stairs, pulling the coat tighter around me and feeling guilt corrode me. It takes me twenty minutes of calculating trajectory and scrabbling around in the snow to find Bear. It's sat in a comfy divot of snow staring up at the sky, its one remaining eye watching the flakes of snow settle on its body. If I'd left it much longer then I probably wouldn't have found it. I brush the snow off and look around.

"Sorry," I murmur and kiss Bear quickly on the head.

"Fuck you doing, pal?"

I turn to see two wraths approaching from down the towpath.

They're about 30 metres away, but when they catch sight of me, they pick up their feet and start running in my direction. I turn and sprint towards the gangway. The snow is up to my knees and it's a simple footrace for who can get there first. My foot hits the bottom step of the gangway just as one of them is level with the stairs about five metres behind, while the other wrath is about 15 metres behind.

My knees pump as I climb up the stairs. I'm halfway up the first flight when I feel the steps judder as the closest wrath mounts the bottom step. Apart from Bear, I'm unarmed. As I hit the top of the stairs, I cast around for anything I can use as a weapon. The only thing I can see is the gangway's control panel - a yellow rectangular box with three buttons marked Up, Down and Emergency Stop. I hit the Up button and turn to see the wrath about six steps from the top. At the press of the button, the entire staircase jerks upwards and he's pitched forward, smashing his face into the side of the corrugated steel.

"YOUS DO THAT FOR?" he screams at me through a mouth full of blood.

I press Down. There's another jerk, then a short scream from the dockside and I see that I've hit the other wrath as he walks under the steps. The nearest wrath still has a fingerhold, so I press Up and then Down several times, and gradually the wrath is shaken free, falling backwards, spinning over and over. I look over the edge and see that the wrath underneath has been pulped by the steps. The one I dislodged is now lying at the bottom, slowly and awkwardly trying to get to his feet. Something about the awful angle of his shoulder makes me think it must be dislocated. I hit the Up button again and with a whine, the stairway rattles up until the bottom step is about three metres in the air. Then there's a loud clunk from the pulley housing and a smell of burning. The stairs stay rooted in suspension above the remaining wrath, refusing to move.

I feel more tired than I've ever been in my life. I'm shivering from the cold and dizzy from the adrenaline. I tuck Bear under my arm and make my way back up to the bridge. I'm frozen and broken and I just want to get warm, or drunk, or both. I open the door and hold Bear out in front of me as a peace offering, and it is promptly seized by a fretful-looking Brown, who appears at my feet. She steals her precious child away, so that she can examine it for defects. Well, new defects. All things considered, it doesn't look like the fall has done it much harm, but I wasn't sure about how much harm it had done to Brown's feelings towards me. I pull on a jumper and thick socks and spend five minutes working blood and feeling back into my fingers and toes.

Once I've warmed up, I make my way to the galley downstairs and defrost a long strip of steak. The smear of watery blood it leaves across the white plate is enough to make me gag, but I hold my breath, sear it quickly in butter and chop it into thin strips, then return to the bridge with my bribe. Brown is angry, but she isn't "ignore steak"-angry. It's a poor apology for a shitty thing, but I stroke her back and whisper words of love and explanation while she eats and gradually the guilt reduces.

After she's eaten, she settles back on the bed and I sit in the captain's chair. I pour a large measure of rum into a dirty mug from the side and sip it, shuddering again as it goes down. After turning the problem over for a few hours, my conclusion is that I'm fucked. Brown's weird non-pregnancy changes everything. My whole approach was that if she had puppies, then she wouldn't be alone. She would have a purpose and she would be forced to go on whether I was there or not. I could focus on dying and I wouldn't feel so guilty about leaving her behind. What am I supposed to do now? By the time I finish the bottle of rum, I'm struck with the exhausting revelation that there is only one way forward.

I have to get better.

***

Even with a thick coating of snow obscuring most of the area, it is clear that something catastrophic happened at Trafford General Hospital. Some buildings are charred, whilst others are gutted almost entirely, leaving only their skeletal steel frames. Nothing inside the structures remain except for a lone office chair, sitting sentinel in a now-roofless room. The landscape leading up to the hospital shows a single giant furrow, ploughed from the car park diagonally across the site.

The drone's camera picks up the cause of the destruction at the southeast corner of the hospital complex – the huge grey wing of a plane stretches straight up 40 metres into the air like a shark's fin. I circle the wing and make out a gigantic oval engine, about the size of a Portacabin, on the ground. I pull the drone's control sticks and gain height. I watch the industrial units and roads of Trafford Park skim by, as the drone returns to the *Our Kid*. I pause to hover briefly over the M60, mesmerised in awe at the thin stretch of the road that holds the two sides of the motorway together. Up close it looks like the metal barrier of the central reservation is the only thing sustaining it. It resembles a dental brace pulling two gap teeth together.

There are two hospitals in Manchester that are big enough to have cancer-specialist departments. The big advantage of Trafford General Hospital is that my *Manchester A to Z* tells me it's only one and a half miles away from the *Our Kid*. But given that someone has parked a large plane there, that doesn't seem like it will be suitable. The reserve option is much better in one sense – Saint James is a world-famous cancer hospital. Unless it has also been destroyed then it's almost bound to have what I need to fight my cancer. The downside is that it's over six miles away. Six miles populated by hundreds of thousands of wraths, who would cure me of cancer by removing my entrails and throwing them in a skip. I sit at the chart tables in the bridge and plot my way, grid-by-grid, through the *A to Z* to try and figure out a route to the Saint James that's least likely to get us killed. I take the drone out on recce flights and push the range as far as I dare to get a better idea of how things look. The conclusion, once again, is that I'm fucked.

The issue is that the snow has rendered most routes virtually impassable. Roads such as the M60, which acts as an orbital around the city, would deposit me handily only a mile or so from the Saint James. However, the roads are buried in snow and choked with smashed vehicles. And, that's before we consider that spending my formative years as a shut-in means that I never learned to drive. I could probably figure it out with enough time and a clear head, but neither of those seems likely. The other factor is that my health is getting worse every day. The diarrhoea which has raged for a few weeks has now depleted me to the point where I find myself nodding off while sitting in a chair. I'm starting to look like a skeleton trapped in a deflated sumo suit. The only thing that I feel like I can eat are the weed custard creams, and they leave me so stoned that I'm a danger to myself. I could wait until the snow clears, but I don't know when that might happen.

I think I have a solution though.

***

As we walk down the steps of the *Our Kid* for the last time, I recognise that we would be dead if it weren't for this ship. It has fed us and sheltered us and I reach over and pat the side of the accommodation block in thanks. I edge nervously down the wobbling gangway and stand at the bottom of the steps as they bounce up and down. I reach over the side and hold Brown out as she silently barks and spins her feet in the air. I aim her at a deep drift of snow and drop her to the ground. She immediately bounces out of the drift and starts leaping around in the snow. I drop my gear and then turn and hang off the edge of the final step and drop down. There's no sign of the wrath who I knocked down the steps, and I try not to look at the body of the other wrath crushed underneath them. Brown starts to sniff at his blue-tinted face until I call her away.

I pass Bear to her from my pocket and she lifts him so I can inspect her golden offspring. I smile politely and say, "Stupid Bear, you're a real piece of shit" in an adoring voice. I look back at the ship and see the safety of the white tower with its cosy home on top and feel a strong urge to remain. *You have no choice*, I remind myself. The snow is up to above my knee and is so deep that Brown starts to look longingly at the steps back up to our home. As far as she's concerned, this is just another in a long line of baffling decisions from the human she's been lumbered with. I pick her up and place her in the red donut. It has a tough plastic floor, which I've covered with a few fleece blankets.

"You know, if mum had got me a husky, this would've been the other way around," I tell Brown. She drops Bear in the donut and stands her forepaws on the side so she can have a better view. We spend a few minutes walking in a circle next to the ship and by the time she's jumped out a couple of times and got lost in the snow she's learned that her role in this journey is to stay still. By the end of our practice, sweat is rolling down my face and I'm winded. Six miles feels impossible. I wonder if I can lighten the load at all but I'm only carrying essential items anyway: binoculars, three knives of varying sizes, the *A to Z*, the crowbar, some spare clothes, custard creams and weed. I've also got a sealed plastic bag of shotgun shells and more stashed in my coat pockets. I've got the flare gun in the backpack, and the shotgun is looped over my shoulder with the safety triple checked. The drone is folded into its travel bag with spare batteries and a controller. I'm as ready as I can be.

Brown is wearing a coat I made from the arm of one of the sailor's fleeces. The cuff is rolled back over her neck like an Elizabethan ruffle and her front feet are poking out of two holes I cut in the fabric. It took quite a lot of wrestling to get her into it, and to figure out how to poke her legs through the holes, but she seems quite content. It's certainly warm enough to stop her from shivering and it shouldn't carry too much water from the snow. I'm layered up in my snow gear and I'm wishing that I'd picked something more subtle. The loud orange of the coat and trousers might be good if you're trapped in an avalanche, but they're not so good if your main aim is to travel covertly. I wonder if I should go back and change but I just want to get started. If I don't go now, I might never leave.

Fortunately, the first leg of our journey is short and if everything goes to plan, this will be the hardest part. We head north away from the *Our Kid* and pick up a service road behind the hotel. The snow isn't quite as thick here, so I get up some speed and Brown learns that she can simply sit in her donut and look out over the side, which she seems to enjoy. Soon she's snatching at snowflakes and having a great time. The trees at the side of the road are brittle and loaded with snow and as we walk, an occasional branch cracks in the cold, which causes me to spin in fear and scrutinise the silent landscape, shotgun aimed along the treeline. After a mile, the path rises and turns right past a Chinese pagoda, where I stop to kick the snow off my boots and catch my breath.

Already I can feel my stomach growling at me – hunger and shards of a wind-like pain mix in my guts, and I sit on the bench at the edge of the pagoda and wait for it to pass. Brown sees ground uncovered by snow and skips out of the donut and sniffs around. I whistle her back as she starts to investigate the water of the canal. She finds something under one end of the bench inside the pagoda and starts to roll in it. Before I can reach her, she's already smeared fox scat into every centimetre of her new wardrobe and across most of her head. The stench is eye-watering and I get my hands covered in it, as I strip her off and rub her coat through the snow, dragging it roughly against the dry wood walls. It still smells, but she seems content enough when I force her back into it. Dogs are weird.

We are at a crossroads. To the left of us is the Barton Swing Aqueduct which, brings the Bridgewater Canal across the Manchester Ship Canal. To the right, the Bridgewater Canal leads in a straight line across the south of the city and should get us to Stretford by afternoon if we're lucky. Just beyond Stretford we can turn onto the River Mersey where it crosses the canal and if we follow it upstream then we should be at the Saint James before nightfall. I shoulder my backpack and throw some chicken pieces into the donut. Brown pounces on it, and we set off down the towpath.

I'm so alert that I feel my flesh creeping with every *cawww* of the crows that are roosting in the top of the nearby trees. They're already accustomed to a newly silent world and this assault of orange moving through their landscape naturally offends them. One flies down and lands on the first bridge across the canal to watch us more closely as we pass. At this point, the canal is about twenty metres wide and is just about resisting the weather's attempts to freeze it solid. In places, small islands of ice have formed a connection with the bank and the water near the towpath has a thicker, slushy quality. I wonder how long it would be before the whole waterway is frozen solid. Under the first bridge, some ancient graffiti declares, "SONYA IS A SLAG, SLUT, ETC." The author's inability to complete the thought disturbs me – did she dictate it to a P.A.? Just beyond that, I find what I've been looking for. I spotted it on my reconnaissance of the area – a red and blue barge, around 60 feet long, with *El Gracias* picked out in ornate letters on the side.

I spin around and check the area for wraths. I can see into a fenced warehouse area on the other side of the canal and there is a pile of bodies mounded in one corner, but no moving wraths that I can see. I unsling the shotgun and throw more chicken into Brown's donut with a hushed command to stay. She shakes the flakes of snow off her head and her ears slap against the side of her face.

The barge is moored to a weathered metal ring sunk into the towpath, I lift my legs over the rope and step onboard. I place the tip of the crowbar in between the sealed steel shutters at the rear of the boat, but as I'm about to lever it open, I notice that there's a tiny thumb hook at the bottom, which I nudge open with my boot, and the door swings back. I duck into the gloomy interior, shotgun first. As I go down the steps, I thwack my head on the entrance to the boat. Obviously, being 6'4" is not ideal for narrowboats. A smell of rot permeates the cabin and as I work my way through the bedroom, bathroom and kitchen it's clear the smell is coming from the gooey remnants in the chair next to the cold log burner. I whistle Brown aboard and she sniffs around while I search for keys, but I find nothing. I even poke through the remains on the chair. I look at the *El Gracias'* control panel. After 10 minutes of chasing pipes and cables, I've got the sort of headache I get when looking at an Escher drawing. I conclude that I'm not going to be able to magically spark the boat into life and that we should move on.

Brown takes some encouraging to go outside again. Despite the spectral mess in the lounge area, she thinks that any version of inside is preferable to going outside and getting snowed on again. I can't say I blame her, but Saint James is calling. Brown leaps into her donut and gently licks the snowflakes that have started to bury Bear. It duly responds with a "I NEED A HUG!" that sounds across the desolate scene. Stupid Bear. I quickly sling the donut's towline around my shoulders and lean into the slight wind that blows along the canal.

I slip and slide through the thick snow, trying my best not to pitch over and fall into the water. After about half an hour there's a car park on the far side of the canal, where I can see the backs of several lorries. Beyond the car park is a long avenue of snow-covered pine trees. On my side of the canal, the towpath opens into an entrance way, which reveals a glimpse of the ruined side of the Trafford Centre dome. It's galling that we've been going for this long and only moved such a tiny distance. Fortunately, there are another two narrowboats moored here.

The first barge, *Libby's Dream*, is empty and looks like it's been ransacked. Cupboards stand open and a glimmering pool of oily liquid is ankle-deep throughout the boat. It smells like the fuel tank has ruptured and there's also a stench of some kind of gas. I can only stand the heady air for a few seconds before I have to get outside. The second boat is moored about ten metres further down the canal. It's called the *Lepanto* and it looks more promising from a quick glimpse at the exterior. Brown is fussing around on the towpath and she disappears into the bushes to sniff after some promising scent. I let her go, step aboard the *Lepanto* and use the crowbar to split the wooden rear doors open. A sudden piercing electronic scream cries out with whoops and dips. I realise I've found the only barge in the world with a burglar alarm. The crows burst upwards from the pine trees and I turn to see Brown scampering out of the bushes to see what's going on. A middle-aged man launches up through the dark interior and grabs at the barrel of the gun.

"Might have known! Might have known! Scallies!" he snarls, his round face purple with anger. His bald crown is surrounded by a long curtain of hair and his wild eyes are rimmed with red. He's much stronger than me and shoves the barrel of the gun up in the air with ease. He reaches past the gun, grabs hold of my face and squashes it. His fingernails rake down my cheek. Brown leaps up onto the boat and the man seethes – froth gathers between his lips. At this range, I can see that his teeth have grown yellow and mossy.

"No dogs on board!" he screams, and swings a leg at Brown who dodges back.

The gun barrel is now just next to his head and the only thing I can think to do is to pull the trigger. The blast is so loud that a puff of blood spills out from his ear and he screams, both hands grasping the side of his head. As he's off-balance I crouch down and force my shoulder into him. He hits the small rail that runs around the back of the boat and topples forward into the canal. He says something as he sinks, but with the alarm it's impossible to tell what that is.

"What do you think you're playing at? On the rob yeah?"

"Look at that big orange fuckwit! What are you supposed to be mate? A beacon?"

"YOU ARE DEAD!"

The voices ring out from the opposite side of the bank, but at least they are on the other side of the canal. But then I notice with a groan a few wraths are standing at the entrance to the car park on my side.

"You a space-hopper?" one of the wraths asks.

"SHUT THAT FUCKING RACKET OFF!"

"WHY ARE YOU BEEPING?" another cries.

The voices grow and I watch more wraths appear as I stand paralysed in deliberation. If I start now, I might be able to outrun them, but I don't think I could do it with all the gear and where would I go? Keeping my eyes on the ones nearest to me, I very deliberately step off the boat and walk to the donut. I pick up the slack towline and untie the mooring rope. I bodge together a knot between the two, figuring this will be quicker than unloading all the gear from the donut. I quickly push the donut into the canal and step back on board. I push Brown down the steps that lead inside the barge. Standing on the bank and leaning against *Lepanto* I manage to push us away from the side and into the middle of the canal.

The wraths are already on the towpath, and some of them try and make the leap to board us, but they either hit the side of the barge or fall short and plummet into the canal. Just inside the barge, there's a covered area and I see a control panel mounted on the wall. Gloriously, sitting in the ignition slot, are the boat's keys attached to a large cork ball. I turn the key round to "PRIME" and then to "RUN" and a red light flashes on the dashboard. Somewhere by my feet, there's a long, considered splutter and finally an engine turns over. The noise is thunderous, but it's drowned out by the rise and fall of the ongoing alarm.

I look up and see three wraths have managed to get on top of the barge by climbing on the front of the boat. As I look closer, I notice with dismay that the *Lepanto* is still attached to the towpath with a mooring rope at the front as well, which is holding us to the bank and threatening to give access to all of the wraths on the bank. I pull the throttle into full reverse and the water froths as the boat moves backwards, stretching the mooring rope to its maximum. There's a jolt as it reaches its full length and stops us in the canal. Two of the wraths on top stumble forward on the slick, snowy roof. I reload the shotgun and fire twice. The shot blasts out the kneecaps and shins of the wraths closest to me, who topple over screaming and pitch into the canal. The other one advances, so I reload and fire again.

The wail of the alarm continues to draw a larger crowd as the barge swings on the front mooring rope. It's clear I need to free us before we can go anywhere. I climb unsteadily onto the roof and crawl on all fours across the blood and snow until I drop into the little deck space at the front of the barge. The wraths on the Trafford Centre side of the canal surge forward and try to leap on board but we're two metres away and they fall into the water. I quickly use the knife at the end of the shotgun to hack through the rope. As the *Lepanto* is released with a ping, the boat is freed from the bank but without anything to tether it, it reverses until we crash with another jolt into the opposite bank. Four wraths who have gathered on the other bank leap onto the back of the boat and crowd towards the roof trying to make their way towards me.

As they climb on top, one of the wraths stands on the throttle and with a lurch the boat starts to speed forward, causing the wraths on top to wobble. I see where we are heading and quickly push through the two smaller doors at the front of *Lepanto* to get back inside. Inside I find a confused Brown frantically trying to work out what's going on. I snatch her up and push into the small bathroom in the middle of the barge just as the front of *Lepanto* rams into the side of *Libby's Dream* with a crunch and ignites the cocktail of fuels and fumes inside. A huge explosion sounds out and the force pushes open the sliding door of the bathroom where we are sheltering. My ears ring for several seconds and I push out of the bathroom to see what's going on. I run to the back of the barge and emerge next to the tiller. The wraths on top of the barge are gone and fire is raging at the front where we broadsided *Libby's Dream*.

The hundred wraths on the towpath have been beaten back in a circle from the inferno but start to advance again, unconcerned by the danger of the flames. While I reorientate myself, I realise that we're now facing in the direction we came from. If I don't turn us around, we'll end up in the Ship Canal, or worse – Runcorn. I pull back on the throttle and leave us idling in the middle of the Bridgewater as I try and think while the alarm sounds out. I pass through the inside of the boat and using a fire blanket from the kitchen, I smother the flames that are trying to take hold at the front of the *Lepanto*. Thanks to the snow the damage seems limited; the engine still works and as far as I can tell, we aren't taking on water.

On my way back to the tiller I search through the boat and can't find a box or a switch to deactivate the alarm, so I have to let it carry on ringing. By the time I've got the *Lepanto* turned around and not on fire anymore, I can just see the outline of the fox-shit-filled Chinese pagoda again. Two steps forward, three steps back. I position us in the middle of the canal and we chug as fast as we can past the throng of wraths on the towpath, whose number has tripled, attracted by the fire, noise and chaos. I remember the donut and pull the towline towards me and wrestle the donut out of the water and onto the barge's roof. I blow out a sigh of relief as I check and see that the rucksack is still there, but then with a panic, I realise that although the equipment survived, Bear is gone.

Chapter 10

4*th* August 2020
The day of the change

This weather is just bollocks – how long has this heat been going on now? Feels like months. I don't know if it's the pregnancy doing something to my hormones or these bloody pills for the toxoplasmosis, but I'd like it if the sun could just go out now. I'm not even at the car and I feel a bead of sweat running down my back. Getting into the car is like climbing inside a toastie. I burn my leg on the seat. Something in me clicks and I smash my clenched fist against the window. The postman is passing and he jumps back from the noise and stares at me – well, what does he expect! Can't a person express their emotions without having to apologise? It's…it's - I take a deep breath and hold my hand up in apology. I wind the window down.

"There was a wasp on the window, sorry if I scared you."

"Oh right, can't stand them either," he says and walks onto the next house.

Being in motion calms me, and the wind rushing through the car windows is warm, but at least it dries the sweat on my back. After a while, the smell of the fumes from the other cars starts to turn my stomach. It's like I can detect every molecule that's going up my nose. I'm either pregnant or turning into a dog. Princess Parkway is an absolute car park, as it always is at this time of day. The repetition – brake on, clutch in, into gear and crawl forward another five yards – seems almost meditative this morning. I flick the radio on.

"–in which case how can they say that they belong here? My grandfather fought and died for this country. I think we can take it as read that he loved England." The voice of the caller sounds like he's talking from a small tin box.

"But should a willingness to go to war really be the benchmark for saying that you're patriotic?" The host asks.

"You can't tell me that some of these immigrants wouldn't choose to fight for the other side if it came down to it, those fucking–"

"Okay, thanks Steve. Lots of voices in this argument, and sorry if any of the language there offended you. Let's go to another caller."

I flick the station and find *Birdhouse In Your Soul* playing on XS Manchester, so I sing along and absolutely nail the high harmonies. For the last ten minutes I've been yo-yoing past a red Sierra. Inside there's a woman with a gigantic perm and I've been trying to think where she would go to get a perm these days. Maybe she does it herself. At the lights, my lane runs faster and I pass her again. As I look across, I notice her fix me with a proper glare and she slowly and ceremoniously raises a middle finger at me. Charming. I give her a puzzled look. Maybe she thinks I've been staring at her? I mean, I have, but I don't think she'd know that. I focus on my lane and cars from the left filter in as we pass a sign showing the start of the roadworks. Hopefully, the traffic will speed up now.

Twenty metres further on, we grind to a halt and I look at the blue skies over the brewery. As always when we pass the brewery, my mind goes back to the drive with Dad that morning. Him weaving across the lanes just because he could. I've got the air conditioning going full pelt, but the air around the road network has a grubby, wavering quality. There's a sudden crunching noise and I scream. I turn to the right to see a man standing behind the boot of the red Sierra, holding the triangular roadwork sign. I watch as he brings it back down onto the Sierra's cracked rear windscreen. The window shatters into crumbs and falls into the boot.

"Dumb bitch, learn to drive!" he screams.

Leaving the sign upside down in the boot, he turns as if he's just going to get back into his car, which must be the black 4x4 with the door open two cars behind, level with mine. There's the rev of an engine and the squeal of a tyre and the Sierra lurches backwards. The man is slammed over the bonnet of the car behind and he roars in pain. His face is jam-red, like a powerlifter in the middle of a rep. He splutters and bangs his fists down on the bonnet. The woman with the perm opens her driver's door and, without looking back, walks towards the central reservation at a pedestrian crossing point. She moves beyond it, never breaking stride, and steps directly in front of a bus. There's a shriek of brakes. Her body is pulled under the bus with a series of thuds. Several drivers, myself included, open their car doors and stand to get a better view of what's going on. One person approaches the man pinned between the two cars and begins comforting him.

"Just hold on, I've rung for an ambulance, they should be here soon."

Despite the Good Samaritan's even tone, they don't seem to want to get any closer. Perhaps it's because the man is pounding repeatedly on the bonnet of the car he's pinned to. His hands look floppy and I can tell, even from over here, that he's broken the bones in his wrists. I look back at the bus, and every passenger inside seems to be dancing. Looking closer, I see an old man and a black woman with shopping bags over each wrist, and realise they aren't dancing; they're strangling each other.

The bystander looks around and catches my eye. He notices my blue tunic and fob watch. He waves at me for help. I wave back but something compels me to get out of here as quickly as I can, so I get back in my car. I look ahead to see where I can edge through, but the road is gridlocked. For a second, I consider flooring the accelerator and just punching a way through regardless of who is in the way. I don't. I get out and wave at him again as I pull my bag out and switch off the engine.

"I need to fetch my things, wait here!" I shout, and he relays this information to the crushed man who continues to drum his sagging hands on the bonnet. It looks like the Good Samaritan is regretting his choice – his expression becomes sour and unsettled and, without warning he pukes over the bonnet, a jet of yellow liquid. I feel my lips purse and my nose crinkles. I don't want to be here. I put my backpack over my shoulder and walk onto the pavement without anyone noticing that I'm going. Another fight starts to my left as a motorbike rider headbutts his helmet into the window of the car next to him. As I walk onto the council estate next to the road and take a path between two houses, the sound of the madness behind me recedes. I turn towards the hospital.

In my head I say to myself, "That should make you feel something, you should be crying, what's wrong with you?" Maybe it's shock. Maybe I'm dead inside.

***

I'm sitting in the break room next when Kelly comes in. She's a student nurse who has shadowed me on a few of my rounds.

"Crazy morning, eh?" she says.

"What do you mean?" I ask, wondering if she knows about the man trapped between the Sierra and the 4x4.

"Oh my God, did you not hear – there's a fire at the town hall, half of it has gone up in smoke."

"Seriously? Was anyone hurt?"

"No idea, there's a full alert though. I thought you'd have heard – they're cancelling any of the chemo patients they can get hold of because traffic is insane in and out of town."

"Okay," I say.

"Are you all right Nat?"

"No. I don't think I am." My eyes tear up and I'm caught between a scream of primal urgency and just blarting out everything that's in my heart. Fear for the babies. Fear that I'm their mum. Terror about where Dad is now. This burning rage I keep feeling. The long stretches of nothingness. All of it. where do I start? What are the words that I can use? The indecision means nothing comes out.

Kelly senses something and rushes over. She takes the coffee mug from my hands and perches on the arm of the chair I'm sitting in. She's so tiny she could fall between the cushions if she's not careful. She grabs my shoulder and squeezes. The humanity is touching, but the pique passes as soon as it comes.

"What's up cocker?"

"I'm okay. I'm just trying to get my head together. As you say, it's been a weird morning. I don't feel all that good."

"Poorly?"

"A bit queasy, but it's more just this feeling. Just really uncertain."

"Ooooh, this is freaking me out, there is *such* a vibe today. It'll be the moon. I bet it's a bastard full moon. It does something to the water in us."

"Is that right, doctor?"

Kelly laughs. The lightness of the sound illuminates the coffee room briefly and I throw the rest of the decaf down my throat.

"Team meeting at the desk, Collins wants everyone there," says Matron, as her red tabard pauses briefly by the open door.

Kelly jumps off and holds out her hand to pull me up, she strains comically as she helps me up and we walk together to the main desk, where visitors are greeted. There's a huddle of various tunics and t-shirts - blues, purples and whites denoting different specialities, all gathered around the large semi-circular reception desk. Collins is the ward manager, a short man with a pate so shiny he could moonlight as a mirrorball. He beckons Loz the receptionist over to him and uses her to steady himself as he climbs on top of an office chair.

"Hello everyone, appreciate it. Quiet please. Qui-et!" The hubbub dies down and the group of nurses, matrons and specialists look at him. He's sweating in the day's heat but he looks nervous too.

"You've probably all heard about the fires in town by now," he begins.

"Fires? I thought there was just one at the town hall?"

"Shush! Please – let me get through this. No, there are a number of fires now. We've just heard that the Lowry Hotel is also on fire."

Lots of people reach for their phones, immediately seeking video evidence.

"Please! People! PEOPLE! Lis-ten, we've been contacted by the area police command and they're implementing an emergency civil order plan. Now obviously we're short-handed because of this vomiting bug going around. *All* nurses – staff and senior nurses – are going to be relocated for today to the Manchester Royal Infirmary."

I think of the man being sick on the bonnet of the 4x4, that explains him at least. I wonder if I've got a touch of it myself, given how queasy I've felt. That's all I need. But right about now, a long lie down in a darkened room sounds pretty good.

A cry of voices goes up in response to the announcement.

"How am I supposed to get my kids from school if I've got to get from town?" A nurse asks.

"Who's paying for us to get buses back out of town?"

Something about the meeting irrationally infuriates me. I feel bile rising in my throat and I think I'm going to vomit. It comes up like a molten burp and I have to turn away from the crowd. I look at a plug socket on the wall and focus on how stupid this all is! What is the fucking point? What is the fucking point? What even is the fucking point? One of the plugs is on, even though nothing is plugged into it. So, we get shuttled around on some minibus that smells of farts; years of training and experience stuck in a bus to the shitty MRI. What about our patients? My breathing is coming in hard gulps and I have to concentrate all my focus on breathing in through my nostrils. I know I'm having a panic attack. There's a swelling feeling in my chest as all of this becomes too much. I walk over to the unused sockets and click the switch into the off position. There, I've returned something to order. The switch is no longer on. My breathing gets a bit calmer. I swallow the bile down.

Behind me, the staff are breaking up into groups to show each other footage they've found. Someone holds up a phone to a group of ten nurses who variously cover their mouths with shock at what they're seeing. I notice one or two of them seem to be smiling though. I find Collins, down from his chair, surrounded by colleagues all pressing him with questions that he's doing his best to avoid answering. I don't bother waiting my turn and just shout over the others.

"I've got that scan Jeff. I'm going to check up on my ward and head up to radiology."

He's already having four or five other discussions simultaneously, but he still manages to respond.

"No, wait Natalie. The police want every available nurse."

"I'm not available," I say and walk off. He starts to say something in response but the lights flicker on the ward and everything goes off. The lights overhead, the computers, the patient monitors. Voices stop and we all hold still. A monitor in the ward nearest to us starts to peep loudly and people dash to it.

"Stay calm, wait for the generators! Don't panic please! The generators will soon–" Collins begins, but before he can finish his thought there's a flicker and everything comes back on. "Thank you, don't rush now!"

My feet find their way to the chemo suite. You can tell it's an odd day because only one of the oversized, wipe-clean chairs that patients can sit in to receive their medicine is occupied today. Margaret is on her third round of chemotherapy for lung cancer. She's 58 and all she wants is to go to her daughter's wedding in September. I keep meaning to check with her daughter if there's any chance of pulling it forward at all, but I haven't seen her and I don't want to have that conversation with Margaret herself. I check the settings on her drip. All is well. Chemotherapy can be scary and painful, but it's also mundane. It's like waiting but with symptoms. When I see

Margaret's face, this anger I'm carrying seems to shrink and it's suddenly the professional me talking.

"Looking good Margaret, you picked a hat yet?"

"I need to pick a wig first," she says. She looks suffused with bliss, but it's more likely exhaustion producing her beatific smile.

"I think blue would suit you," I say. "Not a royal blue, but a lighter colour. Be nice for an autumn wedding too."

"God no, Paula's fella is a red, they'd kill me."

"Can't kill the mother-in-law on the wedding day kid, it's bad luck."

"She's got all the bad luck she needs with him, I'd best stick to reds and oranges."

"You keep well then, I'll have a word with the ward nurse. We're going to be a bit short-staffed today so when you're done get a broom and have a dust around will you?"

"Yes sister," Margaret says and laughs.

It's good to hear her laugh. Maybe she will make the wedding.

Chapter 11

12th April 2021
8 months, 8 days after

As the *Lepanto* chugs slowly down the Bridgewater Canal, I take the drone's travel case out of the rucksack and check it for damage. Fortunately, the bag's waterproofing protected it. I launch it from the roof of the barge and it rises upwards, scattering powdered snow beneath it.

"I'm on the Parish Council and you need to stop all this noise!" shrieks one of the wraths from the towpath.

I can't tell which one it is because there are hundreds of them now, all jostling for position on the narrow towpath. Every few yards one of them loses their footing or gets pushed by the crowd and they fall in and sink beneath the brown waters, out of sight forever. By the time that one has sunk another five have joined in their place. Wraths in shorts and trainers with no shirts, their skin chapped raw by the snow; beefy workers in luminous hi-vis vests;

women in summer dresses, long straggly hair prematurely aged by the snow. An older woman wrapped in a grubby dressing gown with a towel wrapped around her head. It's a snapshot of the world when it changed.

Brown is distressed and is sniffing around the floor looking for Bear. I'm worried that she might slip into the water, so I push her back inside the barge and close the doors. I make sure the tiller is pointing us to the centre of the canal and slip on the drone headset. The camera shows black smoke is still billowing out of the *Libby's Dream*. I steer around the dark column so that it doesn't clog up the rotor blades or damage the cameras. I scout all around the area. I can make out the area of flattened snow where the donut was and the trampled areas where the wraths made their way out to attack us. There are splatters of blood in the snow, and bodies, but no Bear. I even hover over the water, close enough to pick out the lighter colours of skin beneath the surface. Still no Bear.

My theory is that it must have fallen into the canal when the donut was being dragged around behind the barge. Or it was tipped into the water when I was pulling the donut in. I was trying to pay attention to where the barge was going, so I had my attention split. I speed the drone back to the *Lepanto* low over the water to conserve the battery and return it to its travel bag. I could turn the barge around and mount a physical search, but the truth is that we have to push on. It's already afternoon and if I'm going to get us to Saint James before dark then we need to keep going. I open the doors into the cabin and Brown bursts out, frantically sniffing at the floor and looking accusingly at the water. Her mute whimper is heart-breaking. I offer her chicken but she's not interested. I snaffle her up and hold her close as she wriggles. The stench of the fox scat is still strong on her jumper but she needs a hug. I need a hug. I gently return her to the ground and leave her to the fruitless pursuit. I reason to myself that in time she'll get over it and that maybe I can find her another Bear.

Leaning against the rail I pull my hood up and over my head to block out the shouts of the wraths. I hear my breathing trapped in my hood. I feel so tired. If I'd waited much longer to make this journey, I wouldn't have made it at all. But would that have been so bad? Brown would still have Bear and the temporary safety of the *Our Kid*. I could have died in warmth and comfort, stoned out of my mind, listening to ABBA, miles away from the heckling of the wraths. Every part of my body holds pain: my guts churn despite the lack of food, my left knee aches for some reason, and even though my face is close to frostbitten I think I'm getting a fever. Without warning I feel an immediate urge to go to the toilet and I look around to try and figure out how I can make this work. If I stop the barge and use the toilet on board we might drift to the bank and I'll be ripped apart while I'm taking a shit. I'm also terrified of messing with the throttle in case we run out of fuel, or it stalls. So, all I can do is drop my trousers, hang onto the rail and shit over the side of the barge. I try and do it on the side with the fewest wraths. The wraths at the front of the pack recoil collectively.

"What do you think you're doing?"

"This is Trafford, not Salford! We do not shit in our canal here!"

"Please! Please, please fuck off!" I implore. I don't even have any tissues, so I have to lean over and scoop up a handful of water from the canal to wash myself.

"He's douching with the canal!" someone shouts in a disgusted tone and promptly launches himself at the barge. He gets about a foot away from grabbing the side of the boat but plunges into the canal and is instantly gone.

"Please," I plead. "I have cancer, I wouldn't do this normally. *You* wouldn't be like this normally, there's something wrong with you," I say weakly as I pull up my trousers and hold onto the tiller, as a dizzy spell makes the world slide around.

The barge runs on, putt-putting its way through the dead city, as the unstoppable alarm rings out across the streets and fields, summoning ever more wraths. After a while there's no more towpath on the left, so all the new followers from that side simply walk into the canal and drown. It's impossible not to watch the bodies as they writhe and try to deny the water's embrace. They crawl on their neighbours just to get another step towards us, but the *Lepanto* chugs on. I keep our burnt nose pointing at the canal's imagined centre line. We pass barges moored on the sides and thump gently past others that are adrift.

I pull the backpack towards me and take out a Custard Cream. I split it open and use the edges of the biscuit to scrape the weed-icing into the water. Now is not a good time to be stoned. The snow is still coming down and the roof of the barge is nearly covered over again. I scoop up a handful of snow from the roof and turn to the crowd on the towpath. I fire the snowball into the pack. I don't see who it hits, but I hear a cluster of angry shouts. I get another handful and pack the snowball tightly. It goes against playground rules but I feel the situation warrants it. This time it hits someone on the front row – someone wearing shiny black trousers and a short-sleeve white shirt with an Asda nametag. It splats against his shirt and obscures his badge.

"What do you think you're doing?" he shouts at me.

"What do you think you're doing?" I shout back.

"You shouldn't be playing techno music on the canal, this is an area of outstanding natural beauty!"

"No, it's not! It's the arse end of Trafford industrial estate. And it's not techno music, it's a burglar alarm!"

I ball up another three snowballs and let them fly at the crowd. It only gets me more jeers and a chant of "Barge Wanker!" We pass under another bridge where the front end of a bus protrudes over the edge having smashed through the bridge wall. The driver is now a skeleton wearing a luminous yellow jacket. He seems pretty happy with his lot in the afterlife.

Further down the canal, the waterway splits in two and I double-check the *A to Z* to make sure I'm taking the correct route. Left leads to the centre of town and right towards Stretford, and the connection with the Mersey. I push the tiller and we pass under one metal bridge and then another. On top of the bridge, more wraths gather, drawn by the alarm. One of them realises that we're the source of noise and tries to squeeze through a large diamond-shaped gap in the metalwork to get at us. He gets one leg through and then gets stuck. Under the bridge, I look up and see that a graffiti artist has covered the ceiling. Instead of an inspiring fresco, they've just blocked out the words "WHY BOTHER?" I like it.

We pass a long line of narrowboats moored to the canal's sides, then on the right the waterway opens into a basin, where there are jetties with dozens of barges moored together. A sign declares that this is Stretford Marina. Houses line the waterside and, as we pass, I see faces appear at the windows attracted by our noise. Young and old faces press at the window, and their expressions of hatred mimic those in the crowd. Yet more join the throng. On the left bank, a lone wrath in fishing gear stands up with his teeth gritted in fury.

"How am I supposed to catch any fish when you're making this sort of noise?"

"You haven't even got a rod!" I shout. The fishing wrath looks at me blankly. "If I knew how to deactivate the alarm then I would! It wouldn't be much of a burglar alarm if you could just press a big red stop button, would it?"

I lob a snowball at him and in response he jumps towards me and sinks, but then the air trapped in his waterproof coat makes him bob to the surface and he continues to shout as we leave the marina. I consult the *A to Z* again and see that the turn onto the River Mersey is up ahead.

The map shows two blue lines that intersect. The Mersey then snakes around the Sale and Chorlton waterparks and should deposit me in Didsbury, about a mile from Saint James. This stage of the journey was beyond the range of the drone, so I'm going off what the *A to Z* shows me. I see a bridge up ahead and get the binoculars out to examine it in more detail. I scan about to try and figure out how the canal merges with the Mersey.

As we come closer to the bridge the answer is revealed: the two waterways don't connect at all. I power back the throttle to give me time to think and the *Lepanto* slows to a crawl. It appears that the two blue lines may overlap on the map, but in the real world the canal is carried south by a bridge and the Mersey runs some ten metres underneath heading west to Liverpool. And even if there was a way of getting the barge onto the Mersey it's much shallower than the canal at this point. Of course, now I see it, it's completely obvious that a river and a canal wouldn't run into each other. How would that work? What a dumb shit I am. Fuck! There's no way around it – the rest of the journey will be on foot. We have around three miles to go on the Mersey leg of the journey and about two hours to do it before we start to lose daylight. I shudder at the thought of the crowd pursuing us in the dark.

The intersection of the two waterways approaches and I turn the tiller so we're rubbing against the left-hand bank. I dip into the barge to grab Brown who is sitting behind the doors. I stroke her sad little face.

"I know Bear was special honey, but we have to go on. You're special too."

She looks at me and all I can see in her eyes is betrayal. In her mind this is probably just a continuation of my plan to get rid of Bear. I get her to walk to heel and her training over-rides any ill feelings. I shoulder the backpack and shotgun and we walk to the front of the *Lepanto*, where we crouch on the little deck amid the destruction from earlier. The left side of the bridge where we're getting out is just a metre-wide strip of snow and some over-grown bushes. Fortunately, there are no wraths on this side because the towpath is only on the right.

As we pull alongside the start of the bridge, I hop out and skid behind one of the bushes with Brown tucked under one arm. I hold onto her and hope that the bush is dense enough to conceal my orangeness. My hope is that as the shrieking barge sails on, it will take the crowd of wraths with it. Using it as cover, we scrabble across the snowy ground to a thicker bush. Brown looks disgusted, but I get her to the bush and make a sign for her to lie down and wait. I peer through the thick branches and see the wraths are still focused on the noise of the barge and don't seem to have seen us disembarking. Perhaps it's because we're low to the floor that I spot Bear. The stupid thing is trapped at the back of the boat, on a bumper that protects the hull from being damaged during mooring. Some black chains are holding up the bumper and Bear is wedged in the gap, calmly looking out at the world with its one remaining eye.

"Motherfucker," I say and stare intently at Brown: "STAY right here, do not move."

I shrug off the backpack and leave the shotgun behind the bush and try to time my movement. The rear of the *Lepanto* is only about two metres away but it's gaining distance and I've only got about fifteen metres before the bridge runs out and there's no more towpath on my side of the canal. I crouch low and scurry alongside to catch up. The boat is too far out for me to reach Bear, so I step out and grab onto the rail next to the tiller and pull myself onto the *Lepanto*. I squat down and pull Bear from its hiding place. The wraths spot me.

"Hey! What the fuck are you doing?"

There's about a metre left of the bridge. No time to think. I grip Bear and leap for the small spit of land to the left. My feet grip to the edge, but my balance is off. I just have time to throw Bear forwards onto the bridge before I fall backwards into the icy water.

The cold weather gear protects me initially and I just feel a slap to the face as I go under and my mouth fills with dirty water. I can't touch the bottom of the canal but I kick upwards and my head resurfaces. I see Brown skipping along the bridge, she's stood next to the water silently barking at me, full of concern for what I'm doing. How weird, that at this moment I have only one coherent thought: I hope she sees that I did this getting Bear back for her. The thought is fleeting though, because within seconds the water permeates the various zips, hits my skin and stops my breathing. I gasp and gasp and gasp. It feels like no air reaches my lungs. I gasp again. Pain marbles through my entire nervous system and I drop beneath the surface. For a moment the cold signals being received by my brain disappear and I'm just a wash of movement in unity with the canal. I know very clearly that there is an option to stay here. For this to be the end. I raise my hand, feel it breach, then I bring it back below, and I am nothing but water.

Teeth bite into my fingertips. Somewhere above me I'm aware of thrashing and motion. I come to, as if from a sleep, and panic. I beat my feet and arms about and I emerge to the sound of boos. Water drains from my ears and nose and I realise that the wraths are booing.

"Stay down you orange fuck!"

"Prick can't even drown properly."

"BOOO!"

Brown thrashes in the water in front of me, her eyes so wide that the whites are visible. Manchester Terriers are terrible swimmers. She would have been better throwing Bear in for me, but I appreciate the effort. In the end, the booing of the wraths and the panic in Brown's eyes makes me kick my legs. The fear forces my hands over one another. I smash one hand into the stones that line the bridge and something crunches, but I'm too numb to feel anything. I hold onto the side and reach under Brown's belly with the other and unceremoniously fling her back onto the bank. She shakes her whole body and turns to look at me as if unsure if she should "rescue" me again. Just to the left of me is a circular mooring ring. I lie back in the water and lift my foot and jam the toe of my left boot into it. I pull my body back to the bridge and, using the ring as a foothold, I get my hands on the side. The muscle memory of ten thousand pull-ups allows me to heave my sodden body onto the muddy side. Canal water gushes from my coat and trousers and I lie still while the wraths hoot and scream. I hear splashes behind me and I look to see wraths throwing themselves in to try and get me, but also to mock me.

Brown is crouching low in the grass, and she has now reached Bear. She holds herself against it, assuming somehow that it is cold too. With numb fingers I tremble the zip of my coat down and wriggle out of its tombstone weight, as brown frigid water continues to flood from the pockets and sleeves. I crawl to Brown, strip her jumper off and rub her flanks. She's trembling more than I am, so I scoop her and Bear up and hold them to me.

"I NEED A HUG!" Bear says

"F-Fuck off Bear!" I stammer.

On the opposite bank, there must be more than a thousand wraths. Their faces are contorted in rage, and I turn to one side, somehow feeling that the sheer weight of their loathing could crush us. The barge is now half a mile downstream and the echo of the siren is fading. The wraths have forgotten all about it. They just want us. To tear us apart. I shudder with the cold and wring Brown's fleece out and force it back over her head. I look around for the backpack. I crawl over to it and mentally force my fingers to work as I pull out my spare fleece. I strip off my coat and the clinging underlayers until I'm half-naked. The wraths explode anew in a chorus of disgust.

"What the fuck happened to you?"

"It looks like he's melting, that's fucking wrong."

Ashamed, I squeeze the underlayers and slip them back on. I then pull the fleece over my shoulders and its dryness gives me a moment of comfort. My legs and boots are still sodden, but there's not much I can do about that. I find the full bottle of rum in the bag, crack open the seal and take a good, hard swig. The judder of warmth revives me and I can feel the outline of my stomach as the liquid's heat traces its way down inside me. I'm back in the world. The wraths are again launching themselves en masse into the water. They will never stop until we're dead.

Now I want them dead. Not just to leave me alone, or to let us escape and live a quiet life, but to drown and to suffer and to bloat. I should have walked the whole lot of them into the canal with the drone as soon as they appeared, but I was too focused on Bear and escaping. Now I want them to be under the same cloud of pain that follows me. I load the shotgun with cartridges from the rucksack and fire into the crowd on the other side. Some of the wraths on the front are blasted backwards.

"Fuck you," I shout. "Come over here if you want some!"

I watch them pour forward, their red eyes focused on me.

"Bring it on, you braindead fucks!"

I reload and fire again. More wraths stagger backwards. I notice that so many are entering the canal that they're starting to clog it up. At first, it's just that someone floats and someone else stands on his head to get further across the canal. Then another wrath grabs onto someone else. The new bodies that plunge in are caught up in the tangle of the others, and suddenly there's a chain of prone wraths almost stretching to our bank. They can't swim, but they could get across.

"Oh shit," I say and despite the pain in my body I shoulder the backpack and shotgun and grab Bear and jam him inside. My orange coat is still too heavy with water and I reluctantly leave it on the bank. Brown follows me along the bridge to the end. My boots squelch with water and my trousers and leggings are heavy, but the rum and the fear power me forward. At the side of the bridge there's a steep snowy bank that runs down to the Mersey below. I turn and see that the first wrath has now connected to the mooring pin that I used to climb out of the water. Others are crawling across the line of bodies in the canal. A wrath on the other bank shouts "HERE I COME!" with such malice that I pick Brown up, step onto the side of the bridge and jump.

We land in a soft drift of snow and start to slip down the bank until my feet hit the Mersey. The water is only knee-deep, but the second drenching causes actual pain in my leg. The shouts from above remind me I don't have the luxury of time to complain. I wade up the river with Brown tucked under my arm. I decide to cross as the path on the other side looks as if the snow is less deep. I slip on the algae-coated stones beneath my feet and stumble into the water, breaking my fall with my injured hand. I struggle to hold onto Brown, but fear that if I let her go then she'll be swept away so I dig my fingers into her and she wriggles. Pulses of pain shoot up to my shoulder as I scrabble for balance. Somehow, I make it to my feet, struggle to the other bank and launch Brown into the snow. I raise my feet from the water, dig my feet into the snow and slowly pull myself to the top of the bank.

"There he is!"

I turn to see a wrath jump straight off the bridge and land headfirst in the shallow river. He doesn't get up. Others start jumping at various points across the bridge. Some hit the banks of snow and get caught up. Others land in the river with varying success. More and more pour over the bridge and around the sides, all of them fixed on reaching us. I turn and examine the flat, wide path of snow ahead. Brown is bravely trying to leap through the snow but it's still too deep for her. I reach down, grab her and start to trudge forwards.

The Mersey is running deeper alongside me as I've staggered on 500-ish metres, but I'm starting to blackout with exhaustion. I grab a handful of snow and rub it in my face to try and stay conscious. I peek over my shoulder. Not far behind there's a small group of about 15 wraths, led by a man in jean shorts and a Superdry t-shirt. They're gaining on us. I wonder if I should let Brown go and make a last stand. The numbers aren't in our favour though. Facing forward again, I see that the river is shallow for the next few hundred metres, so I skid down the bank and toss Brown into the water at the very edge, where she's able to wade, and drop in beside her.

"Get going!" I scream at her and she looks at me, perplexed by this change in tactics.

"Run!" I shout as the man in the Superdry t-shirt comes over the side of the bank, slips down and enters the Mersey face first. Brown sees the wrath and follows me as I splash fast through the ankle-deep water. It's cold and slippery, but it's quicker than pushing through the deep snow. At every step, I expect to feel steel fingers on my shoulder and I wish I'd had the foresight to get a knife or reload the shotgun. We splash onward, and up ahead I can see a pedestrian bridge over the river, and a few hundred metres beyond it a railway bridge. Maybe we can make it there.

"Come on Brown, run! RUN!"

I glance back and notice that we've opened up a bit of distance. The wraths are now all following the Superdry guy in a steady stream, sliding down the bank into the river.

"RUN!" I urge Brown again.

We go under the pedestrian bridge and I spot another wrath on the bridge, looking like a snowman. They turn as we pass underneath and some of the snow falls off them. The river is getting deeper again, but we have no choice, we continue to wade on until it's waist deep and Brown is once again under my arm, wriggling against the broken bones in my hand. Finally, we move under the railway bridge and I can see that its cover has left a stretch of much more passable ground on the path. I can even see the grass on the bank, muddy and lifeless. I decide the quickest route would be to follow the more passable ground as far as we can. It will take us away from the Mersey, but at this point I've abandoned any hope of making it to the hospital. We need to find somewhere we can hide, or fight one last time.

I put Brown on the muddy ground and with a push she starts to work her way up the slippery bank. I haul myself out of the water and use the shotgun to stabilise myself and the barrel sinks into the wet soil. I take care to drive my toes into the ground at every step, as I struggle to keep my grip in the mud. There's a hope in me that perhaps the wraths will be too uncoordinated to navigate the slippy embankment. I take off the rucksack and throw it to the top just as Brown gets there. We could be okay! I turn and see the Superdry guy about 10 metres behind us. Behind him there are now three other wraths, one is bleeding heavily from a cut on her head. Further behind them, an army follows on. I focus on reaching the top of the verge.

I throw the shotgun onto the ground, drag myself level with Brown and place my foot on the even surface. As I do, I feel the soil give out beneath me. A clump of mud breaks off and my forward motion flings it behind me. A rush of mud takes my feet away. My hands and face slap into the floor. There's dirt in my mouth and a burning pain in my hand. There's nothing but thin blades of grass to grab onto, and I look up to see Brown get further away from me as I slide down the bank, into the water and within reach of the wraths.

"Stay!" I scream at Brown. "DOWN! STAY! DO NOT MOVE! STAY THERE!"

I feel hands on my shoulder.

Chapter 12

4th August 2020
The day of the change

Even a quick visit to the ward helps me get my head in order. Everything is messed up today. I keep seeing that man on the Parkway. I keep wondering why I walked away and left my car behind. Then there's these fires in town, the sickness bug - even that disconnected feeling when I saw the switch on that plug – none of it makes any sense. I think I need to see someone and talk about Dad. I don't want the babies to be affected by the way I've been since he went. I want them to thrive. Being on the ward is good, as I click back into being someone professional. Professional people don't have all these questions and doubts. I check doses of medications. I pick up what the doctors have missed. I smell the oddly comforting mix of bleach and urine that has been the perfume of hospital wards since time began. I fill in the endless bloody forms.

The corridors on my floor are quiet, most of the staff have been whisked off by the minibuses now, off to see the show at the MRI. I feel like I'm skipping school. I swing back round the changing room and consider getting changed into a fresh tunic, but checking my phone I see that I don't have time. I have 15 missed calls, seven from Rick, but the network is down so I can't call him back – there's always been terrible reception in the hospital. I worry that he might be chasing me because the police are angry at me for disappearing from the scene of an accident. I throw my phone back in my bag, shut my locker and head to radiology.

I've been regretting agreeing to help Susie with her exam ever since the word 'yes' left my mouth. There's something unsettling about someone looking everywhere inside me, with no cavity left unexamined. That goes double for the fact that it's Susie doing it. She's a student radiographer and has only been at the hospital for two years, but she's my best friend at work, which I suppose is why I said I'd be Patient X for her. She's got an exam coming up and she's trying to do as much practice as possible before the big day. I spoke extensively to Dr Ranjit about whether or not it was safe for me to get an MRI with the babies, but he'd given me the thumbs-up. I hadn't told Martin though, he'd only worry. Besides, Susie said she'd take me to Sangam and let me order anything I want, so at least there was one positive. Just keep thinking about the chana masala.

I make my way along the corridor and try to ignore my rising annoyance with the sound my trainers are making, squeaking on the floor. It's not like they haven't had generations of nurses and doctors, not to mention the fucking patients walking along this corridor – you'd think they could find some kind of finish that doesn't produce this stupid fucking *EEEEK! EEEEK! EEEEK!* How is that ergonomic or healthy?

"Gaahhhhhhhh!" I shriek in frustration and a patient on a walker about twenty paces ahead spins at the noise.

I look for somewhere to hide and there on my right, miraculously, is an alcove with a vending machine in it. I snuggle in close to try and avoid being seen. I search my pockets and there's only a two-pound coin. I feed it into the machine and get a Double Decker. I notice that no change is given. What a swizz, if they're not getting nurses with parking fees, they're getting them with exorbitant snack prices. If the government wanted to do something for the NHS, they should make Double Deckers free. Never mind all this we're-building-hundreds-of-new-hospitals bollocks.

The chocolate calms me and I squeak on down the corridor. I catch up and pass the patient on the walker and smile at him. He's grizzle-faced and has that brown-grey aura of the smokers who drag themselves down a million miles of corridors to find one of the few smoking shelters in the hospital. He'll sit there in his thin dressing gown, just to give an offering to the tobacco gods, pending a full human sacrifice. I can only salute his dedication, maybe he's got it right, the world could end tomorrow.

I follow the purple line on the corridor that leads to radiology and lean on the intercom. I've never seen the hospital this quiet before, it's so freaky.

"Hello?" comes Susie's voice over the little speaker.

"Hi, it's Patient X, I've had a referral for a full-body MRI. My doctor, like all doctors, knows next to nothing, but I reckon we should do it just to shut him up."

"I'm sorry I can't see you on our system, why don't you get the doctor's secretary to send us another referral which we'll lose and then you can come back again in three months?"

"Susie, I will walk away."

"Oh wait! *Ms* Cross? Yes, I've just found your file. If you want to push the door when you hear a buzzing noise."

I wait for the buzzing with my hand hovering ready to push. I continue to wait. I look at the camera just inside the door and give a little toodle-bye wave and start to turn around. The door buzzes instantly. I hold off turning back until the buzzing goes on for several seconds. I push through the door and scratch my cheek with the Vs for the benefit of the CCTV camera.

Susie meets me further down the corridor with a clipboard.

"Thank you, Ms Cross, sorry about the door. We've been asking maintenance to look into that for weeks."

"Well, I'm just a patient but I heard that they won't work up here because every time they do, they're sexually harassed by the radiologists. Just what I heard."

Susie smiles and makes notes on her clipboard.

"Now I can see from your referral letter that we need to give you a full-body MRI because the doctor thinks that you're 98% genital wart. I'm not going to lie, that's unusual. You must have screwed some real deviants."

"Mostly friends of yours. Do we have to roleplay through this?"

"Nah," Susie turns the clipboard round and reveals a pen drawing of a giant cock.

"So, what will you have to do for the exam?"

"You never know. It could be anything, they give you a test patient and then watch over your shoulder as you do what it says on the instructions. I think as long as you don't kill them then they let you carry on. I'm still shitting it though. Mark is supposed to sit in on your scan to make sure I don't screw up, but he's hiding in the office with a hangover, so I'm flying solo."

"Come on then, let's get this over with. I'm not feeling too hot."

Susie leads me through to a changing room and runs through the spiel of what's going to happen, what an MRI does and what I'm likely to experience. She asks about piercings, fillings, prosthetic limbs and any love eggs I might have left in. Then she asks whether I might be pregnant. She does a good job. I tell her that I am quite badly claustrophobic, which is true, and she explains that I'll be able to hear her during the scans and that there's a mirror on the head restraint which will enable me to see the rest of the room, so it won't feel like I'm just stuck in a tube. Despite my protests she insists that we do need the head and body restraints because she might be asked to do them in the exam, and she wants to practice. I commit. Chana masala.

I change into a gown and she leads me through to the MRI room. To save time she skips the section on explaining more about the scanner and just slaps the table.

"Park your arse here and I'll strap you down. Nothing you've not heard before."

"Is this your normal patter or just for friends?"

I get up on the plastic table which is covered with a disposable paper mat. The room is warm; a source of cool air blows in from somewhere and the breeze feels calming. Susie puts some headphones on me and I position my head in a cage which she clicks into place with a restraint across the chin and forehead, so that I can't move my head. She fastens Velcro straps around my wrists, arms and legs.

"This is horrible, why would you have to restrain someone?" I ask.

"Could be anything. Maybe an Alzheimer's patient who doesn't understand that they need to stay still. It's not often we use them, but we need to know just in case. Anyway, quit moaning. It'll all be over in ten minutes," she replies and disappears from the room. A few seconds pass and I hear her voice clearly through the headphones.

"Okay, thank you Ms Cross, please keep your arms inside the car and scream if you want to go faster. The whole thing will take 10 to 15 minutes and you'll mostly just hear a lot of loud clicking and whirring, but I've got some banging electronic music queued up to drown that out. If you feel uncomfortable at any point then just let me know. For any normal patient I'd stop and bring you out, but you're going to be fine, right?"

"Sure," I lie. My heart is starting to pound. There's a loud series of clicks and then some bleep-bloop music starts and drowns out the sounds. The bed inches smoothly towards the machine.

"Ok, if you're strapped in comfortably then I shall begin with the tips of your delightful little toes."

Susie's voice drops out and I feel the bed move and I am fed gradually into the mouth of the tube. My tension mounts as first my shins and then my thighs edge closer. I try not to think too much as my waist goes in – it's a tight fit inside the MRI machine. My gown doesn't touch the sides of the tube walls but it feels like it does. I feel like a bullet being slowly loaded into the chamber of a gun. The music swells in my headphones and a vocal that sounds like "love crime" keeps repeating as the song progresses.

"Babe? You still with me?" Susie's voice sounds uncertain as it comes through the headphones.

"Mentally I'm at the buffet. Why?"

"You know when I asked if there was any chance you could be pregnant?"

"Very funny," I say and can't keep a smile from my face.

"Nat, I'm not even joking. I am looking at your uterus right now and there is *stuff* going on in there."

"Haha! Got ya!" I shout and laugh. I want to move my hair from my face, but the restraints are holding my hands in place.

"*What the hell*?! Why didn't you tell me! Oh my God! That's amazing! I think? Do we think that's amazing?"

"I thought I'd see how good you were. Be a fun little test for you. Don't worry, I checked with my gynaecologist and he says it's fine to do an MRI."

"Ahhhhh! Oh my God! I'll finish up as quickly as possible and you have to tell me everything. Who's the dad? Is this just random? You've blown my mind."

"Calm down. It's one of two gay men. Possibly both of them."

"I'm so confused right now."

"You muppet, it's IVF. I'm a surrogate for my best friend and his husband."

"Ohhhh, riiiiiight. Oh my word, you've freaked me out. Let me finish this up quick."

The music returns to cover the clicking of the MRI machine and I enter fully into the tube.

"Everything else is fine," Susie says over the headphones. "Kidneys, liver, lungs, throat are all good. You'll live to be 105 and you'll have 14 kids and get your pick of the council flats. I don't know if you noticed but I'm talking too much to try and cover over my embarrassment because I'm currently looking at an accurate 3D model of your tits. Throat and mouth are fine too."

"Good stuff."

"Skull and brain are...what the fuck is that?"

"Please Susie, you can't get me back. I got you good."

"Ohhh, babe. Ohhh shit. Listen, I need to get Mark. Don't worry, I'm coming right back to get you."

"Susie! I'm fucking serious – what the hell is going on?"

"Just wait! I'll be back."

The clicking grind of the machine continues and the music pounds in my headphones. In the mirror on the head restraint, I can see the empty room behind me. Through the room's window I see a section of Susie's legs and chest in purple scrubs. She's running somewhere. I then see two pairs of legs coming back. Her breathless voice sounds in my ear.

"Listen hon, I had to get Mark, are you okay if he advises?"

"What? I don't know! What do you want me to say?"

"You have to give consent. Oh, this is all messed up."

"Fine! Fine! Yes, I give my consent!"

"Mark, what the fuck is that?"

"Ohhhhkay," says a male voice intently. "I do not know what that is. We need to get Mister Doyle down here. See if you can put out a call for h–"

I see a section of somebody new coming into the monitoring room in my mirror, another pair of purple legs heading towards Susie. Their scrubs are ripped, exposing a slab of white belly and dark hair. There's a shout in my earphones that I try and move away from, but they're clamped to my head. I hear a succession of popping and cracking noises that compete with the clicking of the MRI. The music is reaching a crescendo and a wavering voice is singing in a high pitch. The table I'm on judders to a halt and the clicking stops. I hear Susie's voice over the speaker saying "Nick!", then there's the sound of cracking glass and I'm left with just the music in my ears. I can't see anything in my mirror but I can hear someone breathing with a rasp. Then, there's a crunch.

I buck against the straps and the head restraint. In the mirror I see the ripped purple trousers moving around and I thrash against the restraints trying to release myself. I can't move. The only thing that can break free is the anger. It's all too much: the people on the Parkway, the legs in the corridor, the switch on the plug, the greyed-out form. It rolls up and churns away inside me until I feel like I'm coming up on a dark ecstasy. I vomit but the restraint stops me from turning my head so I am sick on my face, a foreign yellow bile, a sickness from somewhere else. I cough and spit and choke, trying to clear my airways. A blackness descends over me. In my head the world is pushed far away and all I'm able to focus on are the dangers and the wrongs. When did evil win? It's too much for me. I'm falling into a sewage tank and the world is stink and shame. I'm lost in the dark and all I can see is the glimmering outline of a huge, undulating hatred. It's good though. We want the darkness. We welcome it, because it is us.

Chapter 13

12th April 2021
8 months, 8 days after

Superdry is on me as soon as I slip back into the water. He grabs me around my shoulders and crashes his entire body onto me, knocking me down into the biting cold river. My right hand is screaming as I search my pockets for a weapon. There are strips of cooked chicken in one, ammunition in the other and the gun for the ammo is twenty yards away at the top of the slippery bank. I'm not good at this.

The wrath forces me under the surface. His fingers weave into my hair and bang my head against the rocky river floor. I raise my hands instinctively to protect my face and then there's a rock in my hand I must have grabbed from the river bed. It's about the size of my palm with a straight, flat edge. I jam it up over my shoulder and it connects with his face. Even underwater I can hear him rage. I push myself to my knees, break the surface and gasp for air. The world is blurred, but I see shapes surrounding me. The wraths are on me. I swipe the point of the rock at Superdry's face and clip the bridge of his nose. He staggers back, but five more are just behind him. I throw the rock at one and miss by two metres.

On some instinct I wade out and launch myself into the centre of the river where it's deeper, and swim hard downstream with the current. I kick frantically and windmill my arms, trying to gain speed and avoid the wraths diving after me. One touches my arm but I shake it off and carry on swimming. The freezing water helps with the pain in my hand and the adrenaline pushes me onwards. Before long, I'm out of my depth and feel myself borne downstream. I daren't look behind me, so I turn towards the opposite bank and splash my way across the river. The strength of the current continues to push me along, and by the time I reach the other bank I'm already back at the pedestrian bridge we passed earlier. Two steps forward, three steps back. I pump my legs through the soft sediment and collapse into the snow and gasp for breath. My heart is racing and I can see my breath pluming from my lungs. I turn to the river and see a tide of wraths streaming down the opposite bank towards me. There are thousands. For a second, I watch in stunned silence as this mass of former humanity comes for me.

As the wraths hit the central current of the Mersey they get swept away at a gratifying rate. But just 500 metres downstream the river becomes shallow again and I can see drenched wraths stumbling onto their feet. They pick themselves up and complete their crossing to my side on foot. I look upstream and see Brown, a dot up ahead on the far side of the river, still sitting obediently waiting for the next command. What a good girl. I climb the bank and head back towards her on my side of the river, moving as fast as I can through the deep snow. My breath billows in the air and my teeth chatter, but I'm alive and the movement warms me slightly. As I stagger on, I consider that since I left the *Our Kid,* I've made every wrong decision and bad move I could have made. No doubt about it, this is one of the worst attempted plans ever. A real piece of shit.

As I come level with Brown I shout again for her to stay where she is. She stands and skitters from side to side but stays where she is, for now. Fortunately, the wraths are focused on reaching me and none of them have noticed her yet. Just to make sure I have their attention I wave my hands over my head and scream at them.

"Hey! Here! Here! Bet you can't catch me you braindead fucks!" The river churns as more throw themselves down the bank and into the water.

I need to find a way to cross the railway bridge over the Mersey. I swing my leg over the waist-high fence which runs alongside the footpath, and hop over. The fence partitions off a woodland, and I move into the treeline heading away from the river. I plunge through the thick forest, tripping over on roots and tangled lines of thorns. Sweat breaks out on my forehead and the frosty water in my boots is gradually squelched out. Fortunately, the tree canopy has kept the snow on the ground to a minimum and I gradually track back, until the bridge is low enough for me to leap up and grab the railing at the side. I try and haul myself up, but my throbbing hand and waterlogged clothes mean I don't have the strength. I drop to the ground and move even further away from the river until I can climb more easily onto the railway bridge. I pull myself up, put my hands on my hips, try to catch my breath and then turn back towards Brown and run as fast as I can.

As I head back, I look down onto the river and some of the wraths spot me immediately. Their screaming soon alerts the rest, who turn towards me. Most of them are in the process of crossing the river, and some are visible at the edge of the treeline, but I have bought myself some precious distance. I finally make it back to Brown's side of the Mersey and realise that if I want the rucksack and shotgun then I'll need to drop down here. I swing my leg over the bridge's railing and climb onto the ledge. I turn and manage to get my foot on another ledge underneath. I'm hanging onto the bridge but I notice that Brown is directly underneath looking at me quizzically.

"Move your arse, you dozy animal!" I shout.

Brown finally realises that I am the voice in the sky, and moves enough for me to let myself go. Even with the foot of snow on the ground the fall still knocks the wind out of me, and a jarring pain runs from my prosthetic leg into the base of my stump. I want to cry, but one look at the hundreds of wraths moving across the river, along the bridge and up the towpath reminds me to get moving, and I grab the shotgun and rucksack. As I pick up the rucksack my leg goes from under me and I feel myself start to slip through the mud, about to slide down back into the river. I hold my hands like claws and dig them into the ground beneath me. I'm just able to keep from repeating the entire farcical loop. I get to my feet and see that there are wraths about 50 metres away now. I whistle Brown and together we lurch onwards, away from the river.

Underneath the bridge is free of snow and we make good time crashing through the long slimy grass and ferns. Before long the height of the bridge starts to drop to rejoin ground level, so once again we're pushed out into the deeper snow. Underneath the snow there are weeds and bushes and Brown is struggling to find a route, so I have to pick her up. We're so slow that again the wraths start to gain. I hear the crash of branches as they push their way towards us.

I'm so tired and cold that I see stars in my vision and my head feels like it's in a vice. Little flecks of light dance as I blink and try to stay upright. My body is trembling, but I'm also sweating. Brown looks in bad condition too. She's covered in cuts on her chest and snout and drops of her blood fall from her nose into the snow. We can't go on. I look around us and see that 20 metres off the path on the left there's a farm, with a large yard in front. There are rows of barrels and pallets covered in snow. There are also several vehicles half buried across the yard. I pick the nearest one and stagger over to it, using the last of my energy to lift Brown above the thick drift. It's an ancient, blocky Land Rover with dull green sides. The old sliding windows are cracked open. I reach my fingers through and find that the locking button is already up, so I yank the driver's door open and throw my backpack, shotgun and Brown inside. Brown instantly shakes herself off and shivers in the footwell of the passenger seat.

I wedge myself into the driver's seat, which is pulled so far forward that my knees have to curl around the wheel just so I can fit in. The first wrath crashes into the yard just as I shut the door. I duck down to the side, hoping I'm out of sight. I sneak my fingers up and press the button to lock the door. My eyes are level with a cubby hole in the dashboard. In the pot are a sweet wrapper and the black bow of a key. I pull it out with my trembling left hand and I reach blindly across and slide it into the ignition. The engine coughs and turns over, then settles into a contented rumbling. A jet of oily-smelling air plumes out of the heater and hits my face. I sit up as much as I can – whoever drove last can't have been more than two feet tall. I look at the instrument panel and see that there's a warning light on the fuel gauge, but that's a nightmare for later.

A wrath smashes into the window and a white feather of cracks spreads across the pane of glass next to my head.

"CAR THIEF! ROTTEN, BLOODY CAR THIEF!" she screams into the air, and smashes her head against the glass again. Blood gets matted into her blonde hair and her nose is squished to one side. She works her fingers into the gap in the window and starts trying to pull it back. I reach my elbow up and push back against her. Another wrath thuds into the bonnet and the wing mirror flies off.

I mash my foot into the narrow accelerator and the engine revs and whines but we don't move. A cloud of black soot coughs from the exhaust. The wrath at the window wins the battle and the gap grows enough for her to stick her head in. She snaps her jaws, trying to bite me. She gets her teeth into the fabric of the fleece I'm wearing. I pull back but keep my foot on the accelerator. I push against her with my elbow until she's jammed against the headrest.

I am not equipped for this. I can't drive and I need to move the seat backwards so I can see what I'm doing, but I don't even know how to make the bastard thing move! This isn't like Mario Kart at all. My right hand now looks like an inflated marigold glove. Using my functioning hand, I start to press every button and shift every lever and stick I can reach. The windscreen wipers come on and the horn sounds out with a cheery *toot* that sounds like it should be greeting the vicar on the village green.

There's another crash and I look in the rear-view to see the back windscreen shatter, as a wrath in a police uniform shoulders his way into the vehicle and starts to climb through the small window. I push the biggest lever I can find forward and with a terrible graunching noise the car lurches forward a metre, but then stops. The jerking movement launches the policeman backwards into the soot of the exhaust cloud but we're still not going anywhere. There's a lever by my left knee with a button on the top. I click it. The lever drops and suddenly, wraths are flying over the bonnet as we jump into action. There's an ungodly moan as the Land Rover mounts something and thumps back down. The snow on the road pushes against the car but the wheels find purchase and soon we're moving at a lightning 10 miles an hour. The back end of the Land Rover slips around like a fish tail. I look in the rear-view and see that our progress isn't being helped by a woodchipper connected to the Land Rover.

I look at Brown and she's cowering in the footwell, panting. I try and aim the air vent with its meagre puff of warm air at her. I glance in the rear-view and see that the wraths are still following us. I catch sight of myself in the mirror and don't recognise what I see. There's a long curtain of blood descending from a cut on my forehead and scratches across my cheeks. My hair is shaggy and a section of a branch is caught in the top. I glance at my right hand, which throbs wildly. I leave the steering wheel wedged between my knees and reach over for my rucksack. I root inside, scoop some cannabis icing out of the tub and eat it raw. It's claggy and sticks to the roof of my mouth, leaving a medicinal aftertaste. I chew the top off the rum and swig more of the amber liquid back. Popeye should have switched to a rum-based diet, because instantly I feel a measure of hope flood my body. I'm still cold and broken and fucked but look at me, I'm leading a conga line of wraths through a dead city and I'm driving a car! Fuck it, if this is how it ends then at least I've had a go.

The roads are impossible to spot in the snow and so I navigate by following the line of cars and mounting the pavement when I need to. At some point the connection to the woodchipper snaps off and our speed increases to 11 miles an hour. The roads are littered with cars and trucks, some with skeletons behind the wheel. Wraths spark back into life as we clatter past them. I focus on pointing the car at any empty space ahead and hope that the engine doesn't explode. If I knew how to change gear then that would help, but I don't want to stall now. I briefly contemplate lifting and re-dropping the lever that got us going to see if it speeds us up, but figure that given my luck on this journey so far it might not be a good idea. On we go.

After ten minutes of driving, I see a road sign that tells me that it's one mile to Didsbury. Up ahead a large lorry is blocking the road completely, so I make a last-second detour and steer us into a mostly empty car park. On the other side is a low metal gate and beyond that a park. I stamp even harder on the accelerator and point the Land Rover at the gate. At the last moment, I see a low bush just to the left of the gate and figure it will provide less resistance, so I jerk the wheel towards it. The Land Rover mounts the bush with ease but a grinding noise alongside the vehicle reveals that it was obscuring a concrete bollard. The Land Rover gradually gets wedged between the bollard and the gatepost.

The engine screams as I jam my foot down on the accelerator and the wheels spin in the snow and thin gravel of the car park. The Land Rover edges forward slowly and smoke starts to chug from the sides of the bonnet. The wraths quickly catch up with us. They start to bang on the back of the Land Rover and I fumble in the footwell for the shotgun. With a jarring pain in my hand, I crack the barrel and jostle two sodden shells from my fleece pocket into the gun. I fire a round into a wrath who has started to climb through the broken rear window. Their chest turns into a gaping wound and they fall backwards. My ears ring with the sound of the blast inside the car and Brown dashes in tight circles in the footwell.

The vehicle shakes as more wraths arrive and hammer their bodies against the vehicle. They can only access the back of the Land Rover though and gradually the accumulated weight of their bodies forces the issue, and with a grind of sparks the Land Rover breaks free and starts to run again, into the deep snow of the park. In front of me is an expanse of white, so I navigate by pointing the Land Rover towards a distant set of rugby posts, a colossal H that looms over the virgin field. As we drive, we establish a small lead over the wraths and again, the hope rises within me that we might get away. The entrance on the other side of the park is wider and the gates are open and I feel positively euphoric when I see a sign at the exit thanking me for visiting Hough End Park.

I turn the Land Rover right onto a long straight road. I dodge cars and navigate our way around spilt lorries and buses. To my left a sign welcomes me to Withington. I spin the wheel as I recognise where I am from the *A to Z*. We continue to work our way down clogged streets until, finally, ahead of us lies an eerily illuminated Saint James' hospital. The lights shine out of the reception area and make it seem like a beacon of warmth and hope. There is a spluttering noise from the bonnet and with a *kek-kek-kek* the engine dies. I turn the key again and the engine starts briefly, but then falters and fails. Turning the key just produces a grinding noise and more smoke.

There's only 100 metres between us and the front of the hospital. I look back at the mob in pursuit and calculate that we won't make it. I rip open the bag and ignoring the throb of my hand I open the drone's carry case and power it up. I switch on the MP3 player and whisper a frantic "Come on!" as it boots up and the wraths close in. I hit play, hold the drone out of the driver's window and launch it into the air. It wobbles slightly from the unconventional launch but it's flying steadily by the time it's 15 feet up. The Vengaboys ring out over the streets of Manchester. I scoot down in my seat and angle the rear-view so I can remain hidden and watch the crowd. As the sound of the song reaches them, the first line of the wraths turns their attention from the Land Rover and focus on the drone. I only have one hand to control the drone but when I'm sure that it's got their attention, I turn the crowd's gaze away from us and I slip from the Land Rover. Once out, I beckon Brown towards me. She reluctantly stands on the threshold of the vehicle and then gamely plunges into the snow once more. What a girl.

I hook the bag and shotgun over my arm and stagger for the line of cars that are stacked up in front of the hospital entrance. Once there I crouch behind a white van. I look at the heads of the wraths captivated by the drone above them. They're raising their hands into the air, hatred pouring from them, but they're powerless to resist. The booming music of the chorus brings even more wraths out of the nearby houses, and I'm now convinced that the entire population of Manchester is here. I swerve the drone over to one side and then back again and smile as their heads turn where I want them to look. I scan around for signs of a convenient canal that I could walk all these fuckers into, but there's nothing. I move the drone away from us so that I can walk to the front door without being noticed.

My face drops in horror as I see a wrath leap and swipe at the drone. They clip the underside of the drone and it pitches over once and then twice and lurches drunkenly first up and then down. It's now within reach of the crowd and arms stretch up. I hit the control and it rises briefly and then pitches sideways directly towards me. A multitude of faces turn toward me and the drone crashes upside down into the branches of the solitary tree in the drop-off area. The drone is knackered but the speaker continues to pump out the Vengaboys as loud as ever. The ground rumbles as the assembled crowd pour towards us. I throw the drone controller towards the front line and step into the hospital's reception as the automatic doors open for me. A wave of angry wraths fills the lobby just behind me and I stagger as fast as I can for the double doors on the far side of the reception area, which are locked. I shoulder-barge them but they hold fast.

Brown is already running ahead dodging a wrath who leaps for her legs. I think I can just make it to the other double doors on the opposite side of the room. I push past spilt tables and wipe-clean green and brown sofas. I point the shotgun at the doors and fire. A hole appears in the door and I dip my shoulder into it. The door swings open and reveals a long corridor beyond with a flight of stairs leading off on the right. I whistle to Brown and start to climb the steps. My heart is hammering in my chest and a flop sweat sheets off my forehead. On the first landing, the doors are locked and I haven't got any more ammo loaded. I hear the wraths filling the stairwell behind me. Their curses resound in the small space. At the second landing the doors are also locked, and I can sense wraths only steps behind. I will my exhausted legs on and make it to the third floor. Miraculously, the double doors open as I push against them. I turn, shut the door and flip the circular thumb lock into place just as a row of faces smash into the doors. They press up against the security glass and something in me breaks. I push my face up to my side of the window. Hundreds of wrath faces, contorted by anger, are illuminated by the sterile lighting in the corridor.

"FUCK YOU! I WIN! FUCK YOU! YOU CAN'T EVEN CATCH A FUCKING CANCER PATIENT. YOU'RE A JOKE! A FUCKING JOKE!"

Roars emanate from the other side of the doors, and I try and give them the middle finger but my left hand is holding the rucksack and my right hand can only make a melted rock shape. It's all in the intent though.

The corridor behind me seems empty. I see a room at the back and make my way there so I'm out of the wraths' line of sight. I walk into the room and a noise by the door makes me turn in time to see a large white gas canister swinging towards my face and that's all there is.

Chapter 14

12th April 2021
8 months and 8 days after

My world consists of a chemo suite, with eight single beds and a comfortable wingback chair next to each bed. Patients sometimes prefer to lie in bed while they have their chemo and other times they'll sit up. Or at least they used to, there are no patients now. The room is at the end of a long corridor with thick security doors at the end. Beyond that there's a corridor that leads to the stairwell and lifts. My daily exercise is to tour this world. I walk around the perimeter of the room, walk to the doors, unlock them and stroll into the corridor. I turn left and walk to the stairs. When I get there, I turn around and walk to the lift. I press the call button and do five squats. The lift never comes, but it's fun to see the arrow light up. When I've done my squats, I turn around and walk back to the ward. I lock the door and come back home to the treatment room on the left. I do that routine at least ten times a day. I'm not sure what it's doing for me, but I think it's important to remember how to move. My ankles and feet are swollen and fat and I've been working my way through the staff lockers to find ever-bigger Crocs that will accommodate my Shrek feet.

I ended up in the left-hand chemo suite partly because it's the one with access to the office and supplies cupboard. I'd double my living space if I could use the right-hand treatment room but it's where I put the bodies and the things I couldn't cope with when I got here. The door to the room is wedged shut now because one night I had a nightmare where the dead were crowded behind the door, singing to me. In the morning I jammed the doors shut, so now they can only come out in my imagination. Up until my third trimester I was doing ten squats at the lift, but these days when I crouch, even a little, I can feel a grinding in my pelvis and I worry that those soft little skulls inside me are being damaged. Being pregnant messes with your head as much as your body.

Breakfast is ten oat crackers, five spread with jam and five spread with peanut butter. I'm down to fifteen jars of peanut butter, so the amount spread on each cracker has been getting stingier with each serving. Initially, that was a joke I told myself – "Whoops! Only fifty jars of peanut butter left, better be careful!" but it's not funny now. I don't know where I'm going after the babies are born. If the babies are born. I don't know when the fucking things are going to come out of me. I don't know how I'm going to do this. At all. I don't know lots of things. I can't think about it because then I start to lose control and have to pull on the nitrous oxide canister until I'm giggling again. Three cheers for Entonox! Breakfast finishes with a little tub of Ensure, a plant-based protein drink. It's a sludgy brown mess, but it washes down the pills: pyrimethamine – a vicious little brown dot; sulfadiazine – a sleek white pill; finally, Pregnacare – a brown vitamin capsule which always gets stuck in my throat. Every time I take them, I see the pharmacist trapped under the shelves in the chaos of her destroyed pharmacy. I see her bulging face and her dislocated jaws snapping at me as I searched through the pills.

After breakfast, I lie on a different bed each day and wait for the indigestion to fire up. Fifteen minutes after eating, regular as clockwork, a wave of heat rises up my back and breaks over my lungs. I rub what I can reach of my stomach and burp. Sometimes they are loud, reverberating belches, sometimes they are sinister, warming vomit burps. After nine months of this I've decided I'm going to let Martin buy me a house after all. A big one with a pool and a chef. As I'm lying on the bed, I massage Vaseline into my stomach and feel the babies respond to the arrival of food through the placenta. Lately, I've been able to see their hands and feet protruding through my skin more clearly. I've learned to shut my eyes and sense the babies' positions. I picture the way they're arranged inside me. In my mind, I watch their dance, their rotations, their fussing and needling of their sibling – a knee jerks and a bottom stretches out of the way. Then I get scared again about how they're going to get out, and I reach for the Entonox.

There's a TV on the ward but it shows only static. It's comforting to have it on but I don't know how long the hospital generators will continue to provide power, so I keep my energy usage to the absolute minimum. My hope is that they had enough fuel to run the whole hospital for several days in case of an extended power cut, so hopefully with just me here to draw power it'll last a while, but I don't want to push my luck. As terrifying as this place is now, if it was dark then...well, I don't want it to get dark. There's a small box of illicit paperbacks – matron used to call them germ hotels, but if someone was bored, we could offer them a Harlan Coben, or a Sue Grafton. I pick up *C is for Corpse* and start the next chapter, one arm wrapped around my babies. Kinsey takes me away for an hour, until I have to wee, so I lever myself off the bed and feel the ache in my back explode again as I stand and make my way to the toilet. I sit on the cold rim and give thanks for hospitals having to accommodate all sizes in their facilities, as the scale and sturdiness of the toilet feels weirdly comforting. I fill the toilet jug with water and pour it into the bowl, diluting the urine. If it's a poo, then it gets fished out with an old Tupperware tub and thrown out of the window where it disappears into the snow. The toilet flush has been feeble since week 10, but the water still flows from the taps and the shower works, for now.

I stand next to the large floor-to-ceiling window at the end of the ward and look out. The tree in the central courtyard is being tousled by the wind and some of the snow is dropping from the branches. The snow is thinner this morning. I hope it breaks soon. It's like being trapped in the Overlook Hotel from *The Shining*, the only thing it's lacking is spectral twins beckoning me to my doom, but maybe it'll have them too when I give birth. One thing that I'm grateful for is that the snow encased the bodies that were lying broken on the floor of the courtyard. I suppose they must have come from one of the windows in the block that faces my ward. There are fifteen broken windows I can see from my third-floor vantage point. I watch the blinds flapping in the wind through one of the windows, I can hear the clack they make as they clip the window frame.

There are three furies that I can see from here. One is a porter. He's sat in the courtyard – he would've been obscured by the snow but the smoking shelter has protected him. You have to marvel at the logic of building a smoking shelter in the heart of a cancer hospital. Maybe the idea was that with all of those people staring at you, it would shame you into giving up. Maybe they just didn't think. The porter hasn't moved since a pigeon landed on the shelter a few weeks ago. He screamed and screamed for hours, but he's still again now. The other two furies are patients, one in a gown and the other in a ripped pink cardigan. The gown lady is standing next to the door in a private room, so I'm guessing that she was wealthy before. She just waits there. I like to watch how her hair is growing. She's like my own little pot of cress. The pink cardigan lady is attached to a wall-mounted drip which she doesn't seem to know how to remove and sometimes she spots me and becomes angry and tries to hammer on the window, only to be yanked back by the drip in her arm.

The snow sets in in the afternoon. I get into bed and pull another blanket off another of the beds. In the store cupboard there are enough sheets and blankets to last until doomsday, which is probably a phrase that can now be retired. I nap for an hour and wake up disorientated. I think that Rick is in the room and he's farted. At home he used to do that. He'd open my bedroom door and I'd just see his arse poke around the door and he'd fart, and then he'd go and shut me in the Dutch oven he'd created. How can I miss something so gross? What is wrong with me that I'd give anything just to see his arse appear around that door? I wonder if he's out there somewhere wondering where I am. My mind takes me down a dark path and I'm imagining his body rotting somewhere. Today he's dead on the doorstep of the house. Auntie Pam is dead. My other brother Billy is dead. Martin is dead. Noam is dead. Dad is dead. Everyone is dead.

The thought of all that waste sparks something in me and I feel the anger shift gears and grow. My head squashes in on itself and I'm back in the MRI tube. I'm hearing Susie being torn apart, I'm listening to windows smashing, to all the different screams, and I'm smelling the smoke as it curls through the hospital. I'm raging and thrashing around, trapped inside the tube for three days with nothing but that dark anger and the looping music. I remember coming to and finally slipping my hand out of the restraint, then bending the headrest enough so that I could escape. I remember the agony of the stiffness in my neck. I remember the thirst and the hunger and the fear that the babies had been harmed. I remember wanting to get back to my ward. My safe place. I remember finding these things that looked human but that wanted me dead. I remember fighting. They were so angry, but they were so dumb. I remember my anger too. I remember my hand wrapped around a piece of a metal window frame and looking at it when I got to the ward and seeing long strands of black hair stuck to the end. I don't remember whose hair it was. I remember more death.

I am disappearing into the anger again. I pull the face mask that links to the nitrous oxide canister over towards me and hold it up to my face. I breathe deeply and feel the cold gas fill the mask and get sucked into my lungs. My head reels and despite myself the gas pulls the corners of my mouth up. A woozy smile appears on my face, and I start laughing. I'm still partly in the dream and partly in the memory of the MRI scanner, but instead of the terror, a sort of drunkenness descends upon me. The gas draws a bubble of a giggle out and I burp, which makes me laugh. I keep the mask cupped over my mouth and revel in the dizziness and how it makes all the memories cartoonish. A foot pushes against the womb and I pinch it lightly. I'm holding my child's foot, I think, and laugh again. If only I could just undo my belly button like a balloon knot and watch them gush out as the gas leaves my body. I laugh until my head aches slightly and I hazily push the mask up over my eyes and let the oxygen sober me up. Only happy thoughts now.

***

Tea is ten oat crackers, five spread with jam, five spread with peanut butter. I wash it down with a bottle of Ensure. After I've finished eating, I pull the remaining pallet of bottles over and spend thirty minutes with a Sharpie changing the S for a D and feel satisfied that my diet will now be bottles of Endure. I take my evening walk early and shuffle my feet from Crocs into fluffy slippers and stand. My head wobbles a bit which is probably from the nitrous oxide earlier. It's safe for the babies, but you tend to get a headache after a while and it can leave you disorientated and cold. But it's better than the alternative. I take my meds and start to make my way around the ward as usual. I visit each bed and pretend that I'm still a nurse and chat with the patients. They're all grateful when I cure them of cancer and right there, they declare me the best nurse in the world. I wonder if I might have the confidence to go and see the other ward tonight, but as my hand touches the door I think of Margaret and the last time we met, this sweet patient frothing with anger and fingers outstretched for my throat. I can't face it tonight. Tomorrow.

Instead, I walk to the double doors of the ward and undo the lock. I turn to the stairway end of the corridor. I turn around and walk the other way to the lift and press the call button. I think back, to try and remember if it was the number two button I pressed earlier, or number three. I think it was two, so I hit the circular three and start to squat. As usual the button illuminates, but no lift ever arrives. I take a wide stance and raise my arms above my head, as graceful as a ballet dancer. Then I lower my butt towards the floor and feel the stretch in my thighs. I rise back up and lift my hands above my head, imagining the hands are the white, black and orange heads of swans. I remember being in the back of Dad's car and Rick telling me that swans always break your arm if you go near them and me crying and Dad having to pull into a layby to shout at us until we stopped. I bend my creaking knees again and, just as I'm at the lowest point of the squat, there's a honk.

I pause in the squat and turn my head to one side, listening intently. Very faintly, I hear it. The sound of a truck's horn and the bump-bump-bump of a drum beat. Is it coming from somewhere? Is it real, or is it the gas and air? I stay so still for so long that a bead of drool forms on my lip and I suck it up noisily. It's real. Not only is it real, but it's the Vengaboys. I turn and as much as my barrel shape will allow, I run up the corridor and push back through the doors into the ward. I listen to see if I can still hear it. It's louder now, and it's definitely the Vengaboys. I can feel my heart pumping faster. Faster even than the beat of the song. It sounds louder from the direction of the right-hand ward and so, reluctantly, I kick the wedges away from the door and open the doors. I try to ignore the dark brown smears on the floor. Instead, I go straight to the window and look out over the front of the hospital. Margaret is where I left her all those weeks ago, thrashing against her bonds and trying to say something to me. I'd like to do something about that, but I can't right now.

The song seems to be coming from up high. It's been months since I saw anyone other than furies. Is this a rescue? Is it the army? Why would the army be playing the Vengaboys? I can only see a sliver of the sky from this window, but as I'm looking up, I see a shape flit across and then it's gone again. It looked like a small helicopter. It was the source of the music. I crane my neck around and push my face to the glass until condensation from my breath obscures my vision, and I rapidly wipe it clear with the side of my balled-up fist.

"PLEASE! I'M HERE! I'M ALIVE!" I shout. Margaret screeches something through her gag.

I listen. I close my eyes and imagine the same way I do when I'm thinking of the babies. I fill in the colour of the picture with my mind. The song is honking again. But there's something else in the mix now. There are voices. They are swearing and shouting. It sounds like more of the monsters, but this is different. It's the sort of crowd noise that you get when football fans find themselves corralled into railway station concourses. They join their voices and fill the space with songs and camaraderie – I think of Dad sitting at the bar starting to sing *Blue Moon* and fifty voices all joining him. But these voices aren't in unison. They're harsh and rude. I see movement and hear the noises of chaos, a smash and breaking glass, like an explosion. This isn't a rescue. I look around and the terror of the room comes back. Breaking Margaret and pinning her down until I managed to wrap her in IV lines and block up her mouth. Staring at what this sweet woman had become and understanding in that moment that the whole world was gone. Then panic at not knowing what to do with the other bodies. Not knowing anything. Locking the door and lying in bed with the blankets over my head.

The monsters are coming. Not just one or two of them, but all of them. My hands are trembling and my breath is shallow. I don't have to strain to hear the crowd now. They will soon be at the door, and they are death. I feel the babies writhing and the anger comes again. They'll never get the chance to eat popcorn in a cinema. They'll never smell fireworks on Bonfire Night. They'll never have a favourite teddy bear. What has happened to this world? There's a taste in my mouth like sick. I swallow hard and run into the other room. I quickly pull the mask towards me and huff deeply on the gas. Despite the terror and the growing anger, I smile giddily and then I'm equal parts crying and angry and high. There's a sound like a vehicle has hit the building. I choke back more of the nitrous and feel adrenaline fighting against the drunkenness. They are coming! They are coming! My hands come to my head and the babies whirl in unison. Another noise sounds out closer this time. Something is in the stairwell. It sounds like an approaching army. I breathe in more gas and tremble.

"I'm so sorry, my children."

My laughter reduces to a whimper and I can't help the tears that are falling from my eyes. The injustice of surviving so long, only to die now, reignites the anger. I will fight. I hear a whistle and recoil at how close it sounds. This is how it ends.

And with crushing dismay and a sense of fatality I realise that I didn't lock the door to the ward. When I heard the music in the corridor, I ran to see what it was and didn't stop to lock the door. My stupidity has killed not just me, but the babies. I reach over the bed and slide the white canister out from its enclosure and silently and awkwardly tuck myself behind the open door. I'm sure that my belly is poking around it and I think of Rick's arse and laugh, but more quietly this time. There's a scream in the corridor outside. My heart pounds and I wrap my fingers tight around the top of the canister so I can get a good grip. I will kill as many as I can, to give these babies even one more second of life.

I hear a thud and then a voice:

"FUCK YOU! I WIN! FUCK YOU! YOU CAN'T EVEN CATCH A FUCKING CANCER PATIENT. YOU'RE A JOKE! A FUCKING JOKE!"

Through the crack in the door, I see a blur of orange as the first fury clatters into the room. I have no thoughts. I pull the canister back and as soon as I see a tall form come within range, I hit it square in the face. It collapses onto the floor in a heap. Then, a small brown and black dog charges through the doorway, its teeth bared to the gums, ears flat to its skull.

I know this dog.

Chapter 15

13th April 2021
8 months, 9 days after

There's something in the back of my left hand. Without opening my eyes, I move my hand a fraction and feel something solid and spiky stuck in it. My right hand feels different too – warm and prickly. My hands are odd. I open my eye slightly and try to take in what's around me. I'm in a brightly lit room, it feels like it's big but currently I can only see one section of it because pleated blue curtains are screening the rest of it. A jumbled thought comes into my head: I'm in the hospital because I needed my leg amputating. They lifted me out of my flat with a crane. That's right. My hands are odd because of the operation. This is a catheter in my hand, which is connected to a tube, which is connected to a drip. I am alive.

There's white paper tape on my face and a piece of blue gauze that sits over my nose. I don't know what that is.

Belatedly, I realise that I'm in a hospital gown and that I'm naked underneath. I have already been fitted with a prosthetic leg, which I don't remember the doctor saying would happen. That seems too quick. I look around, and leaning nearby against the wall is a shotgun with a small knife taped to the top. I look at that for a long time. Why is there a shotgun in a hospital? I see Karl's face going blue and then black as he lies in a shallow pool of rainwater. In a rush my brain starts to fill in the pieces and I remember – the *Our Kid*, the canal, the Land Rover, the drone, the Vengaboys. Everything. Somewhere off on the left, I can just hear the Vengaboys playing faintly. Then I see all of those sad drowned faces in the Salford Quays and I'm awake. The wraths at the doors. Someone hit me in the face.

I lean over to get the gun and I silently lift the shotgun and, using my legs to balance, I manage to break the barrel and see that there is one shell already loaded. I rest the gun on my knees and awkwardly place my right index finger over the trigger and wait and listen. I notice that at the bottom of my bed, Bear is looking at me. So, where's Brown? Bear looks like it's seen some shit. The thousand-yard stare of its glassy eye has deepened and now it looks like it's astral voyaging somewhere. Wherever it is, I hope that it's less awful than here.

I listen intently past *We Like To Party!* to see if I can hear the tip-tap of Brown's claws on the polished floor. Instead, I hear water running and a door opens and closes. I tense and level the gun on my knees. I quickly glance to check the safety is off. The curtain draws back and there is Helen. She's wearing a hospital-issue dressing gown and purple

Crocs, and Brown is standing in touching distance of her legs looking happier than I've seen her in months. Helen's different – she's massively pregnant and a thick purple scar about an inch in length runs from the tip of her chin to the bottom of her lip. But it is Helen.

"Helen?" I say, and the shotgun triggers. The discharge shreds one side of the curtains just to her right. The shot peppers the room beyond and I hear a glass smash and a ricochet as some shot hits something metal. Helen flinches as much as she can, which consists of turning to one side. Brown is silently yapping and leaping around frantically, unaccustomed to being shot at by me.

"Oh shit, are you okay? Are you both okay? It just went off!"

"Ben! What the fuck? WHAT THE FUCK!"

Beyond her the sounds of shouting and raging begin amidst the sound of pounding. Looking shaken, Helen comes to stand next to my bed and takes a clear plastic face mask off a hook on the wall and straps it to her face. She sits on the edge of the bed and takes the shotgun from me, and points it towards the noise. I don't tell her it doesn't have any ammunition in it. We sit in silence as the only sound in the room is her taking deep breaths from the mask and Brown skittering around and leaping on and off the bed, silently barking at the wraths. I sit there and all I can think is: who took my trousers off?

After thirty seconds of huffing on the gas, Helen starts to titter and has to work hard to suppress noisier laughter.

The wraths beyond the doors rage and the sounds of rioting reach us, but after ten minutes the door stops rattling. I start to speak but Helen turns and holds a finger to her smiling lips.

"Let me check," she whispers.

She slips the mask off and hangs it back on the wall. She disappears between a gap in the remaining curtain and Brown instantly follows her. I notice that she doesn't even take Bear with her. Helen reappears and my brain still hasn't caught up with the shock. Why is Helen here? Her hair is darker and longer but she still has those same green eyes, searching me for answers that I'm positive I don't have. In my mind, it's two years ago and Helen is standing in my flat. She kisses me and I don't know where to put my arms, she stands there looking at me, assessing me just as she is now. I notice with a start that she still has the gun. She seems to reach a conclusion in her own thinking and sinks into the wide chair next to the bed. She pulls the mask off the wall and starts to breathe deeply again.

"*Whisper*," she says through the mask.

"Right."

"Quieter," she holds a finger to her lips. "And don't shoot at me ever again."

"Agreed. Sorry."

Brown jumps on the bed and we both just stare at each other. Brown starts to clean Bear.

"Helen. You are Helen, aren't you?"

"No, I'm Natalie."

"What?"

She looks at me as if I'm daft.

"I called myself Helen when I first joined Tinder. It seemed sensible to use an alter ego in case it turned out to be the sort of degenerate place where weirdos would pretend to be wonderful human beings and then ghost you with no warning."

Ohhhhhhh, right.

"I'm sorry Helen,"

"Natalie."

"I'm sorry, Natalie. I'm sorry I ghosted you."

She just looks at me, assessing me and I sit back in the bed and wince at the various pains across my body.

"I fucked up. I wasn't well. If it makes you feel any better, one year after that I got ghosted by everyone in the entire world."

"You have to stop using the end of the world as a way of covering up a relationship faux pas."

She sits in silence and looks at me.

"Is that what this is? Is this the end of the world?" I ask.

"The furies? I don't know. I don't think so. I think it's just the end of humans. The world will go on. Maybe the snow will cover it all and it'll be like in those Bugs Bunny cartoons when he'd run onto a blank page."

"Furies? That's a great name for them. I've been calling them wraths."

"Potato, potahto."

"Tomato, tomahto."

Natalie takes a final pull on the gas and lifts the mask onto her forehead. Her eyes are glassy and unfocused. She smiles to herself. Then she looks at me and snorts with laughter, snot flies out of her nose.

"Oh, bumblefuck!" she says, doubling over with laughter.

"Is that safe for the baby?" I ask.

"Bab*ies*. Plural, two of them. Not that it's any business of yours. This is strictly between me and my husband," she defiantly pulls the mask down over her mouth and draws heavily on it again, as if to prove a point.

"You're married?" The disappointment in my voice is all too obvious.

"Of course, do you think a lieutenant general in the Queen's army would have a child out of wedlock?"

She smiles drowsily and exhales the invisible gas as if she's blowing out smoke rings. "Relax Benjamin, it's gas and air, it doesn't cross the placental barrier – that's why they use it in labour. Besides, it's safer than what happens if I don't have it."

"Why?"

She pauses before answering and her face becomes sad.

"Because I'm one of them." She gestures casually over her shoulder towards the wraths, then she brings her hands up as if they're claws and makes a face. "I'm a fury."

"A wrath? How can you be? You can talk! You can... do things!"

"Oh, I can, if I stay calm. If I take my drugs. If I keep myself fucked up on this stuff. Then so far, I've not gone as far as them, but it's never far away."

"How do you know?"

"Well, Benjamin, when this all began, I was in the middle of getting an MRI scan, which is how I know that something in here-" she taps her forehead hard "-is wrong."

She takes another huff of the gas.

"And I feel it, too. I look at them sometimes and I find myself agreeing with them. I get it. I feel every grievance that they have. I hear the same voices inside me telling me that things are wrong. I want to…I just know."

"What do you mean "something in here?" You mean there's something in your head?"

"The technician doing my MRI saw something when she scanned my head. Then everything went mad and I spent three days and nights trapped in the MRI machine. And the only thing I wanted during those days was to get out and to break everything. I have to stop talking. Tell me what happened to you."

She breathes heavily in the mask again.

"Um, well, when it happened, I was supposed to be going to the hospital for an operation. I got stuck as well. Then when I got out, I was stuck in my flat. I lived off water and a single pack of Bourbons. I lost over 35olbs."

She bursts out laughing at this.

"That's…not the reaction I was expecting. If you like that, you'll love this: I had to amputate my own leg."

Helen guffaws so loudly that she turns to see if the wraths have heard, but she can't help the tears of mirth pouring from her eyes.

"Brown was nearly killed by a wrath so I eviscerated him with a drone and then strangled a fireman who tried to kill me."

Helen holds up her hand to make me stop talking as she continues to laugh. She pitches forward and laughs into the bed to try and muffle the noise. I look nervously at the door.

"Ohhhhhh Ben, that's priceless!"

"For the last month I've been living on a cargo ship, waiting for Brown to give birth, but when she went into labour there were no puppies. Or there were and they just disappeared, I don't know."

"She had a phantom pregnancy?"

"Is that a thing? Why is that a thing? Yes, it was probably a phantom pregnancy."

She tries to stop laughing, but it's too much and she starts to pound the bed with her fist. She pulls Brown towards her and cuddles into her neck murmuring, "Little mother." Interestingly, Brown doesn't resist and licks the tears from Natalie's face.

"Stop talking or I'm going to wet myself!"

"Oh yeah, and I have colon cancer and I frequently shit myself."

"YES! You'd shat yourself....when I knocked....you out!" her words come in painful bursts through the laughter.

"That explains the missing trousers."

"Oooh! Oooh! Oooh! And your nose is broken, and some of the bones in your hand too!"

She inhales painfully as her body tries to cope with the onslaught of hilarity I'm providing her. To be honest, I'm not even sure how to feel, here's Helen – Natalie – alive-ish and real. There's someone else in the world. Maybe there are others.

Despite my mind spinning out trying to make sense of it all, I feel a sense of calm for the first time in months. It's partly the joy of seeing Natalie again and knowing that I'm not on my own, but there's more to it than that. I feel like I'm just starting to glimpse the outline of a bigger picture, drawn by a greater hand. The one thought that keeps going over and over in my mind is there has to be a reason for this. Out of everyone in the entire world, the one person I find alive is Natalie. That can't be chance.

"And I'm a monster!" she manages to say in a croak.

"A drug-addicted monster," I point out. "A *pregnant* drug-addicted monster. The Daily Mail would have a field day with you."

"Ohhhhhh, it's too good. It's too good! We're perfect. This is perfect. Don't talk. I can't take it anymore."

I smile at her. She presses the heels of her hands into her ears and closes her eyes. She breathes very deliberately through her nose and exhales through her mouth with an *AHHHHH* noise. I look at Brown, who is gazing at Natalie with great interest.

"You get that she's pregnant right?"

Brown looks at me with her head tilted.

"I mean actually pregnant, not just cosplaying with a teddy bear." Brown picks up Bear and lifts it to show me.

"Good girl," I say and Brown yawns.

While Natalie is restoring her equilibrium, I examine my bandaged hand. I try and wiggle the fingers. They move stiffly but I don't feel much pain. With my left hand, I probe the tape and gauze on my face. My nose feels bigger and I realise that I'm breathing through my mouth. Natalie probably thinks I'm a mouth-breather. I gently snort and try and clear my nasal passage but my nose is resolutely blocked. I try and smell myself but I just smell the medical twang of gauze. I bet I need a bath. Maybe she gave me a bath. Oh, God.

"Where's your husband?" I ask.

"He's in Monaco," Natalie replies, but doesn't elaborate. She looks at me, immediately very focused. "Ben, listen to me. If I turn into one of them then I want you to kill me and take the babies to him in Monaco."

"But..."

"Shush, you need to do this. If I turn then I don't know what will happen. I don't know if I'd hurt them. Or you. Or Brown. Or whatever that thing that used to be a teddy bear is. You need to promise me that you'll kill me and take the babies to Monaco."

"Okay."

"Promise."

"I promise," I lie.

"Thank you."

"Do you know if your husband is alive?"

"I don't. But if there's anyone on Earth who I'd put money on surviving, it would be him."

"What happened to your chin?"

"I don't want to talk about that. It's so strange, seeing you thin."

"Better?"

"Different."

"I don't know. While I was stuck in the flat, I got into fitness. It's nice to have a body that does something. It's just a shame I look like a giant skin tag."

"You don't."

"Cancer and the apocalypse are a potent weight loss combination. I should market it as a diet plan."

"What, you weren't joking about the cancer?"

"No! Why would I joke about cancer?"

"Ohhhh, I'm so sorry. I thought you were just making everything sound worse to make me laugh!"

"No! That was all true. Just before the change, I was being brought into hospital for the amputation and the doctor told me. That's why I came here."

"What were you going to do? Have a go at some DIY chemo?"

"I don't know. I didn't think I'd get here. I was hoping there'd be a pamphlet or something." Natalie hoots with laughter.

"What type is it? What stage?"

"I don't know for sure. The doctor said that he did a blood test which showed it up. He said he guessed it was a colorectal cancer, but he wanted to do more tests."

Natalie is stood at the side of the bed now and she starts to pull my blankets down.

"Show me your stomach."

"*Okay.*"

I lift the gown and once again I'm struck by the horror of my flesh. Seeing it through Natalie's eyes, I can't ignore how horrid it is. Pock-marked by old scars from ulcers, lined with stretchmarks and stringy and clammy to the touch like a burst balloon. Natalie doesn't flinch though. She pumps foam from a dispenser on the wall and rubs it into her hands. She gently starts to probe and push at my stomach. It feels weirdly intimate. I'm aware that I'm naked from the waist down and only covered by the blankets. I'm really, really concerned I'm about to get the most inappropriate erection ever.

"Does this hurt at all?"

"It feels tender."

"Tender like painful?"

"I don't know, like I'd rather you weren't doing it."

"Any place worse than any other?"

"Not really." She pulls my gown down, squeezes more foam into her hands and sits in the chair again. Her tone changes and she bites at her top lip with her lower teeth.

"What are your poos like?"

"This feels more like a second date conversation."

"Poos. Tell me."

"Runny, bloody."

"What type of blood?"

"I don't know, B I think?"

"Not what blood type, what type of blood? Is it a darker red? Brighter? Streaks? Drops?"

"Oh, lots of red blood, like quite a fresh-looking blood, I think."

"Okay – the next time you do one I need to see it. If that's right then it sounds more like the ascending colon than descending. And the doctor said they'd done a C-reactive protein test?"

"I can't remember exactly what he said, he just said that there was some blood test that they could do which picked it up, yes I think it was a protein test."

"Ok. So that was eight months ago. That's not good."

"Oh."

"Well, we don't know what it is – but we need to get started."

"Started with what?"

"Chemotherapy!"

"You can help?"

"Ben, I'm a specialist cancer nurse. This is literally my job."

"Well, okay."

"Give me a minute." She disappears once more through the curtains and I look again at the blast hole in the fabric on my right. That was too close. Natalie returns and passes me a small cup with seven pills in it.

"What's this?"

"That's your next dose of dihydrocodeine for your nose and hand. You had some a few hours ago, so you're good to go again now. The little pink ones are capecitabine, which is the chemo. There's also an anti-emetic as well, because buddy you're going to want to barf like never before. You might get mouth ulcers and weird feet too, but we'll deal with that if it happens."

"What, so this is chemotherapy? I thought it was all drips and machines or something?"

"A lot of chemo is oral therapy these days. I wish I could do a DPD test to make sure you're not going to cark it, but unless you've got a gene scanner in your rucksack then we're just going to have to cross our fingers. Ready?"

She offers me a carton of drink and I read the label to check it's vegan. The drink is called Ensure but it's been amended to read Endure. It seems like a good suggestion.

"Chin, chin," I say and hold the cup up in a toast and tip it back into my mouth. I start to swallow the pills as I chug the drink back.

"Just the one chin these days," she says.

And just like that, I'm having chemotherapy. Brown shuffles up the bed with Bear in her mouth and rests herself on my leg. Her weight is comforting and the silky touch of her fur makes me smile. I realise that I am warm. I feel happy. I look at Brown and a sense that something greater is at work fills my heart. There are too many coincidences. Too many choices that could have led me in an infinite number of different directions. But my choices brought me here and that has to mean something, doesn't it?

Natalie sits back and puts her feet up on the bed. She picks up a well-thumbed book and starts to read. I look at her and remember the endless scroll of messages that we sent to each other on Tinder. My mind takes the conversation back to the very beginning, to when she told me that she was a nurse.

"That could come in handy," I'd said.

The ceiling tiles start to waver in my vision and a gilded heaviness creeps across my body. I want to sleep for an eternity. If this is the end, then I'm glad that I died in this place. I'm glad Brown isn't alone. That's good.

"Helen?"

"Natalie."

"Sorry, Natalie?"

"Yes?"

"I wanted to go with you. To America. I just couldn't make myself leave. I'm sorry." I feel tears welling in my eyes. The shame of what I did to her.

"It's okay Ben. You were jammed in pretty tight. I knew it was a big ask. I didn't want to make you feel uncomfortable, but in some ways, it seemed like what you needed were people who were okay with making you feel uncomfortable."

"I wanted to go to Disneyland with you so much."

"Me too."

"What was it like?"

"I didn't go in the end, life got in the way."

My eyes shut and I hear the rasp of my breath coming in and out through my mouth. Somehow, despite the wraths at the door, the ward feels warm and safe. A big mouse in white gloves comes and sits on the bed. I smile at him and he smiles back. He's always smiling. I feel a hand in mine, and I drift away.

Chapter 16

15th April 2021
8 months and 11 days after

The chemo has kicked in and Ben is wiped out today. He lies in bed either staring at the ceiling in a stupor, or he's sleeping. I'm not surprised, he's on a full dose of capecitabine, which a patient once told me made her feel like she was wading through treacle. I didn't want to make too much of it but there was an 8% chance he would have been lacking the DPD enzyme. If he was, then the medication I gave him could have been toxic. The balance of risk in doing nothing was greater though. Maybe I should have told him. I don't know.

Brown only leaves Ben when I go to the toilet, when she leaps off the bed and trots alongside me. She seems determined not to let either of us out of sight if she can help it. She scratches at the door if I leave her outside, so instead I let her in and she sits obediently about a foot away from me, maintaining eye contact while I use the facilities. I don't know if it's because she can't make any noise but eye contact seems to be more important to her than other dogs. If you move your head even slightly while you're sat down then she's looking at you. Sweet Jesus, she's cute. She knows it too though. Once I've flushed and washed my hands she herds me back towards Ben, who is snoring. I pinch his nose and he snorts.

"It's not a go-kart if you have to push it," he says and swats at some dream bees.

"That's your best friend," I say to Brown, and she eyes me as she curls in a tight circle at the bottom of the bed and flops next to Bear. I reach over for my pill cup and down my next dose. I shudder as the Endure reluctantly pushes them down my throat. I put my bare feet up on the bed and let them rest against Brown, who gamely begins to lick them, but almost immediately thinks better of it. I haven't been able to reach my feet for several weeks now, so I don't take offence. I wonder how long you have to wait before it's acceptable to ask someone to cut your toenails for you. Is that period of time longer or shorter in an apocalypse? I'll bet that Debrett's covers it.

I look at Ben's face, his slack jaw and the dark purple circles that have settled under his eyes from the broken nose. It's strange but I don't feel any guilt about hitting him. He was just in the wrong place at the wrong time. When he's conscious Ben won't shut up about our meeting being a divine intervention – he thinks he was in the exact right place at the right time. I told him that using that logic meant that God wanted him to be smacked in the face with a gas canister. I understand the temptation to overlay meaning on this, but it's just a coincidence. We live, well – lived, on a planet with seven billion people; the only surprising thing about chance meetings is that we're surprised by them. You bump into your dentist in an airport lounge in Egypt, so what? You're on a conference in LA with someone you went to school with, who cares? That goes double for Manchester too – it's one of those cities that acts like a village. You can't go anywhere without bumping into someone you know. Any meaning we add to those moments is just stories we tell ourselves to obscure the truth: we're on our own and the universe is random and mostly awful.

***

Fighting my way back to my ward after I escaped the MRI scanner was a sort of homing instinct. I was spinning in and out, more fury than human at points. But some unconscious internal mechanism kicked in and brought me back here. It's like how Dad could have ten pints and not know his name, but he would still turn up at home and find his way to bed. I'd picked up some Entonox as I'd come through the hospital, mostly because I was in such pain from being stuck in place for three days and it was the first thing that could numb me back to reality. When I got back to the ward and finally locked and barred the doors, I wasn't ready to face what was in here. Someone, I'm guessing Margaret, had killed two of the nurses – Sonya and Phillip - and she was *paused,* looking out of the window. I didn't know then that that's what happened to the furies when they weren't disturbed. She seemed so calm that I didn't know she was a fury, but when I whispered her name, she turned and her smile dissolved into a screech, and then a sprint towards me with her arms outstretched.

"Margaret, it's me – Natalie!" I shouted as I tried to hold her at arm's length.

"You're the bitch who sticks me every time I come in. Learn to hit a vein, you fat sow," she replied as she kicked her slippered foot at my knee.

I got angry then and my intention changed. I went from restraining her to pinning her. As my fury mounted, I'd slammed her to the ground and knelt on her arms. I felt the bones break. Her feet and thin legs wheeled in the air, but I had her restrained. I could have left her like that but I had to go on. So, I punched her. Again and again. Over and over. For the first time in my life, I balled my fist up and drove it into someone else's face. It felt great. It felt like the first glass of wine after a week of double shifts. By the time I stopped, her face was pulped and bloody and she was gagging on her false teeth which I'd knocked loose. I somehow dragged on the gas and found myself coming back by turns. I wanted to cry as I looked at what I'd done. How I'd hurt a woman who I'd spent the last few months desperately trying to give more life.

Her breath rattled and a string of blood poured out of the corner of her mouth. I tipped her on her side, found some IV cable and tied her hands up and gagged her, and with both hands over her head I dragged her into the right-hand ward. I pulled the bodies of my colleagues in after her and shut the door. I mopped the floors and straightened the room out and then I studiously avoided thinking about it for weeks at a time, until the inhabitants of the ward started to populate my dreams. Guilt is a seed that always blooms.

Now Ben was here I'd been wondering about the opportunities that the other room presented.

"No way," Ben says.

"We have to," I reply.

"But what will it prove?"

"It could prove everything. It could explain everything: don't you want to know what caused the end of the world? I don't want to do it either, she was a patient of mine, but we have to do this, Ben. We might never get another chance."

"Why not?"

"You could die. I could die. Any minute, if one of us coughs too loudly a thousand furies could come through those doors and tear us apart! I need your help."

Ben winces and looks conflicted.

"Look, I'll do the nasty bits," I assure him. "I just need you to do the first bit. I also need to borrow your crowbar."

Ben looks paler than ever. I help him get up and wrap another of the thin hospital gowns around him. He holds onto his drip stand and we shuffle him to the edge of the ward. I look down the corridor and the wraths are still pressed up against the door, but they're in a sort of group standby state, they seem to be swaying together very slightly in time to some hum that only they can hear. Fortunately, the batteries on the speaker have finally lapsed and the Vengaboys no longer ring out across South Manchester.

I put my arm around Ben and support him. We walk swiftly across the corridor, removing the wedges and barricade to the other ward. Inside there's a musty smell, like old towels and raw mince. I try not to look at the decaying corpses in the hospital uniforms in the corner of the room. I know I left Margaret behind the last bed on the left and I point Ben in the right direction.

"Hold Brown," he says, and I reach down and tuck a hand under her stomach to keep her from following him.

Ben slowly makes his way down the room with something metal glinting in his palm. I watch as he stops at the end of the bed, like a doctor checking the charts, and I hear shuffling and a very muffled growl. Ben lets go of his drip stand and advances, holding a scalpel out in front of him, and disappears behind the bed. There's a high-pitched squealing noise which makes Brown try to run towards Ben so I hold her tight. The squealing rises in intensity, then there's a bubbling sound.

Ben holds up his hand, telling us to wait where we are and he hops onto the bed. I see a red puddle emerge beyond the end of the bed and gradually extend to the middle of the room. Ben swings his legs over the other side of the bed and reaches for his drip stand which he wheels back towards us. I notice the drip stand has tracked four dark, slick lines of blood across the floor. Ben looks dangerously pale.

"Done."

"Go back if you want," I say to him.

"No, I'll stay. Moral support."

My hand is sweaty around the crowbar and I make my way to the end of the room. Margaret is almost unrecognisable. Her body looks tiny and frail. She's lying motionless in a large pool of her blood. Ben slit her throat from ear to ear and a gaping flap lies under her chin like a hideous necklace. I feel my breakfast swill in my stomach, but years of nursing has made me resistant to most gore. The difference is that this is gore that I created. I tap Margaret's foot with mine to make sure she's dead and wait for a few seconds. Then I reach over and drag her out into the middle of the room. Ben lifts Brown onto the bed and he sits and watches. She leaves a wide crescent of blood above her head like a rainbow from Hell. As I'm pulling her, I can feel the babies wake up and start to kick each other.

I tell myself that this is important work, this is priceless information. I tell myself that this could help the babies and I have to do it. So I put aside my revulsion and place the tip of the crowbar against her nose and brace my arms against the bar and let it take my weight. There is resistance for a moment and then with a *crrrk,* the bar sinks into Margaret's nasal cavity. I place a foot on her head and turn the bar through 180 degrees. My foot holding her skull still isn't enough to get leverage, but Ben sees the problem and stands unsteadily, putting his foot on the other side of Margaret's head. Between us, we pin it in place with enough force, that when I apply the crowbar there is a noise like a crab claw cracking and my journey into her brain begins.

***

It takes 20 minutes to find it. If Susie hadn't told me there was something in there, I don't think I would have kept on looking. By the end, our arms are caked in brain and blood up to our elbows. There are sections of skull littered across the floor. Brown scratches at the other side of the bathroom door, annoyed that we put her in solitary confinement after she started licking blood from the floor. The Entonox mask is over my face the entire time and I have to change the canister, but even off my tits, the rank horror of what we've just done sits heavily on me. Margaret's head is spread across the floor in pieces. Ben has been sick several times, which just adds to the organic smells in the room. In the end, we only found it because the pale white colour stood out against the ruddy pink of the brain tissue.

"Whatever it is, it's fucking revolting," he says. He starts to prod it with his finger but I hold his hand back.

"We don't know anything about this, we need to be careful."

The centre of it is barely bigger than the tip of a ballpoint pen. Extending from all sides are spindly tuberous threads, some several centimetres long. There are more on one side than the other, but I figure I must have ripped some of them off when I was extracting it – this is why you don't do brain surgery with a crowbar. The little shoots remind me of the growths from potatoes. Some of them are almost hairlike, others shorter and stouter.

"You think this is what your friend saw in your brain?"

"I think so." The thought of one of these sitting in my brain makes me feel odd, like I want to itch a spot five centimetres behind my eyes.

"What is it?"

"A parasite. If I'm right it's toxoplasma gondii, or a mutation of it. It's the only thing that makes sense and it would explain why I'm not quite one of them. I was diagnosed almost exactly at the point when I caught it and treated, so maybe that's why it behaves differently in me. My doctor said that it was incredibly common. He said that up to 70% of the population have the parasite."

"In Manchester?"

"In the world."

"Wait, so 70% of people *in the world* have one of these sitting in their brains?"

"Well, they did have – but the point is that they never did anything before, they just sat there, like it was asleep. There's no real reason that you'd know if you carried it or not."

"So, what, it grew?"

"Ben, I don't know what happened! Maybe it was the heatwaves, maybe it was limited edition Orange Kit Kats – I don't know! I think it's safe to say that it woke up."

We sit in silence and look at this little speck of evil and contemplate the destruction it has wrought.

"Think about how dumb the furies are. Look at the little shoots this thing is sending out. What if it's making its way into other areas of the brain. If it's changing brain function then it may be responsible for that weird hibernation they go into."

"So that's why they don't need to eat or drink?"

"Maybe, I mean this is all speculation, but it's the best we've got."

"But why didn't I get it?"

"Well, 30% of the population who don't have one is still billions of people, you're not that special. It's mostly caught through contact with cat faeces, undercooked meats or unwashed vegetables."

"So, I was protected because I was a shut-in? A vegan shut-in with a dog and a diet of ready-meals?" he says and he looks at me. "I was saved."

"Well, if you want to look at it like that then 30% of the population were also saved."

"But then the other 70% killed them. But again, I was saved."

"Ben, get over yourself. This isn't proof that God has a plan for you. Look at this thing. What possible point could our all-loving Father be trying to make with this shit?"

"But we could do something, couldn't we? Why can't we get the same drugs that you're on and give them to the wraths?"

I'm starting to get frustrated. I've never seen someone so oblivious. Sometimes Ben's flashes of idiotic optimism tries to bypass all of the obvious problems, but that doesn't mean that it solves them – they're still there.

"Ben, do we look like we're ready to save the world?"

Ben looks wounded and seems a bit unsteady. I grab his hand and help him to the edge of the nearest bed. His face seems drawn and I can feel my anger mounting again, so I grab the Entonox and start to pull on it. Ben recognises that this is a sign that things are getting out of control.

"So, if none of this makes any difference, why did you want to do it?" he asks.

"I needed to know. I wanted to know if the babies were safe. I want to know how to keep you safe. We can't save the world, but we can save ourselves. That's the priority."

***

It's deep into the night. Snow is falling outside the window and all I can hear is the snuffling of Brown's breathing and Ben's snoring. My hands are splayed on my belly and I'm feeling the babies fluttering. A memory comes to me of when Martin first moved down the road from us. He wore this mad purple smoking jacket. Kids came from streets away to see it and as sure as night followed day, they'd punch him. But that little psycho wouldn't stop wearing it. Instead, he doubled down and bought a cane. That kid could take a beating.

One day Barry Faulkner was going after him and was stood over Martin who was curled up in the gutter. I came up behind him and kicked Barry in the nuts in a pair of princess shoes so pointy that I'm amazed it didn't get stuck up there. Barry pissed himself a bit and everyone called him Barry FuckedNuts from then on. Martin smiled up at me from the gutter with a mouth full of blood, then he got to his feet and turned to the assembled children and screamed in a weird old crone accent, "Let that be a lesson to yez! Alllllllll o' yez! Come for me again and I'll sic my harpy on ya!"

The point is that I have this very bad habit where I pick broken people and stand in the way of everything that tries to hurt them. It's why I chose to specialise as a cancer nurse. Most of my patients are doomed. A very large anvil is falling on their heads from a great height, but every time I stand next to them, hold their hand and put up the biggest umbrella I can. It doesn't often help, but I do it again and again and again. It's just part of who I am.

I'm aware that I love Ben. He's broken and that's part of why I fell in love with him, but as I got to know him, I saw that he's just as odd as me. He's broken and he knows it, but he wants to fix everything *apart from himself*. That's why his first reaction when we looked at that shitty parasite was, let's save the world; God has a plan for us to save the world rah, rah, rah! I knew I loved the dozy arse when I asked him to come to America with me and I knew it when he ghosted me. I knew it when I stood at the crematorium watching Dad's coffin go behind those horrible gold curtains and I knew it when I've been stuck in here for the last eight months. Sitting in the chair listening to him snore, I know I love him now. I don't buy into his bollocks that this is all according to some great plan, but I do believe something just as daft. Somehow, I think that my love brought him here. It's like how birds follow a thin magnetic field to find their way home. I think he's here because I pulled him here. The difference in our bullshit theories is that I'm smart enough to keep mine to myself.

But the universe can't give me a happy ending, can it? It's the Monkey's Paw – you get what you want, but not in the way you wanted it. Ben was brought to me and now I have to watch him die. Even before he said about the cancer, I knew he was dying. It's the same way Dad would tell you that a car needed new tyres from the other side of a car park. It's professional instinct.

I stand as quietly as I can, but Brown looks at me and lifts her head off the bed that she hasn't left for hours now.

"Meds," I mouth to her and then wonder why I'm explaining myself to a dog. She stands and stretches, then drops off the bed to accompany me. I reach down awkwardly and run the back of my hand along her muzzle. Her softness and warmth bring me more comfort than I can believe. Since she arrived, I've needed the gas much less. She is next to my feet until I reach the counter. I pop two pills from their case and wash them down with water. Brown looks at me appealingly and I open a pack of crackers and feed her one. She eats it without much joy, leaving half of it on the floor.

"Same," I say and force a cracker into my mouth in the hope that it will stave off the indigestion.

I feel restless so I walk across the ward and open the door a crack so I can peek around the corner. Furies are still pressed against the door. A giant smear of blood obscures one of the glass panels but through the other I can see the horde – it runs back to the elevator and possibly beyond. The weight on the door must be incredible, if it wasn't held by the security lock they would be in here in an instant. I look down, and realise that Brown has sneaked out and is sniffing around in the central corridor right in front of the furies.

"Brown! Come here!" I hiss, but she continues to sniff around in the main corridor investigating some ancient smell memory. I open the door and walk quickly towards the main doors. One of the fury's eyes open and the ripple effect spreads instantly as she starts to scream. The doors rattle on their hinges and the lock groans. Then Brown is stood between me and the doors, her lips pulled back over her teeth, ready to fight to the death. Something about the furies' anger resonates with me and I understand. I know what they want. I want it too.

They want silence.

They want darkness.

I pick up the fire extinguisher from its station by the door and struggle with the safety tab. It snaps off just as I hear the door creak louder from the weight of the anger behind it. I'm not scared. I pull the pin, point the hose at the door and spray. A thick curd of foam splatters on the door's windows and I keep spraying until the glass is completely coated. Parts of it slide off but a thick membrane stays on the door and obscures us from the furies, and vice versa. Brown skips away from the hissing of the extinguisher, but I'm weirdly rooted to the spot. I hear my thoughts as the furies bay at us just metres away. They want me to agree. I stand still and just listen. I feel my arm involuntarily rise towards the lock. It would all be so simple. So quick. I jerk myself out of the reverie.

I walk back to the ward and tear down one of the privacy curtains and fix it on the doors with some micropore tape. Even if the foam slides off, we will hopefully be obscured by the curtain. Robbed of the visual stimulus, the furies start to go quiet. The door holds and the mist in my brain clears as Brown rubs against my ankles. As the babies play tag in my womb, I feel my focus turn inwards again, I see my heart beating and the gush of adrenaline as it slops around my body. I watch the burning origins of the indigestion as it erupts in my gut like the gloop that gathers around underwater volcanoes. I see the parasite in my brain, stuck in arrested development by a coincidence of drugs.

I walk into the right-hand ward, past Margaret's dismembered body which we covered with a sheet and up to the window. I lean on the slim ledge and crane my neck so that I can see an angle of the outside world. There are more faces there now. A sea of post-human rage, all drawn in by the lights of the hospital, the loop of the Vengaboys and the rest of the crowd. I'm caught between hopelessness and annoyance at Ben's insistence that this isn't all chance. What sort of plan is this? What am I supposed to do with him? I feel a wet nudge and look down to see Brown tapping her nose against my shin.

"Do you know? What are we supposed to do?"

Brown sits down and looks at me hopefully.

"Don't ever fall in love Brown," I say. "It's the worst pain in the world."

In the main corridor the hastily erected curtain is still holding up and the wraths beyond are silent again. We are free to use these two rooms and the corridor, but more beds don't help us much. We need more if Ben stands a chance of surviving. I decide to talk it out with Ben. I've become so used to processing everything in my head that it's strange to have someone else who can help me decide things.

I head back to the other ward and pour a big glass of water. I take a bottle of Endure to Ben and put them on the table next to his bed. I place a hand on the back of his arm and he smiles in his sleep and gradually comes round. It takes a few moments for understanding to return to his eyes and then his smile gets wider.

"What time is it? Where's Brown? Are you okay?"

"I'm fine, indigestion is keeping me up."

I pass him a drink.

"Breakfast in bed? And people say the service in the NHS is getting worse," he says.

"We need to talk."

"Okay," he says and takes some sips of water. He tries to push himself into a sitting position but struggles because of his hand, so I help to sit him up in the bed. He smells of sweat and industrial fabric conditioner.

"Give me the bad news first, doctor."

"What if there isn't any good news?"

"Oh."

"You're dying Ben. I can't say how long you have left, but even if the world hadn't collapsed, I'm not sure we'd be able to save you. You need surgery and I can't do that. I could try but I'd kill you."

"I saw you with Margaret, I'll pass on the surgery option," he says. He looks wounded, but we don't have the time to waste. *He* doesn't have the time. "How long do you think I've got?"

"I don't know. Maybe months?"

"Huh. I thought it would be more. What can I do? What do you suggest?"

"This has to be your choice. What do you want to do?"

"I want to help you. I want the babies to be safe. I want Brown to be safe. I want to go to Disneyland. I want to help you get back to your husband. I want more time."

"Ben, I wouldn't blame you if you didn't want to fight this. It's okay if you want to just sit here. I can make it comfortable for you. We'll be with you."

Ben smiles and opens his Endure and takes a considered sip.

"When I was stuck in the flat – let me clarify, when I was stuck in the flat *after* everything changed, I realised something most people figure out when they're children."

"What's that?"

"You can't build a fortress with biscuits."

"Wisdom for the ages."

"It seemed more significant when I first thought it. I decided I needed protection from life and biscuits was how I did that. What I didn't know is that nothing can protect you from pain in life, not even bourbons. Avoiding pain isn't the point of life, it's finding a way to deal with it. I know I'm going to die, but I'm going to die going forward. With you and Brown."

I feel relief coursing through me. The idea that Ben could have found me and then decided to give up would have been too much.

"Right, we'd best start to pack up."

"Where are we going?"

"We're stuck fighting your cancer blind, we can't do blood tests or imaging scans. It's like fighting a ghost in a heavy mist."

"Sounds cool."

"The chemotherapy will buy us time but it's really only going to help us to stand still. Plus, we can do that anywhere. If we want to claw back time then we need to get to radiotherapy."

"And radiotherapy can help? It can kill the cancer?"

"If you could have it with a proper radiotherapist who was guided by diagnostic scans and trained technicians, then absolutely. In our situation, we're going to do our best. Again, it's like firing a gun into the mist and hoping we shoot the ghost."

"And you can do that?"

"Well, I know how to switch the machine on and how to start it up. After that, we're going to have to play around with some of the fine details."

"You're not filling me with confidence."

"What do you want me to say Ben, "You're going to be 100% fine"?"

"Yes."

"You're going to be 100% fine."

"Hell yeah!" Ben says and pumps his fist and then winces as it jostles the broken bones in his hand. He starts to pull back the covers and get himself out of bed. "Let's get going."

"Not tonight! We need to think about how to get there." I say and picture how many corridors, over-run with a horde of furies who want to pull us apart, we need to take to get to a machine that might not even be there anymore. We're going to be 100% fine, I'm 90% sure.

Chapter 17

17th April 2021
8 months and 13 days after

After a breakfast of pills and two bottles of Endure, I go into the bathroom with supplies from the ward's storage cupboard. I set three razors down next to the sink, put the plug in and run the water to the top. I dunk my head into the freezing water. I lift my head and the water runs down my face and into the towel around my shoulders. I lift one of the large flaps of skin that used to be my chest, which now sits like an elephant's ear on my body. I wash awkwardly with my left hand. I make sure I get in every crevice, which takes a while because most of my body is crevice these days. I don't know when I'll be able to shower again and so I revel in the clean, refreshing water and rinse my body free of the hospital residue it's acquired.

When I'm clean, I *koink* a few squirts of the all-purpose body gel from the dispenser onto my hand and froth my hair up. I gingerly use my right hand to sweep it back so that I can see the roots. I hold the safety razor against the hair and look in the mirror. I pull the razor through the tangle of hair and lift it up to see a clump jamming up the blades. I use my thumb to unclog the blades and run the razor back through. After five minutes I can see my scalp. After ten I'm as bald as an egg. There are several thin cuts on my scalp that are stinging from the shampoo. They show on my head as thin slits of blood, but I continue to rinse, shave, unclog and repeat. The full shape of my skull appears, I'm alarmed to see it's more pronounced than it was the first time I shaved my head at the farm. My skeleton seems to be coming to the fore. With a final swish of the blade, my head is naked and cold. I place my palm and fingers across my scalp and marvel at how tacky it feels.

Natalie said that it could be a few weeks before the chemo took my hair. She also said hair loss was not guaranteed with capecitabine, but that patients often said that it helped when they chose to shave their hair first because it felt like them taking control, rather than being a victim. I liked the thought of that, so even though Brown won't like it, I felt a full shave might be the way forward. I leave my beard intact, so that I don't look completely like a thumb, and unlock the door. Waiting on the other side are Brown and Natalie. I jump because I wasn't expecting anyone to be there, but also because Natalie is completely bald too. It takes me a second to work out what's going on.

"Why did you shave your hair?" I ask.

"Solidarity," she says and holds up her fist. "I asked Brown if she wanted to be shaved too, but she said she doesn't like you enough."

"Can't blame her," I say and bump her fist. "Won't you be cold?"

"I like it," she says and runs her fingers across her fresh pink scalp. "I thought it would itch, but it feels smooth, like glass."

"We look like a buy-one-get-one-free on Ross Kemps."

"Are you ready? We should get going."

"Yeah," I can feel the cannabis starting to pull funny shapes in my stomach and a sense of lightness dances through me. Natalie reckons that the cannabis isn't going to do much harm, but she's not sure about how it will interact with the chemo drugs, so I'm saving the remaining biscuits for special occasions. Today feels special, the next step in our journey. I still have no idea where we're going but maybe that's the point of a journey sometimes.

"Will you be okay?" I ask.

"We'll be fine," replies Natalie, and she gives me a measured look. "You're sure you want to do this?"

"Well, in the grand scheme of things, no. But there isn't another solution. Unless you've thought of one? Because I'm open to late-breaking, eleventh-hour solutions that don't involve me facing off against a thousand wraths."

"To be fair we don't know yet if this *is* a solution."

"You'll look after Brown if anything happens?"

"Nothing is going to happen. This will work."

I don't say anything else. There's so much I can feel inside me that I want to say and share with her but she's right, we need to get going if we're going to be in radiotherapy by the end of the day. I don't know if it's the weed or just a general sense that I can't have come this far to be killed now, but I feel oddly calm. This will work.

I walk to the edge of the ward and shrug on an anorak I've taken from the staff lockers over my fleece. It's a bit snug, but at least it's something to protect me from the weather. It hangs heavy on my shoulders as the pockets are full of bits of tile that we've taken from the bathroom. Snow has already begun to mount up on the lip of the building and ever since we took the window out, we've been shivering and wrapping up in double and triple blankets. Brown has taken to sleeping under the sheets with me, poaching the warmth from my body. The whole side of the left-hand ward is exposed now. It took us a day working with the crowbar to loosen the fixings around the oversized window, and to work enough bricks loose around the sides until eventually the window simply fell into the courtyard below, with a crash that sent the porter from the smoking shelter into a top-volume tirade.

The next step was finding a way of suspending me in the air, outside the window. Fortunately, that was made easier by the fact that above the ward's roof were a network of pipes and foil-insulated tubes, which ran the water, electricity and internet around the hospital. A series of wire cables also dangled from the ceiling and by pulling some of those cables from other areas of the roof, we had wires which were secured to the joists somewhere way above us. We removed a sturdy 15-metre wooden handrail from the corridor and secured it to the cables. We then lashed it to the remaining frame of the window. By the time we'd finished, we had a piece of wood, which jutted about eight metres out of the window at ceiling height. Over this, we hung a bariatric sling that was strong enough to support me on the pole.

The whole thing was Natalie's idea. It's such a stupid contraption that I laugh as I hoist myself into the sling and test it can hold me for the hundredth time. The handrail bows slightly and creaks if I move all the way out to the very edge, but it feels secure enough. Before I hoist myself out of the window, I call Brown over and she sniffs at the bandages on my right hand. I pet her ears with my left hand and she sniffs at the unfamiliar scent of the shampoo. I grab her by the scruff and pull her to me. I kiss her head and push her backwards onto the ward away from the open void. She scuttles back and stands behind Natalie. Natalie smiles at me.

"Ready?"

"No."

"Good luck."

"Natalie."

"Yes?"

"Thanks for everything. If I don't make it then I hope you get to Monaco. Your husband's a lucky man, I'm sure he'll be okay."

She smiles curiously and walks towards the corridor. I reach up, take hold of the handrail and slowly edge my way out of the ward until all that lies below me is the ground, thirty feet away. If I fell the snow would cushion my fall, but it would still be an ugly death. Or worse, it would be a miraculous survival with just an array of broken bones to show for it. Natalie would have to put me down. I try not to think of that. Snow settles on my face and beard as I work my way to a distance of about five metres from the window. I wonder what will happen if any of the wraths take the time to stop and think about how or why I'm suspended in the air. My job is to make sure they're too angry to think and keep their focus on reaching me.

As I look back at Natalie, I see Brown barking as I inch out into the air. The fact is that our time is limited – Natalie could give birth any day now, we don't know how I'll respond to the treatment as I go on. With so many wraths outside, there was no hope of fighting our way through. Natalie's too big to sneak and I'm just too weak. We needed a plan for getting the wraths out of our way. This is it. Natalie gathers up the two rucksacks – mine and another one we found in a patient locker. They're stuffed with food and everything we might need – Natalie's toxoplasmosis medication, surgical supplies, enough capecitabine to take me through more rounds of chemotherapy than I could ever want or need, Bear, clothes, two Entonox canisters. We thought about taking water but we figured that we'd need to carry so much that it would slow us down, and then it still probably wouldn't be enough. Natalie says that we should be able to find a supply over that side of the hospital, if we make it.

Natalie returns in a few seconds to gather up the wheeled drip stand that's hung with the containers of Entonox and the shotgun. She turns to look at me and she smiles, and holds up her hand in a part-wave, part-salute. She's so beautiful when she smiles. Her face is normally so serious, with her brows forever etched in enquiry. Even in the ice of today's snowstorm, her face brings me warmth. As I raise my hand in return, her smile widens. A drugged laugh escapes from between my lips. I'm terrified but elated.

Natalie moves out of my line of sight and I picture her doing exactly as we rehearsed. Brown and our equipment will be stored safely in the bathroom in the other ward. Our hope is that the wraths will be too angry with me to explore where else they can go. If they're not then the wraths will kill her and Brown and I'll have to watch, while I dangle outside the building. Natalie will walk down the corridor and poke the shotgun around the curtain and fire both barrels at the lock. She will then speed-waddle back down the corridor, lock herself in the other ward and pull the curtain from across the door. Then it's my turn. As I'm imagining her movements a snowflake finds a path through my clothing and slides down my back. The chemotherapy is making me more sensitive to the cold and I shudder for several seconds.

"Mum, me and God haven't been talking for a while, so will you have a word? This is his plan after all. Not for me, for them. Amen."

I see the cord on the floor jerk and the corner of the blue curtain trails on the floor. I hear screaming and thousands of footsteps. We talked long and hard about who should be out here on the pole. I only won by reminding Natalie that technically she's three people now. If that hadn't convinced her then I was prepared to explain that I wasn't sure that the pole would even take her weight. I've been on the other side of too many of those types of discussions and it's not fun. Fortunately, she gave in when I mentioned the babies.

I see the first wraths appear through the ward doors. The very first one I see is wounded and bleeding heavily from the stomach. She's leaking blood and her hands are clasped to her waist. I can only assume she was on the other side of the door when Natalie shot the locks. She's wearing a uniform that looks like she works in the cafeteria – her long grey-blonde hair is held in a net. More wraths appear skidding down the hallway, searching for something to focus their hate on. Some are running, one of them rolls on the floor wrestling with the blue curtain, but the older café worker is now level with me and turns to look in my direction. I can see her trying to figure out how I'm hanging in the air. She's trying to decide if I'm a target or not. Her head turns to one side, like Brown does when she's trying to deduce where a noise is coming from. I think of what Natalie told me and how when she's not in control, she can understand their anger. She said the only way she could describe it is that it's complete – no other feelings: pain, hunger, tiredness, can make it through the anger. The older lady starts to turn, perhaps because I'm not moving, and she starts to look around for something to focus on. She looks at the other ward door.

"I LIKE TO PARTY! I LIKE, I LIKE TO PARTY! I LIKE TO PARTY! I LIKE, I LIKE TO PARTY!"

I scream it so loudly and so out of tune that pigeons that had settled on the roof of the hospital take off and disappear into the squall of snow above. I'm terrible at remembering lyrics, so I instantly forget what comes next and skip to the next bit of the song I can remember.

"Your Vengabus is something and people here are jumping. New York and San Diego, let's all have a disco! Dur dur dur dur dur duuur dur."

I pump my arms and legs, and the sling wobbles unnervingly. I take a handful of the broken tiles from my pocket and lash it at the wraths I can see. One wrath catches a piece in the face and wails. The rest whip around and instantly their hate is on me. I hear someone wail; "NOT THAT FUCKING SONG!" There must be twenty wraths in sight now and they're all screaming, pointing at me, spitting, pulling things off the wall, destroying whatever is near them. I need to keep their focus.

"Your Vengabus is der der and did I mention jumping? Dur dur dur dur durr durr! Come on you fuckers, want it a bit louder? THE VENGABUS IS SOMETHING, AND SOMETHING SOMETHING JUMPING!"

The cafeteria lady sprints at me. Her head is down and she doesn't even pause to consider it. She just leaps when she comes to the edge of the building. I stop singing and watch mesmerised as she sails through the air. She falls at least three metres short of where I am and plummets to the ground below, her hands clawing at the air. There is a crunch and I look down to see her sprawled on the floor below. She moans, "Fucking gravity," then another body drops on top of her, then silence. There's an inhuman rattle that comes out of the next faller that sounds like someone gargling. I start to sing again.

"HEY THEN, HEY THEN! HEAR ME SAY WHEN. HAPPINESS IS JUST AROUND THIS CORNER. YOU LOVE TO SEE THEM JUMPING, HONG KONG AND SAN DIEGO, WHAT RHYMES WITH DIEGO? I LOVE TO EAT SOME MAYO, IN TRINIDAD AND TOBAGO, BUT ONLY IF IT'S VEGAN, I ONLY LIKE IT VEGAN, DURR DUH DURR DURR DUR DURRRRR DURR!"

They keep coming. They keep jumping. A tide of wraths pours into the ward. I swear I recognise some of them from the Trafford Centre. I keep singing, but as the weed takes hold all I want to do is sleep. I yawn as I'm singing. I think of Brown and Natalie stuck in the room, not sure what's going on outside and not daring to peek out. All the while I carry on singing. For variety, I fling tile shards at the crowd. The wraths keep leaping to shut me up and the pile of bodies grows bigger. Some of them are only incapacitated, and they add their screams of pain to my Vengaboys hellscape remix.

Despite the cold, I'm sweltering and have to try to hold my coat with my teeth as I use my left hand to pull the zip down and feel the cold air touching my odd body.

"I'VE GOT A MESSAGE TO TELL YOU, I'VE GOT NEWS FOR YOU, THERE'S A REALLY BIG PILE OF BODIES BELOW ME IN THE SNOW. DURR DUR DURR DUR DURR DUR DUR!"

After five minutes the push of wraths hasn't abated and I'm cursing myself for not bringing water to moisten my throat. Five more minutes and I can't hold my stomach any longer. I shit myself while watching a waterfall of people careen to their death. All the while, I goad them with solid gold Europop. I hold out my hand and start to collect snowflakes, and when my palm is full I push them into my mouth and lick the drops of water off my coat sleeve. So much time passes that it almost becomes boring. I start to worry that the mound of bodies will reach such a height that they might be able to get me from below. Fortunately, any wraths that do survive the fall are so broken that all they can do is twitch and shout.

After what feels like a full morning of singing, there are just a few stragglers in the ward now and the occasional wrath rounding the corner looking lost. I feel so depleted that I wonder if you can die from exhaustion.

"AMAZING GRACE, HOW SWEET THE SOUND!" I sing, quite possibly as out of tune as it's ever been sung.

"Not fucking hymns!" A wrath shouts and jumps for me. He lands on his head and I hear the snap of his spine. On the signal, Natalie peers out from behind the curtain and cracks the door.

"Hey! Everyone! I just want to get your attention, so please look over here!" I say, and the wraths that are in the ward look at me. Most are too injured or brain-dead to do much of anything. Natalie places the shotgun to the back of a wrath's skull and vaporises it in a spray of bone and blood. Natalie calmly fires again at the one nearest to her, quickly cracks the barrel and reloads it as we'd practised earlier. Before any of them can get within a metre of her she's shot them all.

"Nice shootin', Tex," I say. She just looks at me.

"I've never killed anyone before."

"You get used to it," I tell her. She grabs me as I pull myself in towards the ward. My right hand aches as I lean forward and tip myself off the sling and into the ward.

"Before you ask, yes: I have shit myself."

"Come on, we have to hurry."

Natalie takes me by the arm. It's nice to have someone warm and human – even part-human, to be near. She's so solid. In comparison I feel like a crisp packet; like I could just blow out of the window and away into the air. We grab the bags, the drip stand and Brown, who's been asleep on a bed in the ward. Natalie reloads the shotgun and pockets a handful of our remaining ammo. I have a knife in my pocket and the crowbar in my hands.

With Brown between us we move silently down the corridors, leaving only footprints and a waft of shit as we pass. We kill a handful of wraths as we go, mostly with the knife on the barrel of the shotgun, but I also bludgeon one we come across. We shoot two more hospital workers-turned-wraths. At the second one, without much emotion, Natalie says, "That was my boss."

By the end of the journey, I feel like an infant being carried from the car after a late-night party. I'm leaning on Natalie so much, but without her I'd be sprawled on the floor. My feet trip over themselves, and the lights of the wards seem blurred and starry. Natalie props me against a wall while she scouts the area. I look at the large glass windows of the department in front of us. Just the letters "THERA" hang in the air, suspended by a slender network of glass, "RADIO" and "PY" have already been dashed on the floor. I hear a rumble of sound and walk forward to the edge of the landing that we're on. If I crane my head around, I can get a view of the larger side entrance of the hospital. It's a sea of wraths stretching as far as I can see. Scrummed together, faces and bodies, a humming hivemind, swaying in the carnage. Fighting, screaming – it looks like Hell. It is Hell.

As I stand and survey them someone points at me, and a section of the crowd surges closer. I hear smashing glass below and the entrance to the hospital collapses under the press of the crowd. Another large window shatters, and a section of the frame falls onto one of the wraths and splits her head open. I turn away in horror, just in time to see "THERA" fall and scatter into fragments on the ground. Natalie returns and puts my arm over her shoulder. She says something but I can't make it out. I steady myself on the drip stand. She pushes me into the main waiting area for radiotherapy. She tries one of the doors that says TREATMENT on the front. This one is locked, and she goes in turn to the other six doors leading off the waiting room. The noise of the wraths is getting closer. The seventh door she tries opens. She looks in, cautiously at first, then bursts over the threshold with the shotgun in front of her. I hear a shot, then she emerges and returns to my side, her newly bald head glinting in the light. Everything around me seems weird and gloopy. She awkwardly scoops me up and clicks her cheek for Brown to follow her.

She pulls me into a new room with just one small clouded-glass window, high up on one wall. There's a wide medical bed in the centre of the room which has a large machine raised over the top of it. The letters LINAC are embossed on one side. I sit on the bed while Natalie locks the door into the treatment room. She cups her ear to the door and listens. She looks scared. Even from the bed I can hear the chants and screams of the wraths as they get closer. Natalie backs away and sits down beside me. Brown leaps onto the bed. Natalie loads the shotgun again and points it at the door. She pulls the Entonox mask over her face and starts to take deep breaths until she's stifling her mirth. As the din outside intensifies, she reaches out her hand and tightly grips my hand in hers.

Chapter 18

26th April 2021
8 months, 22 days after

On my nursing course, we had an American tutor and she insisted we recited the Nightingale Pledge when we qualified. I didn't realise that we would get a little card to read it from at the ceremony, so I memorised it. I think I was having flashbacks to school when I was one of the shepherds at the Nativity and rather than saying my line: "We shall look for Him in the stable," I stared out at the audience, got spooked and emitted a sort of high-pitched white noise. Dad never forgot that. If I ever zoned out, or took more than a second to answer a question he'd say, "Oh no, we're losing her in the high frequencies again!" and try to tune me back in. It never failed to make him laugh. Ha-ha-ha Dad.

I've been thinking of the Nightingale Pledge a lot recently, specifically because of the line, "I will abstain from whatever is deleterious and mischievous, and will not take or knowingly administer any harmful drug." The real question I'm facing now is am I being mischievous or deleterious? Would Florence look at me and think I was producing a net negative or positive effect? I suspect that, were she alive, she'd be so amazed by the whirling, automated LINAC machine that she'd have more important questions.

Of course, the truth is that I don't know if I'm being mischievous. I'm pressing buttons and hoping. The only reason that I even know how to switch the machine on is that all the nurses from the cancer ward do a rotation on radiotherapy if they're interested in progressing to senior nurse. Consequently, I've worked in radiotherapy for a cumulative period of about eight weeks. I remember the guy I trained with telling me that the machine does most of the calculations these days, but I suspect he was just playing it cool. He did then ask me if I wanted to go and see the new Jason Bourne film and then he didn't talk to me for a week when I said no.

The important thing is that Ben doesn't know the limits of my knowledge. He's been so much more positive since we moved into radiotherapy. Even if the only thing he gets out of all this is a placebo bump, then I'm determined to let him have it. Since we arrived, our world has shrunk to encompass the treatment room, the maze entry into the treatment room and the monitoring room. Fortunately, there's a sink in the monitoring room but there's no toilet, so we've created a composting bucket near the exit which we've been throwing out of the door once every few days. You get used to the smell after a while. The chemoradiation treatment is obviously affecting Ben. Most of the time he's asleep or so whacked out that he just stares at a wall. I've been forcing him to eat as many custard creams as he can, so that's probably not helping with the sleepiness. His appetite is so reduced that I think Florence would agree with me that the potential harm of not eating anything, and wasting away to the point where his organs fail, is worse than the impact of some THC on his system.

I'm hoping that Florence would also agree that guessing a treatment regime is acceptable, if no other authority exists. Essentially, my gamble is that giving Ben a course of radiation treatment over a wider area of his body than we'd ever usually dream of doing offers at least a chance of hitting the cancer. That then gives the chemo more of a chance to do some good. That's the hope anyway.

"Ok Ben, I'm going to start, give me a thumbs up," I say into the microphone, and on the closed-circuit camera I see Ben wearily raising his thumb. He's lying on the treatment couch and the loose skin of his formerly-fat body is pooled about him. I've used some positioning cushions to pin the flaps of skin down so that I can see what I'm doing. The billows and folds of his body are fascinating, I know he's embarrassed by it, but I think it's incredible. Again, I feel an inconvenient pang of love for him. A desperate need to protect him and hold him up, away from the river of filth.

"Ok, stay very still," I say and hit the button.

The LINAC machine spins around and, once again, I'm thankful that the machine is cutting edge. Its movements are pricelessly quiet, some of the older machines would be noisy enough to summon the furies from across the hospital. The machine revolves around Ben and casts a square beam of white light onto his stomach. It's been several days since we started the treatment and his skin is starting to show some signs of damage. It's apparent in the cherry-red and dry patches appearing where the linear accelerator focuses the X-rays on his abdomen. I watch the square of light touch the hideous tattoo of Mickey Mouse on Ben's stomach and concentrate my hope that this light will seek and destroy the invader in his body.

When we first arrived in the treatment room, we went through every cupboard and did a thorough inventory of anything that could be useful, or that we could use as a weapon. Amongst the piles of vomit bowls and rolls of tissues we found a bottle of tattoo ink and several sterilised needles. I explained to Ben that patients usually have a few dots tattooed on their skin to help the radiotherapist line up the machine with precision. Ben said he wanted a tattoo. In the end we decided that if we couldn't be that precise with our version of the treatment it wouldn't matter if his tattoo wasn't exact either. We both had some Entonox and by the time I got round to doing the tattoo, we were laughing so much that my hand shook.

I did my best stick and poke tattoo of Mickey Mouse from memory, and I put his nose roughly where we'd decided that the cancer lay beneath. I'd been quite proud of the two perfect black circles of his ears and the V shape of his hairline. I knew that his snout was supposed to look shiny and 3D, but I was buggered if I could get the effect right. Consequently, it looked more like a parsnip extending from the face of a shocked badger/bat hybrid. By this point, we were laughing so much that Ben insisted I carry on and finish the job. As I did the white circles on Mickey's shorts, they looked so much like displaced testicles that I had to stop because I thought I'd cackle myself into labour. I thought it would only be fair to let Ben do one on me, so he drew Minnie Mouse on my shoulder. I still can't see her properly because we only have a tiny mirror, but by pulling the skin of my shoulder around I know the bow in her hair is garbage. Ben said she's also boss-eyed. It is my first tattoo and I love it.

The monitors create a fascinating sectional picture of Ben's stomach and organs, and there is an automated targeting programme that runs through a series of checks and activities each time. This is where the extent of my knowledge lies though. I can switch the machine on and set it going on the programme, but I don't know if the beam is hitting the right part. I might simply be irradiating another part of him which will cause another cancer in the future. The giant machine spins around until it's upright again and then with a buzz, it announces the end of the session. I wait until the green light shows in the treatment room and open the door and go in. I pass Ben a bottle of water and he woozily props himself up on his elbows and takes a long sip.

"Did you get it?"

"Yep, burned the balls right off that mouse."

He smiles and then lies back on the treatment bed. Normally, I've been helping him to the bed area we created in the monitoring room, but today I sense that he needs a moment. My ankles feel full though, so I drag over a plastic chair from the side of the room and cautiously lower myself into it, fully expecting it to buckle underneath me.

"You ok?" Ben asks, his eyes closed.

"Grand, never better."

"I want you to know I'm grateful Natalie, I don't care what happens. I would have died on my own. I know that now."

"Hey, come on, I know you'll make it," I reply, and Ben smiles as if he's just come up on MDMA. "What?"

"I never told you, did I? I found my mum's grave, and the inscription said, 'I knew you'd make it.' She knew that I'd make it out of the flat. Or she knew that I'd carry on and survive, I don't know. It just made me laugh, you saying the same thing."

"My dad died when he was taking me to the airport to go to America. We pulled over because we were both crying about me going and when he pulled back onto the motorway, a truck rammed us and he was killed. That's where I got this." I point to my chin.

Ben has propped himself up again and is looking at me intensely.

"Nat, that's awful. I'm so sorry that happened."

"For the longest time, I looked for someone to blame. I blamed you, because if you'd just come with me then maybe it wouldn't have happened. Then I blamed the driver of the truck, but it was early and raining and Dad probably didn't look closely enough because he'd been crying."

"I blamed myself when Mum died. I should have been there for her. I should have left the house to support her in the hospital and be at her funeral. I should have been there for you."

"You couldn't have known. It's strange, though. When I feel myself going towards the furies and the anger is rushing in, I know that the one I'm angriest with is me. Is that something you feel sometimes?"

"It's certainly how I felt when I was at my biggest. I don't know what changed that. I think in part, having Karl there saying all those things about me meant that for once, the nastiest voice in my head wasn't my own. Does that make sense?"

"It does."

"I NEED A HUG!" Bear interjects, and I see that Brown is up and about. During the treatment time, she's been moping in the bed, cleaning Bear and sleeping. Ben walks her around and around the rooms, but you can tell that she's feeling claustrophobic. I'd like to run the treatment for as long as possible. It seems unlikely that we'll find another functioning LINAC machine, so we should use it for as long as we can now, or at least until Ben is braised nicely on all sides. I remember my pills and pop one into my hand, choking it back with a sip of Ben's water.

"Eurgh, these are the worst-tasting pills I've ever had."

"Not had much chemo medicine then? It's like they coat them in earwax."

I laugh and Ben smiles at me.

"When did you meet your husband?" he asks.

I've been studiously ignoring this topic since I lied about it before. I don't know why I lied; maybe I just felt like hurting Ben. I look at him, and the naive innocence shines out of his face.

"I'm not married Ben. You need feelings to get married and I've not had many of those since Dad died."

Ben stares at me and reaches his hand out and I go to take it.

"I NEED A HUG!" Bear says again, and I decide that right at this moment the fucking thing is just too much. I reach down and yank it from between Brown's teeth and throw it towards the wall. Brown speeds off in pursuit. It's ridiculous! You shouldn't have a fucking talking teddy bear when you're hiding for your life. It's all too stupid! And you shouldn't have a dog in a treatment room, we're trying to cure cancer in a room where a dog is shitting!

"Fuck all of it!" I yell, and I feel the rage swelling like a panic attack. Short waves of intense pressure on my brain, and my ability to think and process is faltering. I can't deal with this.

Ben appears by my side holding the plastic mask to my mouth. I get a whiff of the sweet air and, for a moment, I just want to hurl the mask and bottle across the room, but I turn and Ben is looking at me, weak and fearful.

"Come back Nat," he says kindly. So, I breathe in. And I look at his face as I breathe out. I breathe in. I breathe out.

"Talk to me Nat, tell me good things. Tell me about the babies. Tell me about their dad."

"I'm a surrogate mum," I say, and I feel the gas reach my brain so I can't suppress a smirk as I say: "I'm *allllll* alone."

Chapter 19

3rd May 2021
8 months, 29 days after

If a genie gave me three wishes right now, I'd ask for a toilet. A really solid, stable toilet. If I could pimp it up, it would have a footstool and a backrest, maybe one of those beaded covers that mini-cab drivers have on their seats. It would also have a cupholder so I could have a brew at the same time. *Ohhhh*, a brew. My second wish would be for a brew. Got to be a big mug, two tea bags and enough oat milk so that it goes past orange, into being a light brown. Old me would have wished for six sugars, but new me just wants the brew. A brew and a lovely comfy toilet. That would leave me one wish, so I suppose it would be for all the wraths to return to normal and for humanity to join forces to rebuild the world while retaining the hard-won lessons of this nightmarish nine months. Or some Pringles. I don't know, it's so hard to choose!

As is my life these days, I'm sitting on the shit bucket. My tip is that if you're going to subject yourself to amateur chemoradiation, make sure you don't have to shit in a bucket. I've been squatting so much that I can feel my thighs burning and there's a constant imprint of the cheap plastic rim on my arse. So much so, that it's now calloused and bruised. The good news is that the diarrhoea has given way to another catastrophic type of bowel movement. I squat and strain as if I'm going to shit out the *Lepanto*, I can feel my stomach muscles clenching and driving something southwards and then at the culmination of all this effort, a tiny pebble of poo drops into the bucket. This process affords me ten minutes of relief before my arse starts twitching again. Not since Brown got fake-pregnant has so much effort been expended to produce so little.

The thing that's making it more bearable is that today is my last treatment. Nat says that she'd like to keep going for as long as possible, but I think we've reached a conclusion that we can't take any more. Something has to give. We've been in the same tiny space for just over two weeks, living amongst each other's piss and shit, sleeping, whispering, trying to keep Brown from going insane, trying to keep Bear from killing us all by shouting about needing a hug. The food is nearly gone, so we've reached the point at which we either make a break for it, or we die locked in here. Quite how we'll make a break for it is another question. My head is fuzzy, and answers haven't been forthcoming recently.

I fill the bucket with some water. I take it down the maze entry and throw the contents out of the door. The first thing we have to be careful of when we leave is that we don't slip on the massive slick of turds and piss out the front. It would be a glorious, poetic end to humanity if the very last people died on a skating rink of shit. The glimpse of the world outside the treatment room door is brief, but it's enough to confirm that the snow is still falling, and that I can still see a glimpse of the horde outside. We know that more are inside. They never made it to radiotherapy, but you can hear them in the hospital. Natalie says she feels the mass of rage. We've been so lucky to get two weeks here. It's odd, but it's felt more secure than the ward. Perhaps because the walls are thicker and there's little natural light. It's such a small space that it feels like sitting in a snug cinema on a wintry day.

I walk back around the corner and see Brown splayed out, resting against Natalie. They're both lying flat on their backs. Brown definitely understands that Natalie is pregnant. She keeps bringing Bear to Natalie so that she can play with it. Part of me wonders if she's preparing Natalie for the arrival of the babies. Dogs are weird, so it could be anything. Natalie's shirt has ridden up and I can see the dome of her stomach. A couple of nights ago she took my hand and held it on her belly. I'd wanted to touch it since I saw it but it felt too intrusive. I remember too well when people would gawp at me or take surreptitious pictures of me when I was at my biggest. I closed my eyes as I held my hand to the warm skin and felt the fluttering beneath. The push of a limb against the taut flesh. A sense of contained joy.

These children will be the first to be born into a new epoch of the planet. *Homo sapien* is dead, long live *homo furious*.

Their days will be spent avoiding predators on every street, living in a world of decaying bounty that gradually disintegrates around them. They will see the scattered pieces of planes but never fly in one. They'll only know dark and broken computer monitors. Or perhaps their lives will short and painful. I don't know. I don't even know how they'll get here yet. In the last two weeks, I've grown to believe that there is a far greater purpose for all of this than I understand. Back at the *Our Kid,* I wanted to see the plan and to have it all laid out so that I could understand and approve it. But I realise that was arrogant. It's not my place to question what happens, it's my challenge to have faith when it does.

I've been thinking a lot recently about how odd it was that Brown was debarked. It's such an unusual thing for someone selling puppies to do. I mean, maybe he was just a crackhead and wasn't thinking. But how many times would Brown and I have been killed if she had an audible bark? Too many to count. If I'd known when I got her, why her silence would be so important, what would I have done differently? Could I have coped with that knowledge? It's so easy for humans to focus on what's at their eye level, without thinking that there are other levels that things can be seen from. When I think about this I then start to wonder about the cries of a baby, or the screams of a labouring mother. The conclusion is simple: we cannot stay here. Every minute we remain risks disaster.

On cue, I see the skin of Nat's stomach stretch a little under pressure and a penny-sized patch raises by three centimetres. Nat's hand comes up to the point and she strokes it, soothing the baby. She notices me watching and smiles.

"Perving?"

"Just witnessing the miracle of pregnancy. And emptying the shit bucket."

"Nice."

"Breakfast?"

"I'll take an Endure and some crackers, sure."

I take one of the small drinks from the cardboard tray and pass her a pack of crackers. We both know we're running out. We've not talked about it.

"I'll share them with you," she says, reading my thoughts.

"No, I'm fine. I had a Dominos last night and it's sitting heavy on me this morning."

"How did you not share a bloody Dominos with me!"

"I didn't know you wanted any!"

"What did you have?"

"Oh, it was insane. I massively over-ordered."

Natalie shuts her eyes and shivers with anticipation. She opens the crackers and puts one near her mouth ready to eat. "Okay, I'm ready, tell me."

"Well, I'm a Diamond Club customer, so they make things expressly for me that aren't on the normal pleb menu that people like you have to order from. So, first off, it was a 42-inch pizza."

Nat laughs with a mouthful of crumbs, "Wow! That's like a tractor tire."

"That's exactly right, two delivery men had to carry it in and, rather than folding it, we took out the wall in the mystery room," The Mystery Room is what we call the back room – no more than a short corridor that contains the workings of the LINAC machine.

"And I just slept through this?"

"Like a giant, pregnant log. Brown helped me eat it though, that's why she's so tired today."

"Okay, what was on it?"

"Vegan cheese and instead of a tomato sauce I had them coat it with the garlic and herb dip. Then there were little dots of the BBQ sauce all over it. It looked like a Jackson Pollock. It was a thing of beauty."

"Oh God, that sounds so good."

Nat keeps her eyes shut as she places another cracker in her mouth. "Mmmm, delicious. You not having one?"

"I've told you; I'm processing 42 inches of primo Italian."

"Oh stop! It sounds just like the nurses' city break to Milan."

"*Okay*...fancy nuking me one more time?"

"Sure thing, give me the bucket, the babies are tap-dancing on what's left of my bladder."

I hand over the bucket. Brown rolls over into the warm hollow that Nat leaves on the bed when she hoists herself up. I give her my hand, but I'm not sure how helpful I am. I'm not stupid enough to say this out loud but I weigh a lot less than her now. Once she's on her feet, I walk through to the treatment room and heave myself onto the bed. I shrug off my shirt and pin my melting body under the cushions so my skin is flat. I look at my odd form with despair. I look at the wonky Mickey Mouse on my stomach. What a strange story my body tells. I hear a click from the Mystery Room; the cue for the LINAC to start humming and repositioning itself. It smoothly rotates as it hovers over my torso. A small square of light appears on my stomach and focuses on Mickey Mouse.

Nat taps three times on the thick window between the two rooms and I lift my thumb. That's her signal that I need to stay still. According to Nat, I'm something of a fidget. I place my hands down by my side and listen to the beeps of the machine as it moves. It's like being scrutinised by an inquisitive photobooth. I find the quiet beeps it emits comforting. It's a reminder of a time when qualified people existed to make machines that were guaranteed. If they didn't act the way you wanted them to, then you just took them back and they gave you a new one, or gave you your money back with a profuse apology. Beeping was a key feature of late-stage *homo sapiens*. Oven timers. Google Home. Watches. Fire alarms. Life support machines. Open fridges. Cars. Reversing trucks. They're all quiet now.

There's no pain or sensation as the treatment is going on. Afterwards, there's a faint sensitivity, but I could be imagining that. I lie still and wait as the machine spins itself back into its resting position, then there's another beep and it becomes dormant, perhaps forever. Enjoy your rest and thank you for whatever you've done, good or bad. The door to the monitoring room opens and Natalie comes in. Brown also snuffles her way in as she takes Bear for a mooch. Natalie stands by the side of the bed and smiles at me. She pretends as if she's holding something behind her back, then she reveals it and says, "Celebratory fizz?" She mimes the motion of removing the foil from a bottle. She picks at the invisible cage, discards it, tucks two thumbs under the cork and pops it off.

"Wooo!" she shrieks as quietly as she can.

"Champagne? Fancy."

"Well, it's Asti Spumante because I couldn't find any champagne. I thought it would do because we don't have a bell for you to ring to celebrate the end of your treatment."

"Couldn't you just have mimed giving me a bell to ring?" I ask, but Natalie ignores me. She pours from the bottle and then passes me a glass. I pretend to hold it and raise it to her in a toast.

"Champagne for my real friends, real pain for my sham friends," she says as she pitches her hand towards mine. "*Clink.*"

"Candy is dandy, but liquor is quicker," I reply, and I drain the glass of the thin gold liquid. It tastes like heaven.

I'm still focusing on the pretend champagne, eyes closed in mock satisfaction, when I suddenly feel Natalie's lips on mine. I instantly tense up, then soften and kiss her back. I wonder if I'm doing it right. As she keeps kissing me, an unconscious rhythm takes shape between us. I find my lips reach an agreement with hers After ten seconds, my internal monologue melts away and I'm just there, suspended in a moment, kissing the woman I love. I throw my champagne glass at the wall and reach up, running my fingers over her shoulders. I cup my hands softly under her jaw, gently exploring the velvety down of her scalp with my thumbs. She places her hands on my cheeks and squeezes my face into hers. The bulge of her stomach fills the space between us and presses into my chest.

"I NEED A HUG!"

"Not now Bear!" I shout between kisses.

Natalie laughs – a genuine one, unblemished by the gas. It's clear and pure. As it subsides, she seems so human that I can't believe there's anything wrong with her – that there could ever be. She takes my hand and pulls me down to the treatment room floor with her. Our kissing grows intense, clumsy even, as we erase our shared history: the wraths, the loneliness, the pain, me letting her down over America, her dad, my mum. We're together now, and that is enough to heal us. Natalie doesn't stop kissing me as we cross the floor and close the door into the monitoring room. I think the champagne must have gone to my head.

***

We're lying in bed and Brown is scratching at the door. I'll let her in in a minute, but for now, I'm content to lie here, getting squashed by Natalie's stomach. We didn't speak a word while we were having sex. I always thought it would be embarrassing or ungainly on my part, and that I'd fill the embarrassment with stupid words, but it wasn't. It was beautiful. She took my broken body, with its one leg, fractured hand, broken nose, loose skin and marauding cancer, and shaped it into something new and worthy. Natalie is holding onto me as if she's scared I'm going to be washed away by the sea. My left arm is under her head and my fingertips are stroking the space behind her ear, tracing along the arch where her smooth, milky skin meets soft stubble. I keep thinking of questions to ask her. What are you thinking of? Does it hurt when the fury arrives? What will you call the babies? How are we going to get them out of you? Can we have sex again?

The turmoil fades away as I reach a decision. My wish before was that I could protect Natalie, her babies and Brown. Even if I recover from the treatment, my future is that I'm going to be a short-lived impediment. What could I give her – one year? Three? Natalie and her children are the future of humanity. If I want to save the world then saving Natalie is what that means. I wonder if this is the meaning of love – a complete understanding that the other person is the meaning of it all. They are the reason. I inch closer towards her and kiss her forehead. Her skin is warm and perfumed. I want to exist in this instant, on this hospital floor, with her, forever. I'll get Brown in a minute, but just now I want to hold onto this woman and this moment. I want it to stretch to eternity and I'm so grateful to God for the chance to experience this happiness.

Chapter 20

4th May 2021
9 months after

I turn over and my face squashes against something crinkly. I open one eye and see a piece of paper on the bed. It must've slid off the pillows and tumbled down under our makeshift covers of dressing gowns and airflow blankets, where I've crawled in the hope sleep claims me for another hour. In a haze, I waft the paper onto the floor. I squeeze my eyes shut again and try and will myself to sleep, but the fuse of consciousness has been lit and I instinctively begin scanning the mental checklist. Bladder. Pain. Babies.

I'm lying on my side and can't help but feel like one of the babies is being crushed. Even though I know they're suspended in amniotic fluid, they're so big now that I can imagine the press of limbs and tubes and it makes me feel claustrophobic on their behalf. After the MRI I don't think I'll ever be able to think of tight spaces again without breaking out in a sweat. I sense the pulsing fullness of my feet. The way they have swollen overnight makes it feel like I'm wearing novelty slippers. Rick has a pair of Gromit ones. Had a pair. My back aches. My neck is cricked. The usual wash of indigestion lies on my chest and it burns as I swallow. I resolve to punch Martin in the face if I ever see him again. When I see him again.

I then realise that Ben is not in bed, so I lift the blankets above my head to see if he's buried at the bottom of the bed. He's not. I squint into the gloom. I hear a faint nose whistle from Brown and sense that for once she's not on the bed, but under the desk where she sometimes hides with Bear if she wants some personal space in our cramped home. I still can't hear Ben though.

"Ben?"

Nothing.

"Ben?"

Fear starts to creep in. I get up as quickly as I can, a process that consists of rolling onto all fours and then placing my hands on the wall to walk myself upright. My head throbs with the sudden change in position and I have to take a moment to make sure I don't blackout. Brown is at my legs, either wanting food or stroking, probably both. I fumble my way around the walls and click the lights on. Harsh strip-lights flicker into life and illuminate the empty room. I tip-toe across the cold vinyl floor in bare feet and peer out into the entrance corridor. Nothing. I open the door into the Mystery Room and try and look as far inside as I can, but it's apparent that there's no one else here. Why would he be in there anyway? What's he playing at? A surge of irritation comes on and I'm not sure if it's just a legitimate annoyance, or the fury within me rising to the surface. I nearly trip over Brown who has come to sniff at the Mystery Room.

"Brown! Give me some space! Where's that stupid man?"

I leave her to investigate the Mystery Room and walk back into the monitoring room. I scan under the desk and behind the door. There's a small supply cupboard, which absurdly I open and shut when I see it's still full of plasters and spare cardboard sick bowls and not Ben.

"Ben?"

I risk a louder shout, but all I hear in reply is Brown skittering back into the room to sniff around. Then there's a noise that comes from the direction of the Mystery Room, a very loud *WHOOOOMP* and then a crashing noise. Looking into the treatment room I can see dust falling in vague linear patterns as it is dislodged from the edges of the ceiling tiles. Distantly, several alarms sound out. I'm frozen in terror. What was that? I need to find Ben. What if the building is on fire? We might only have minutes to get out. Something is starting to form in my mind though, a suspicion. I look on the floor for my crocs and slip them on. I reach over to the desk and grab my meds. As I swig them down unthinkingly with some stale water, I see a notepad and pen on the desk. That wasn't there last night. It's notepaper from Saint James. Within seconds I'm scrabbling around on the floor, looking for the piece of paper I shoved off the bed. I find it and unfurl the scrap to discover a spidery black scrawl in which Ben explains exactly why he's gone, and what he's going to do.

"FUCK!" I shout, immediately blinded by tears. "FUCK! FUCK! FUCK! YOU FUCKING PRICK!"

Brown looks around nervously and starts to chase her tail. I pull the nearest Entonox container to me and huff on the gas. The babies spin seemingly in time with my mind as it spirals.

"You stupid bastard Ben, I'm going to kill you!"

Ben has concluded that without someone to lead the horde of furies away, there's no chance of escape. He's going to take them all to the north of the hospital and clear a path for us to the south. He knew I'd object if we discussed it, but he also knows he's right. He loves me. He loves me and he wants me, Brown and the babies to survive.

BOOOM– CRASH.

Another explosion, this one bigger. One of the ceiling tiles falls into the room. Brown runs under the desk. I dress quickly and realise that Ben has already packed the rucksack with the last few bottles of Endure, the ammunition and another note, which I can't open right now. I pick up the shotgun and see that it's loaded, both barrels. I edge my arms into the straps and scoff a packet of crackers and crunch up a couple of Rennie. I hold a cracker out to Brown, which she very reluctantly nibbles with her lip curled.

"Fine! I get that it's not bastard haute cuisine, but it's what we have. Do you understand? Listen! Listen to me! You are going to have to follow me. You have to stay with me, do you understand? Ben is being an idiot, us girls have to stick together. Do you understand?"

Brown fetches Bear from her desk hidey-hole, I take it from her and tuck it in the rucksack.

"I NEED A HUG!" it appeals as I jam it callously inside.

"Shut the fuck up, Bear!" I scream as a panic sets in. What are we going to do? How are we going to survive? I'm going to kill him. Brown is looking at me with her head to one side. "I'll keep Bear safe, don't worry."

We walk through the maze entry and I take a breath as I touch my hand to the handle. Here goes. I pull it open, and we edge out into the corridor. Already my nerves are failing me. I want to go back to the safety of the room. The adrenaline makes it easier to move, but I'm not going to be able to outpace any furies. Why didn't Ben think about this, or talk it through with me? I could have told him how stupid he was being.

The entrance to the radiotherapy department is now destroyed and my crocs scatter crumbs of safety glass as we edge out onto the walkway that runs around this section of the hospital. I can see where the big glass frontage used to be and all I can see beyond it are bodies. Hundreds of bodies in various phases of decay. Some are skeletons, others are withered, some are still fresh. True to Ben's plan, the horde has left, and in its place are the remnants. So much destruction. I stop and lean my back against the wall. I'm going to go back to our room. Ben may come back. Maybe we're going too early. Brown bumps into my leg and I look at her staring up at me. She assumes that I have answers. I pull up the mask that's hanging around my neck and take three measured breaths. I'm fine. On we go.

I keep my back to the wall and waddle as fast as I can. We shuffle our way past the various wards and only hear the scuttle of movement a few times. As we move Brown keeps close to heel. Then, there's another explosion, this one bigger than all the others so far and from wards around the building, I can hear crashes of falling glass and the clattering as items collide. What the hell is he doing? More to the point, what the hell am I doing? I'm skulking around here hoping to escape from the wraths when it's futile. I escape this horde, what am I going to do? There isn't anywhere safe from them. I am one of them. Wherever I go, I take that hate with me. And what is the point of trying to keep a fucking dog alive in an environment like this? Why should Ben give me this responsibility? At this time? Who the fuck does he think he is? He's a fucking idiot, that's who he is. A peg-legged, melting man who needs his face smashing in if he thinks he's going to be some big hero.

"Get gone dog! Get away from me!" I scream at the little black animal tailing me. My voice rings too loudly in the corridor and I can hear a smashing noise nearby. The animal backs away, unsure about the tone of my voice.

Oh God, oh God, oh God. I breathe into the mask but see that the small canister is already depleted. I wrestle the rucksack from my shoulders and get the other canister of Entonox from the bag and hook it up to the mask with trembling fingers. I get it in place, suck the gas down and wonder if it's already too late. I start to hyperventilate, sensing more keenly than ever that this is hopeless. This gas is just a plaster on a gaping wound. I breathe in and out.

"I'm sorry Brown, please come here," I say in a hushed, giddy tone, and Brown cautiously edges towards me. I reach out my hand and smooth her cheek. "I'm so sorry. I'm not well, honey. I'm trying so hard."

As I'm bent over stroking her, I feel a blow and a spike of pain spirals from my bottom up my back, and the force sends me sprawling. I manage to take the weight of the fall on my hands and knees as I land on the debris covering the filthy corridor floor. I gasp as a fresh jolt of agony scythes up my legs and into my back, and the babies flip inside me. I look over my shoulder to see a soldier in full army fatigues. He's pulling his leg back, ready to kick me again. He's yelling something incomprehensible because his face is caved in from some ancient battle.

"YAMMMMMMM ETCH ENN!"

I see his boot pull further back in slow motion, and then there is a black blur. Brown is attached to his hand and she is whipping her body from side to side. She's not strong enough to stop the kick from coming but she causes him to pitch to the left. He scuffs the kick and just clips my right hip. The soldier's intent changes and he takes hold of Brown and tries to rip her off, but she's clamped her jaws tightly and I see blood trickling from the corner of her mouth.

"AAANNNT INNNN DEEESH!"

The soldier makes to wail again but before he can there's a bang, a flash, and he flies backwards, his head misted by the shotgun smoking in my hands. As his body hits the floor, Brown lets go and trots back to my side as if she's playing fetch. I crawl to the side of the corridor and heave myself up using the handrail, which creaks under the strain.

"Good girl," I say with awe.

I snap the barrel of the shotgun and pop another shell into the gun. We reach the edge of the wards and after glancing through the window I move us into the stairwell. We head downwards and make our way to the lobby of the hospital. On some intuition, I decide that we should move to the back corridors that the porters and food delivery staff use. I'm hoping that they'll be less populated. I've still got the Entonox mask clamped to my head and I've been inhaling more and more nitrous oxide as we go. I'm breathing heavily from the exertion of the movement and the pain of the kick in my back, but as I push at an external fire door, I glance at the bottle and realise that it's empty. By this point, I'm high enough that the idea of running out somehow just makes me laugh again.

"This isn't good Brown!" I say with a giggle.

We stumble through the door into a side road behind the main hospital, and the cold instantly hits me. After eight months of being inside a warm building protected from the elements, the rawness of the snow and the piercing wind takes my breath away. Goosebumps bristle on my arms and I pull my weird wardrobe of hospital gowns, coat and surgical stockings tighter to me. My Crocs sink deep into the snow which soaks my stockings. My freshly bald head gets it the worst though, and with only a small crop of stubble as a barrier against the elements, I feel practically naked. I wish I had a hat. These are all the preparations you can make if someone tells you in advance that they're about to sacrifice themselves for you. You can find a fucking hat. Brown leaps into the snow and has to bounce to make any progress. She looks thoroughly miserable. I laugh at the sight of her depressed pogoing.

"You can't use that door! That's not for you, you fat heifer!"

I turn and see a knot of furies at the top of the alley. They look like hospital porters. They look as if they're frozen in place from another time, their shoulders dusted with snow. They're about 20 metres away, and without saying anything I turn in the opposite direction and start striding back down the alley, lifting my knees out of the snow. The pain in my back flares and I reach around, putting a consoling hand on the small of my back, but do so with a sharp intake of breath.

"Don't run away, you fat cunt!"

"Oi! What gives you the right to ignore us?"

"Stuck up bitch!"

The opening of the alley into the street beyond is about 30 metres away. I breathe in again and hold my belly up for support as I go. Brown hops along by my side but she's turning and keeping an eye on the group of wraths, so she doesn't see the approaching stairwell and trips, sliding down the stairs that lead to an underground section of the hospital. The staircase is clear from snow because it's covered by a canopy, but the steps are slick with ice. I watch Brown slip down three steps and fail to get any purchase as she attempts to skitter back up. I can't bend over to grab her without fearing that I'll fall in too.

"Waiting for us, are you? Dirty bitch."

I unsling the shotgun and brace it against my shoulder. I aim at the first fury who is now only ten metres away. I shoot and his stomach opens up. I fire again and hit another in the chest. He stumbles into a sitting position and then falls onto his back. Another two furies pass them. I drop the rucksack, reach in through the zips and pull out a handful of ammo. I open the barrel and in a blind panic I try and thrust two shells into the gaps, but they're the wrong way round. Brown is still trying desperately to climb the slippery steps while I fumble the cartridges around. I place one in the right way and close the barrel just as a hand reaches and grabs the end of the gun. I blindly pull the trigger and the closeness of the sound shocks me as the round hits the wrath in the shoulder and arm. At this distance, it shreds the flesh and bone is exposed. He collapses to the floor, emitting a primal shriek.

Another four are just behind him though, so I pick another shell, jam it in and fire. Two of the wraths are hit and spin. The last two are on me though, and as one reaches for the shotgun I bring the gaffer-taped bayonet up and swipe it across his throat. The fury grabs at his neck as a jet of blood squirts across the alley. The last one swings a punch at my head. It glances off my scalp, which dazes me, but he is slightly off-balance from the punch so I swing the barrel of the gun and knock him toward the steps. He just manages to grab the handrail next to the stairs, but looks confused as his fingers find slide along the icy metal rail, and he slips backwards. Brown barely jumps out of his way as he collapses into the tight stairwell. She jumps on his chest and uses him as a springboard to leap out into the alleyway. The wrath wriggles on his back but like Brown, he can't find any purchase to right himself. I reload the shotgun and point it at him. He doesn't even blink.

"Big woman when you've got a gun, eh? Come in here and I'll fuck you up you fat whore."

I hover my hand over the trigger and feel saliva pooling in my mouth. How nice to have the option. I hear more voices from the same place that the porters came from, so I purse my lips and spit the mouthful of drool I have over the helpless wrath and turn for the top of the alley moving away from the hospital. We hit the road and I finally understand where we are within the hospital grounds. We've come out just next to the new research centre that was being built, and to my right stands the entrance to the construction site. I know that we have to find somewhere to hide because we can't run from the furies. I point the shotgun at a double-width chain-link gate and blast a hole through the padlock securing the doors together. Leaning my full weight into it, I manage to shift the snow on the other side and push Brown through the gap. I lean into the door again and then I'm through too. Various lengths of steel rebar jut from the ground through the snow. I place my feet with care as I head towards the nearest thing I can see that might serve as a hiding place - a huge yellow bulldozer with ASHBROOK written along the side in blue and white letters.

The large yellow blade of the bulldozer is down on the floor, and I have to step over a hydraulic arm to grab the railing and take the steps. Brown leaps athletically up onto the caterpillar track. As I get to the top of the steps, I feel a cramping pain across my stomach and I gasp out loud. With tiny movements I shuffle to the centre of the bulldozer, yank at the black door handle and haul it open. Brown needs no invitation, and gladly hops into the dry cab that smells of oil and dust. Inside the cab is a central dashboard, a huge worn grey seat and controllers that look like the gaming joysticks that Rick had for his PC. On one side of the cab is a large display with a keypad to the right of it. Underneath, sellotaped in place, is a scrap of a post-it note that says "JAMES – 6969". I scan the keyboard but can't see anywhere to enter the access code.

I look up as five wraths come into the yard and scan the landscape. Almost as soon as I spot them, one of them spots me, points at the cab and shouts something inaudible. I look for a lock on the door but find nothing. I look again at the keypad, this time pressing and holding a green button. There are two loud beeps and the numbers on the keypad flash brightly. The little screen starts to work through a login procedure, then it displays the CAT logo and then the ASHBROOK symbol. Each screen seems to freeze, and I urge the computer to go faster. The wraths are nearly at the bulldozer now, and with agonising slowness, the screen flashes up a message: Enter PIN. I stab in the code, "6-9-6-9," but nothing happens. The first wrath leans up onto the caterpillar tracks and begins to drag himself up. I stare at the keypad and frantically wonder what it is that I've not done. The wrath lies on his front along the tracks, and punches at the lower portion of the glass in the door, which splinters as he pounds at it. Brown starts to scrabble at the fracturing window on our side of the door.

I notice that there are various symbols on the keypad, and that one of them looks like a 'Return' key. I slam my thumb into it and the screen to my left lights up with images of dials and various information. A prompt on the screen says, "PRESS IGNITION KEY". I look at the pad and opt for another one of the green keys. I stab at it and there's a rumble from beneath me as the bulldozer shakes itself awake. I take a second to look at the various controls but the arrows on the controllers make it all seem blissfully straightforward. I push my left hand forward and with a jerk, the machine jumps a few feet forward and I feel the blade dig into the snow and earth in front of us. Two of the wraths who were trying to climb up the front are jolted off and one is skewered on a spike of rebar in the snow. The wrath on the bulldozer gets his arm pulled into the caterpillar track and he screams, his torso gradually gets fed into the mechanism as the bulldozer growls forward.

I nudge the controller around and squash the last of the wraths and figure out how to lift the blade of the dozer up. I bring the machine to a halt and sit in the driver's seat, thinking about next moves. I have no clue where I could go or what I can do that will help to solve all the problems I have. Without warning, I feel a crush in my chest and grief rolls over me and I really, really miss my dad.

Chapter 21

4th May 2021
9 months after

I wish I had a hat.

I'm wading through knee-high snow on the flat roof of the hospital as a thick flurry continues to fall, so even if I had a hat I'd probably be freezing anyway, but still – I wish I had a hat. I'm wearing my fleece and the anorak zipped up to the top and over that I've stretched a red-and-brown checked dressing gown I pulled from a corpse, so the top half of me is warmish. I didn't want to risk waking Natalie or Brown by rustling my trousers on, so I'm wearing thin pyjama bottoms. From my knee downwards the paper-thin fabric is wet and heavy and they keep falling down, so I have to keep stopping and yanking them up or my arse pokes out of the top. I stop to retie the dressing gown cord tighter, so I can get on with my mission at a reasonable speed. Somewhere under the snow, a pair of scavenged Ugg boots are absorbing more water than if they'd been made of sponge. They make me think wistfully of my waterproof walking boots, or really any other footwear at all.

It's been an hour since I crept out of the treatment room, not daring to breathe. Brown had stirred and I blew her a kiss as I left. Beyond that, there was no time for emotional goodbyes. Outside the door, my fear had counter-acted the weariness I felt and it propelled me along the corridors. The lower hallways of the hospital were full of wraths, so I found the first stairwell I came to and made my way upwards, towards the roof. The top levels of the hospital were quieter, and on my way through the corridors, I stopped at a janitor's storage cupboard and filled a supply trolley with anything from the cupboard that had a flammable symbol on it. I also took a large red axe from a fire hose cabinet. As I pushed the trolley through the wards, I loaded gas containers and anything that looked like it might explode onto the trolley too. I worked my way as far north as I could within the hospital, trying to put as much distance between me and radiotherapy as possible.

As I went, I realised why there were no wraths in this part of the hospital when I saw that a fire had ravaged a section of the building. I guessed that the overhead sprinklers must have put it out, but not before it attracted all the wraths in the area. I've seen wraths around fire before and they are drawn towards it, oblivious to the danger that it presents – they just want to shout at it or fight it, and that never ends well. The cold wind blew through the broken windows, and I edged as close I dared to figure out where I was. I took a flight of stairs up and used the axe to break into another flight of stairs that lay behind. At the top was a locked exit to the roof and I swung the axe against the hinges of the door and the vibrations of the strike almost shook my teeth loose. Eventually, I managed to get the axe into a gap and lever the door open onto the roof.

Before me lays a flat, untouched white plain. Here and there a vent pokes out just above the snowline. I carefully wade to the edge of the surface and look down on a deserted road, opposite a church and a Texaco petrol station. Even though the street has been buried in snow it's clear that the horde of wraths has come this way. They have left a characteristic path of destruction, with trees uprooted and cars flipped on their sides. Stomped and broken bodies are scattered through the streets, gradually being hidden by the endless snow. I blow on my hands and wish I had gloves – and a hat. To keep frostbite from setting in, I take ten minutes shuttling between the supply trolley at the bottom of the stairs and the side of the building, bringing up my collection of flammables. My theory is that if I can get a big enough fire going and make a big enough noise it should attract the horde who will ideally display their characteristic lack of fire safety and fry themselves to a crisp.

By the time I have all my supplies at the roof's edge, I realise that the one thing that I don't have is anything to start a fire with. Wheezing and numb-fingered I retrace my steps and search the bodies in the ward looking for any smokers who might have a lighter on them. I finally find a black powdery corpse with a silver Zippo in the back pocket of his or her jeans. It's embossed with a picture of a dragon and the words "You're Hot, Chiles". I test it, holding my fingers over the broad flame until the hair singes on the back of my fingers.

I make my way back upstairs and peer over the side of the building and see about 10 metres from the edge is an articulated lorry. The trailer has spilt on its side and it has pulled the cab over with it, exposing the mechanisms underneath. I take three of the gas canisters that I've found, open the valves and throw them as close as I can to the truck. Two of them fall short and poof into the snow with a muted clang, disappearing from sight, but the third strikes the front wheel, bounces and finally comes to rest on the side of the trailer. I think it might roll off, but the layer of snow holds it in place. I move 15 metres away from the store of flammables and rip a piece of cloth from a light blue cellular blanket. I jam it in the neck of a bottle of drain cleaner, which smells so strongly that even in the open air it makes me feel light-headed.

I look again at where I'm aiming and flick the zippo open. I grind the flint wheel and hold the cloth in the flame. It burns slowly, but then it catches the fumes of the cleaner and erupts into a raging bouquet. I stand quickly and fling the container towards the lorry. It falls towards the trailer and with a *woof* it splits and sets the side of the trailer on fire. The snow limits the inferno, so I return to my store of ammo and select another bottle. This time I open the bottle and shake some of the fluid onto the outside of it. I pitch the bottle and it lands in the centre of the dwindling pool of flame. This time it explodes with a quiet growl. I look for what I can hit next.

After 10 minutes, I've used all of my flammables and only succeeded in starting a few small fires, while the side of the trailer burns slowly. A small contingent of wraths have spotted the flames and gathered near the trailer. They are shouting, but I can't hear what they're saying and none of the main horde from the front of the hospital have been attracted. I need to think bigger. I look at the crane that soars 30 or 40 metres above street level. I can see the jib of the crane is about 60 metres long and is frozen in place with a large skip, suspended from the end of a long chain. I gingerly step back towards the very edge of the building, look over and see scaffolding that could lead me straight to the crane.

Before my stupid brain gets overly involved, I climb over the security rail and scuff the snow from the roof's edge. The scaffold is only a metre away from the edge of the building, but my anxiety seizes me at the worst possible moment and instead of stepping out, I cling onto the rail. In the end, it's only the thought of Natalie and Brown and my freezing fingers that decide it for me. I close my eyes, let go, take the step out and land in the padded snow on the scaffold platform. I catch my breath and start to work my way across various ladders and sections of the scaffolding, until I'm able to duck my head and step across onto the crane and walk over to the ladder that leads to the top.

I shake the blood back into my hands, stamp my feet and look up. The top of the crane blends in with the thick, formless clouds and before I can psyche myself out, I grab the first rung in front of me and start to climb. The mishmash of healing bones in my hand and the wetness of the rungs means I lose my grip and bang my wrist trying to grab hold of something to steady myself. Somehow, I painfully ascend the first section of the ladder. This opens out onto a platform, with the next ladder accessible by walking around to the other side. This offset system means that if you slip and fall, you're only going to be smashed to pieces on the platform below rather than falling all the way to the floor and dying. It's a comforting thought as I grab the next ladder and climb up.

I try to keep looking outwards rather than down, and as I ascend the skyline of Manchester is revealed. Before long I can see the entire gathered horde at the front of the hospital. I risk a look up and see that there are only two more ladders to go to the top. I suppress the exhaustion and find a rhythm to scale the rest of the way up. I step out onto a flat platform with a rail around it, and a cabin to one side. The city is so far below me that bile rises in my throat, and again I have to fight the urge to hold onto the railing as I look at the buildings looming through the blizzard. Adrenaline is coursing through me. I open the door to the cabin and scream, as an obscured face with a long, matted beard wheels round in the seat.

"Oi! What are you doing up here?" bellows the wrath.

He's a huge guy in an oversized hi-vis safety jacket. I'm so close I can see that his eyes are bloodshot. He lunges over the back of the seat to grab at me and I slip backwards. As he stays in place and continues to grasp at thin air, I realise that he's strapped in a safety harness that secures him to the seat. The belt is keeping him in place and presumably, he doesn't have the cognitive ability to unclip himself. I visualise the little tubers of the parasite reaching into the various parts of his brain and, even now, I can't help but feel a pang of sadness for him. He didn't ask for this. None of them did. The ones I filled Salford Quays with were victims of the parasite, just as this man is. There's a small fire extinguisher clipped to the side of the wall and I pull it from the clips.

"Oi! Fuck off, that's mine!" he shouts and again he writhes in his seat, trying to find a way to escape his bonds. I lift the extinguisher and club him solidly on the forehead. He spits and emits a loud gurgling noise, and again I club him on the head. The skin of his brow splits and a thin spray of blood coats the inside of the window. I hit him on the back of the head and he slumps to the side, still held in his seat by the harness. I try not to think too much as I unclip him. His body slides forward off the seat and onto the thick glass floor. As I roll him away, I see a picture of two school girls stuck to the window both smiling awkwardly at the camera. The older one is wearing braces.

I slide into the driver's seat and look around to get a sense of how to control the crane. Fortunately, it's not complicated and I'm not looking to do things safely. There's a green start/stop button on the dashboard and two joysticks on either side of the chair. I take a breath and push the green button. The only sign I have that anything has happened is that the crane vibrates slightly. I lightly touch the left-hand control and the jib moves. With the right controller, I push forward and the load at the end of the chain starts to lower.

"Time to make a scene," I say, and look for what to smash first.

I move the jib further to the right and line up the height of the skip. I then swing the crane arm fast and watch as the skip is sent rushing effortlessly along the skyline, smashing with an immense shattering noise through a large glass section of the hospital. I smile grimly and lower the full weight of the skip on a motorbike. A small fireball escapes from beneath the sides of the skip, then it's on to the next potential explosion. I turn the crane all the way around so I can see down the road, and at last, I notice a chunk of the horde peeling off and turning towards the chaos. I wait until they're close enough and then drop the skip on the smouldering lorry in a satisfying burst of steel and sparks. There's a delay and I raise the skip again to drop it, but as it's rising there's a huge explosion. The fuel tanks of the lorry go up in a fireball. Wraths are blasted sideways and more start to sprint from the front of the hospital.

I look at the Texaco.

With the crane at full extension, I use the skip to clumsily swipe the metal roof from the forecourt and it falls with a clang, exposing the pumps and dry ground underneath. I calculate that the fuel tanks must be buried somewhere beneath the pumps, so I sit the skip on the floor and drag it back towards me, like running a match against the sandpaper strip. As the first pump is effortlessly knocked over, the sparks from the skip ignite an underwhelming, localised fire along the top of the upturned pump. I see the wraths move towards it and smile, ducking in the cabin just as the windows of the crane shatter from the force of an explosion. A mushroom-shaped inferno is unleashed into the sky. I look up to see a dark black cloud propped up by crimson wildfire reach higher than the crane itself and the heat pushes me back into my seat.

"Come and get it," I say to the approaching wraths.

The horde is rampant now. They pour around the corner of the building and out of the hospital windows in their desperation to get to the source of the disturbance. The wraths nearest to the blaze are pushed into the flames by the weight of the crowd behind them. They windmill their arms and fall to the floor. More are pushed onwards. I lower the skip into the throng and scoop more of the wraths into the flames. Some of them climb into the skip and again I brush them into the fire. At some point, the skip comes off the crane's hook, and when I try and move the crane arm it no longer responds to my commands. I watch for as long as I dare and lean back in the seat, utterly spent. My skin is crawling with a cold sweat and my head is pounding. I would be content to sleep here forever. It's certainly warm.

"Dear God, please get Nat and Brown away from here. Please. Please."

If I fall asleep, I'll never wake up. So I stand up and bang my head on the ceiling of the cramped cab. I pull my trousers up and cinch the cord even tighter around my waist. I open the door and, even among the nearby flames, I feel the icy wind creep through my clothes. I start the long journey down the ladder.

Chapter 22

4th May 2021
9 months after

I sit in the bulldozer with Brown at my feet and watch more furies get pulled under the tracks. As we move forward, a red mulch spins past on the tracks. It's almost funny to me now. Fragmented thoughts enter my head.

My dad died in a car crash.

The world ended.

I was trapped in the scanner, screaming.

Ben is exploding things.

I'm supposed to be running away.

It's *almost* funny. The dog leaps up and pushes her paws against the door of the bulldozer. This dog is called

Brown. She's barking but not making any sound. I can't hear anything anyway. There's just the sound of the inside of my head. I'm diving into the deepest pool at Martin's house. Martin is my friend. The water pressure becomes punishing as I challenge myself to go deeper. I feel the water get colder at an alarming rate as I kick further downwards. My ears start to hurt and my lungs tighten. I turn back towards the light that exists somewhere above and frantically push to the surface. A warming spread of bubbles, sounds and sunlight return as I get closer to the surface. My lungs are screaming. A fist smashes through the bulldozer window and Brown leaps up and grabs at it.

I ignore the fist. It will either get me or not. I realise that I've stopped driving the machine, which is why we're at a standstill. A furious face is pounding on the door and I look at it in surprise. What an odd thing. This is a monster called a fury. There is blood running from his nose and teeth. I push forward on the controls and the face goes away. I pull the right-hand controller to see what it does and the blade in front of the dozer raises up. I try pushing the other one and the tracks spin in the snow, but suddenly we're facing 45 degrees to the right. I reflexively reach for the gas, but it's not there. I should be worried but it's fine: I'm not there. I'm coming to the surface in the pool, and there is no noise in my world, just the certainty of what happens next.

I idly push the controller onwards. I realise that it doesn't matter if I steer, the bulldozer just moves forward. Its certainty matches my determination. Everything falls beneath its blade. I can tap the controller to steer or I can leave it and we push onwards anyway. There is a group of furies on the road, dead ahead, which makes the decision for me. Tons of machine carves a path through them and the deep snow as if they don't exist. As we pass by, furies launch themselves at the spinning tracks and all are pulled under. The noise of the machine mounting the cars overpowers thought. We grind onwards towards the explosions and fire. That's where Ben will be.

A black pall of smoke is rising upwards and I know that there I will find Ben. I see now that he is a vector of destruction. It follows him, or it is him. I don't know. My thoughts aren't even. The black and brown dog is subdued by the cranking noise of the bulldozer and she sits and pants as she looks out at the furies falling beneath us. We round the corner of the hospital and onto the main road and ahead I see the gathered masses. Ben did a good job of creating a diversion for us to leave, but what he didn't consider is whether we wanted him to leave. He didn't give us that option. He chose not to have that discussion. He thinks he's following God's plan, and it's precisely because of that bullshit that I have to kill him. I won't have it.

I flick the switch on the panel that has a picture of a horn and a *CRRRROOOOOOOONK* sounds out from the machine, joining with the *TAKTAKTAKTAKTAK* beat of the caterpillar tracks on the concrete. The tail end of the crowd turns towards us and the blade doesn't hesitate as it cuts them down. The horde is thick here, like a crowd packed in at the front of a concert. The bulldozer doesn't care. I don't care.

I see that in the middle of the destruction is the crane. Something is hanging from the end of the chains amidst the flames and I connect the dots. He used the crane to destroy the petrol station. I look up at the ladder leading up to the crane and see a speck moving, three flights down from the top. I recognise him instantly. I focus on him and sound the horn again and again. Wraths leap onto the moving tracks of the bulldozer and get pulped. We're fifty metres from the base of the crane, it's surrounded by boards screening off the building site, but the weight of the crowd has pushed these to the floor. I angle the bulldozer to the left and we continue towards the crane.

As I maintain pressure on the horn I watch him. I see him reach the next landing of the ladder and look around. He spots the bulldozer and raises both hands. He looks like a lunatic in a dressing gown and Uggs, his bald head glinting in the light. He's waving and pointing the other way. He's crossing his hands as if he's cancelling us out. He descends another flight of stairs. He slips as he's coming down and falls, landing on his back. He's up again and as we get closer, I can see his face. I smile at the expression of horror etched onto his features. He's shouting "GO! GO AWAY!" He's waving us off as if he can brush us up like dust. I beckon to him. One finger, crooked towards me.

He screams with exasperation, and I can see a plume of vapour escape his mouth as he bellows. He comes down another flight and now, as we get closer, I watch his face and see the disappointment and fear more sharply. He's 20 metres away and I continue to call him to me. Another flight of steps and now he's close enough to touch. I circle the bulldozer underneath him and we turn in a tight circle twice, ploughing a dark furrow of soil and crushed bodies. I will circle here until you jump, I think to myself. I take the bulldozer as close as I dare to the base of the tower crane and on our third pass, I point to him and then to the front of the dozer. Jump. We pass underneath, and out of the sky drops an unwieldy heap of flesh and fabric. The bonnet of the bulldozer bounces as he lands on his knees. He's thrust against the black exhaust pipe, and he holds on to stop himself from falling, but then screams as he feels its heat. The voices of the wraths are baying for him, desperate for him to slip and pitch under the bulldozer with them. The dog is stretched against the glass of the windows, frantic for him to return to us, her claws scratching at the glass of the cab.

I don't know this dog.

The man pitches forward and flattens himself onto the bonnet. I see the pain in his expression as he slithers himself onto the platform outside. I open the door, and with a yelp of pain he slops down into the cab. I grab him with a strength I don't normally possess. I pull this cold remnant further inside and slam the door behind him. My hands dig into his dressing gown and then his flesh beneath.

"I told you to go!" he whimpers through his shivers. "I said to go!"

"I did go," I say, as my fingers find his throat and interlink. He struggles, but he's weak and I can feel the cartilage of his throat under my thumbs. The man makes a *glurk* noise and I push him back against the dashboard. The dog is pinned under him but she worms her way free and tears at my arm. I don't feel any pain. He looks confused and scared, but I think I see a glimmer of recognition in his eyes. He knows what I am now. The dog is jumping up and trying to bite my face. The bulldozer goes on. I can't steer it now. It knows that the way is onward. Only onward. Finally, the certainty is here. I can see the crowd fall as we travel on. My people cheer this last death, they shower their screams upon us like confetti. The man reaches out for something. He takes hold of the dog and pulls it to him. The man looks at me and his bulging eyes start to close as the colour of his face deepens to purple.

From somewhere deep inside me, somewhere ancient, a tearing pain rips through my body and reaches out to where I am, where I've gone. The man in my hands is still and smiling and the dog wriggles from his grasp. I don't know where I am. I look out of the window and I don't recognise any of this. A supernova of agony erupts inside of me again. I look down and see the front of my clothes are soaked. I touch it and the liquid is warm. I don't understand. The dog is angry, and I stare at it as it bites at my arm. It snarls and opens its mouth again but there's no noise. I know why it doesn't bark. She had an operation when she was young. She is debarked. Brown is her name. The pain tears through my stomach and back again. I reach the surface of the pool and I gasp for air.

"BEN!" I scream. I look at Ben and I see that we're moving slowly forward. Wraths are everywhere around us and we're pushing a large tree and some gates across the middle of a park.

"BEN!" I shout and slap him.

"Ben! Come back to me!" I slap him again and he doesn't move.

"You said you'd help me! I need you now. Ben. Be with me. Please!"

He suddenly shudders, takes a pained breath, and then a deeper one. He looks at me with a groggy focus. I shriek at him.

"BEN!"

He sits up on the floor of the cab looking confused. Brown licks at his face and he looks at me with a fearful awareness.

"I can't go again," I say in a wretched little voice.

"It's okay. You're okay." He reaches out for my hand but the pain rips again. I scream and the sound fills the tiny cab. What feels like a volley of knives fires across my stomach, and I remember that there are babies inside me.

"Ben, please – you promised. Kill me if I hurt them."

"I wanted you to get away," he says.

There's a crunch and the bulldozer grinds as it comes up against a building. I look up as bricks and cement dust fall from the corner of a pavilion onto the bonnet. A pall of white smoke is billowing out of the engine compartment.

I try to reach for the controllers but my hands are pulled back to the sides of my abdomen. My stomach feels stretched tight like a drumskin and sweat beads all over my naked head. I feel sick and I need to stand, despite the grinding, drunken motion of the bulldozer and the low ceiling. I have to stand. I grab at the looped door handle and pull myself to my feet. It releases something within me and a warm gush of fluid runs down my legs. I'm suddenly aware that the furies are climbing over the back of the bulldozer. Too many to count surround us.

"Ben, they're coming!"

Ben scoots out of the way and pulls himself onto the seat. He takes the controls and I feel myself swing around as he pulls back on the sticks, and we move away from the building. I squint my eyes shut and dive again into the deep pool at Martin's. My ears block out the sounds and I feel the anger coming back in waves. The wave of anger meets the wave of pain from my stomach and all I can do is howl. Brown skips around, terrified of the noise. I howl and moan. I tentatively sit on the edge of the seat and lean forward onto the loop, which creaks under my weight.

"Hold on," Ben says, and I grip harder onto the loop. The blade flattens a series of railings, and we're out of the park and back onto the road. I turn and see the horde behind us. The dashboard says that we're going at 9 miles per hour but furies surround us still. They throw themselves at the machine as it runs on. The road opens up. We make speed up slightly; a supermarket and a cinema complex pass in a blur. I feel sick with the rocking motion and the pounding noise of the tracks.

"Where are we going? The babies are coming!" I say.

"I know. I'm thinking," Ben says.

I scream again as pain pumps upwards from my womb and I feel myself pass into a nowhere state, where the pain is simply all there is and I am a greyed-out form.

"Ben, please help," I say in a strained voice.

"We need to lose the wraths, we'll never outrun them in this and if we stop, they'll swarm us."

"Please, Ben?"

"We could try and get back to the ship, but I don't know how I could get you on board. If I put you on the blade at the front, maybe I could lift you up."

I shriek with pain, and incredulity, at the thought of what he's suggesting.

"No. Not that."

"Okay, okay. I've got another idea. Just hold on."

As we travel, it seems like every bump in the road and car that we smash into forces another half pint of fluid out of me. I scream with venom at Ben to drive smoothly. At some point, Ben's hand reaches out to my back and he rubs hard against me and I feel like it helps.

"More," I command. He does it more.

I open my eyes and we're on a motorway bridge. I can see the frosted tops of trees and the ranks of white roofs from a housing estate below us. From here the world looks pure and calm. I start to pant to control the pain. We drive onwards. Memories of my previous life come to me. I remember Dad holding my hand outside the school gates. I see Rick dressed as a Mighty Morphin Power Ranger at Christmas. Martin putting Little Martin on the Christmas tree. The babies inside me want to get out and I can no longer stop them. I'm not sure I can help them though. I'm not sure of anything.

"Nearly there," Ben says softly. "I know you don't want to do this, but in a moment, we're going to have to move. I promise you won't have to move far. Natalie, you need to trust me."

I nod, because that's all I can do now. My face is fixed in a rictus of agony. I hear Ben gathering the rucksack and the shotgun. I feel him cradle my face and kiss my forehead tenderly.

"Brown, you have to stay with me, okay? Trust me, Nat," he says again.

I feel him push past me and open the door. There is the sound of a shotgun blast, then he grabs my hand and pulls me out of the door and onto the caterpillar tracks. I open my eyes and behold the world. We're so high up. I can see a stretch of river, and on the right, I see the slope of a large building and beyond that, I recognise the Trafford Centre.

"Please Nat, we have to move," Ben urges me. I step one foot in front of the other and feel another relieving rush of liquid, as blood and fluids are jostled from my insides. I feel like I need to poo or be sick, or both. I turn to the right and once again see the advancing mass of wraths. We're about 50 metres ahead of them but they're closing ground fast. I look at Ben and he smiles, almost serenely.

"Trust me," he says, and I step down into the deep snow on the road. He sweeps Brown unceremoniously off the track and she lands in the snow beside me. He turns me to the left and with his hand under my arms, he propels me forward. The road lies before us, only it's not a road at all. The road is gone, both sides have been destroyed and all that remains of the road is a thin strip about a foot wide near the central barrier. It's covered in snow and Ben keeps pushing me towards it.

"What are you doing?"

"We're going to walk across there."

"Why?"

"It's the way, Natalie. Trust me. Don't be afraid."

I want to split his head open with an axe. I want to put my foot in his arse and send him skittering off the edge. We're close enough now that I can see what lies underneath the road. Far below is the dark strip of water, the rubble of the original tarmac, and a jumble of cars and lorries. My eyes focus on the broken vehicles far below and I feel myself stumble towards them as the world sounds fainter in my ears.

"Nat! Stay with me! WALK! NOW!"

Ben is in front of me and we're out over the edge. There's a metal barrier rubbing against my left leg. I'm not going to look but I think I can sense Brown behind me. Ben is facing me, walking backwards across this thin strip of land as if he's done this a thousand times. He's holding both my hands and I'm drawn to look at him. He smiles at me. I look down and see my Crocs sliding forward on the tiny partition. If I slip then I will die. If I die then my babies will die. I hold onto Ben's hands and look at his face again. His nose has healed and the bruises are nearly gone.

"Natalie, I love you," he says, and he laughs. "Just one second."

He lets go of my right hand. He pulls at his sagging trousers and hoists them up to his chest. He smiles at me again. We shuffle on and soon I can feel the strip of road broadening beneath me as it rejoins the other side of the motorway. And then we're across. Brown skips past me and bounces around on the road. I realise that I've been holding my breath and I turn to see where we've come from. Some furies are trying to cross the thin strip of road, and as I look one loses her footing and slips into the void. At the other side of the road is the abandoned bulldozer and the furies who are reaching the edge and simply tumbling away into the wreckage below. I remember the penny waterfalls I used to play at the arcade. We continue to watch the crowd press forwards, over the edge and into nothing.

Chapter 23

5th May 2021
9 months, 1 day after

I check to see that there are no wraths on this side of the road and lean Natalie as gently as I can against the wheel of a truck. Her face is twisted with pain and her hands are clenched on either side of her belly.

"Hurry," she whispers.

I return as close to the edge of the road as I dare and find a suitable car – an ancient red Ford Fiesta. The door is open and snow has piled up in the driver's footwell. I briefly wonder where the driver went. I think back to the Land Rover and look for the lever in the centre. I press the button in and lower it to the floor and feel the car rock slightly. I turn the steering wheel, which is made easier by the snow underneath the wheels. Then I lean into the door frame and gradually push the car to the end of the thin footbridge. Most of the wraths are spilling over the side of the road and away into the Mersey below. It's mesmerising to watch. From this distance, they look like lemmings casually pitching themselves into oblivion. A few of the wraths, though, are trying to balance their way across the same strip of road we came over on, and I don't want anyone following.

One young wrath wearing an acid house t-shirt is about 20 yards across the gap. I reach into the back seat of the Fiesta and pull out a dog-eared road atlas. I rip out some of the pages and go to the back of the car and unscrew the petrol cap. I jam several pages in the mouth of the tank and smell the whiff of fumes rising to my nose. Using the Zippo, I light one page of the atlas and then hold it to the others in the tank. They catch fire and I turn and move as quickly as possible to grab Natalie and our things. I whistle Brown to my side, and with my arm supporting Natalie, we make it to the back of the truck just as the fire catches in the Fiesta's petrol tank and a ball of flame rises above the car. A thick pall of black smoke pours out and consumes the vehicle. I see the acid house t-shirt flutter as the wrath falls. I turn away, and we push on into the snow.

Natalie is feverish by the time the road has dropped level with the ground. We turn left and follow a path through some trees and emerge into the car park of the rugby ground. I've used the drone extensively over this area so I'm confident the wraths will be in the canal already, but I keep the shotgun ready. We pick up an access track that leads to the shed that I prepared for Brown. Following the line of the brook keeps us under the trees and away from the snow and it's easier for Natalie to stumble along. She still has to pause frequently as the contractions hit her. Her cries make me daunted by what is to come but a quieter voice inside me tells me that this is good; it is the final jigsaw piece slotting into place just as it must. I push open the white doors of the storage shed and settle Natalie onto the platform of the fertiliser bags. I wrap duvets around her and prop her up with the pillows I brought to this place a lifetime ago. I rip open the bag of kibble and Brown falls on the food, delighted to eat something that isn't crackers spread with peanut butter. I build a small fire just outside the doors with the wood I cut from the door and branches I scavenge from nearby. It doesn't do much to warm the room, but just the sight of the fire feels comforting.

Natalie's breathing is thin and quick, shallow pants taken mechanically. I fetch water from the brook and bathe the sweat from her forehead. Gradually, the feeling returns to my feet and hands, and I can focus fully on Natalie. She's sprawled across the makeshift bed at the back of the room and a dark red circle emanates from her groin across the duvet she's lying on. Her belly is exposed, and I dip a clean strip of cloth in the water and hold it to her lips. She sucks gratefully and I repeat the process until she's had her fill. I find more wood and build up the fire outside, even though her skin is slick with sweat. I use the cloth to wipe her forehead again and she looks at me as if she's seeing me for the first time.

"You'll kill me if I turn?"

"I don't know," I reply.

I shake my dressing gown off and re-tie the braided cord holding up my trousers. Like Nat, my t-shirt is drenched with sweat. It stinks. My skin sags freely under the bottom of the shirt and I try and scoop it into my pyjama bottoms. Natalie grunts and pants. I reach out and hold her hand.

"You did great, Ben," she says before going quiet. After several minutes she concludes the thought: "This is a good place."

I try and remember *My Dog Is Having A Dog!* and summon forth any transferable knowledge, but unless Natalie intends to chew through the umbilical cords then I suspect there's not much I can do, except to be here and do as I'm told. I search out the tools that I left here and wonder if the saw or the hammer will prove to be of more use. I take the short knife from the barrel of the shotgun and hold it in the fire until the blade shines red, to purge it of any germs. I use the saw to gather more wood for the fire and collect water from the brook. Time takes on a sludgy, unreal quality, but as the night reaches its darkest point and the orange glow of the fire is the only thing giving us light, I estimate that Natalie has been labouring for over 10 hours. Brown alternates sleeping by the fire and standing on the bed to examine Natalie solicitously. At one point, Natalie reaches out and runs her hand over Brown's head and I see tears brimming in Natalie's eyes.

"I'm sorry I scared you, baby," she says. Brown licks at her hand and Natalie grabs her and squashes her to her side.

Just as dawn is starting to bring definition to the trees outside, Natalie starts to scream again. Unlike the other cries since the labour began, which all reached a crescendo and dissipated, this stays at a constant level. She looks at me with urgency in her eyes.

"Help me get on all fours," she commands and I feebly provide her with an arm to help her flip over. She screams twice in quick succession and angles her bum towards the ceiling and the first baby crowns. I stare dumbly at the circle of dark hair that appears in her vagina. The baby's entire head appears and then stops. There's a pause where Natalie is panting like a dog and I don't know what I'm supposed to do – is the baby stuck? Should I pull? I decide I should, but Natalie growls as I approach and so I stand back and leave the baby lodged there. Instead, I say, "You're doing great!" with as much conviction as I can muster. After another scream, the baby turns slightly and at the next scream, a slurping shape is deposited into the pillowcase that I somehow have ready in my arms. I lay the baby on the bed and in a second the baby issues a series of coughs and then becomes war-red and angry, its tiny arms raised in defiance. I wipe a string of spit from its raspberry-sized mouth.

"Hello baby girl," I say. "Nat, you have a daughter and she's perfect."

"A daughter," Natalie says as if she's trying to figure out what that means.

"What do I do with the cord Nat?" I ask. A twist of white-blue tubing stretches from the baby's belly button and reaches into Natalie's vagina.

"Tie it and cut it," she says in a dreamy voice. "Once near me and once near her tummy. Hurry up."

I should have asked about this before and I look around the shed to see what I could use to tie it off. There's a spool of green twine on the floor which I fetch and quickly tie a tight granny knot about five centimetres from the baby's tummy. I then leave another five centimetres and tie another knot in the cord. I hold the knife up to the cord and panic at what I'm doing. What if this is wrong?

"Are you sure I just cut this?" I ask Natalie.

"Cut it," she commands and I instantly pull the razor-sharp knife through the tough cord. Immediately a jet of blood fires from the cord. The girl screams and I feel like I'm going to pass out. In a second the pulse of the blood stops though and I'm able to wrap the baby in the pillowcase and make her warmer. Brown leaps onto the bed and I show the baby to her and she sniffs at its head. I then shuffle along the bed and hold it under Natalie's face.

"I think she's ok, Nat. I think you did it."

Natalie cries in unison with her newborn daughter. I cuddle the little bundle to me and kiss her warm cheeks. The smell of her! Oh, the smell! I hold her so Natalie can smell her. She takes a deep breath and seems calmer as she exhales. The baby's eyes are an impossible blue and her hair is dark and silky. I crook my little finger and hold it to her mouth, and her hard gums pinch down on it. She suckles on the finger for a few minutes. Natalie doesn't move position and I keep wondering if I can somehow attach the baby to Natalie's breast to feed, but I don't think it would be a good idea to break the sphere of concentration that Natalie is projecting around herself. In time Natalie starts to shriek and a large mass of blood and flesh slips onto the bed. Fortunately, *My Dog Is Having A Dog!* had prepared me for the existence of afterbirth otherwise I would have fainted. I move the placenta out of the way before Brown has a chance to eat it.

"Do you want to move? Are you cold?" I ask but Natalie shakes her head.

"This is good. I want to stay here," she says and remains steadfast on all fours.

I dip the cloth in water and hold it to her mouth. Steam rises from her body as the room gradually cools with the fire burning down. Natalie shifts her position slightly and without warning, the second baby appears. I push Brown off the bed so I can lay the first baby down, she doesn't like the change in position and her face wrinkles as she screams. Natalie doesn't make a noise. Instead, she grunts with resolve as she pushes against the next baby – bigger than the last by some margin.

"You can do it, Nat. You're the strongest woman alive," I say, aware that it might actually be true.

After a minute the baby breaks free and joins its sister swaddled a pillowcase. I tie the cord again and slip the knife through, almost like I know what I'm doing. Their cries mingle together and the small shed is full with noise. Brown retreats to the outside. Natalie slumps into the bed and a deep shudder runs through her body. I help her to turn around and she collapses back against the wall of the shed. I scoop up the babies, who are now plum-coloured with anger and hold them out to her. Natalie pulls the children in close to her. She instinctively shuffles them in her arms and pulls them out of their makeshift covers and lays them across her naked chest.

"You did it. You have daughters," I say. She looks confused and then smiles at the babies' faces.

"I don't know what I'm doing," she says with a wobble of her lip.

"I think that's how it starts," I reply.

***

We take a week to reach the coast.

The Manchester Ship Canal becomes the river Mersey, becomes the Irish Sea. The barge we take first becomes a fishing trawler, then that becomes a footballer's yacht. The girls learn to feed and gain weight. With a familiar pleasure I place them on digital scales and make a careful note of their measurements in a red notebook. We realise that the oldest baby is blind when her eyes don't move like her sister's. In time, we start to suspect that the younger twin may be different developmentally. Natalie thinks it's connected to the toxoplasmosis, but we can't be sure. All I know is that both girls are perfect. My heart swells and sings when I see them, even at 3am, and I know without question that the meaning of my life is to protect these children, to give them the world.

Natalie feeds and sleeps and eats. Gradually, she deflates and regains mobility. She walks gingerly for the first few days after the birth and her path around the ship can be tracked by drops of blood. For some days she hardly speaks, and eyes me warily. We don't seem to know what to say to each other. Somehow, we don't seem to know each other. She keeps the babies close to her and only Brown and Bear are allowed to come near. Once she gets over the shock of the noise, Brown is smitten with the new arrivals and as the babies' pudgy arms flail around and poke her in the face she takes it all with saintly canine patience. I know how fragile our family is, but I can't contain my joy. It connects to a deeper well of happiness; songs return to my lips and I acutely feel the connection between everything. This is perhaps helped by the exceptional weed I find in the footballer's yacht, but maybe it's also because I am starting to see how it all fits together.

It's a time of primal silences and gentle action. I keep the vessels warm and steer us to safe ports. We chance upon a full first aid kit in the fishing vessel and the painkillers help us to cope. My right hand is usable again, but it's set at a funny angle and whenever I accidentally knock it, the pain spreads through my whole arm. For a few days I find it hard to eat because of the bruising around my neck. It's only when the bruises start to fade that Natalie starts to talk to me again. By the time the bruises are gone, we are together again.

The babies are christened, Anne and Kate, named after my mum and Natalie's mum. Natalie announces this as a done deal one night as we settle down to try and get some sleep. I look at the girls and wonder what their world will be like. Anne is the older and more vocal of the two. She feeds voraciously, and whenever she's not feeding she's screaming, or just vocalising in a pitch-wavering chatter. Kate is quieter and sleeps more, she is the first to smile but Natalie says it's just wind. I'm not so sure. It's too soon to tell if they are wraths. I don't think they are. Natalie hasn't needed gas to control herself since the birth. She says that it's still there, but that it's in balance. We scavenged some more Entonox anyway, and I can tell she's feeling something is off when she reaches for her mask. Sometimes though, she just wants to get high and laugh her arse off.

We sail south. We never leave sight of the land and when the weather is bad, we don't leave whatever harbour or inlet we have found. Viewed from the water, the world looks rugged, white and beautiful. Most of the time at sea, it's easy to kid yourself that the world is the same. The waves swell dark blue and crash over a different world. Sometimes we pass by ghost ships, impossibly large tankers that are adrift. We see a spill of oil emanating from a ferry wrecked on the coast near Ilfracombe. We round the Longships lighthouse at Land's End and make our way east along the south coast. We upgrade ships when we find better ones, or when they start to run out of diesel. We scavenge weapons and clothes. We accumulate food and supplies. I read manuals on seacraft and gradually learn to sail. Natalie teaches herself how to shoot. The girls learn to babble, the first sound either of them produces is "Beh". Natalie and I agree that they can't possibly mean Bear.

When we are ready, we cross the English Channel in the village-sized vessel of a billionaire whose wrath form chases a drone into the sea. As we cross the channel, the dorsal fins of dolphins accompany us nearly all the way to France. Natalie thinks she sees a whale breaching.

We trade our ships down in size as we navigate the Seine, from Le Havre through Rouen and on into Paris. The wraths are here too. We sleep safely anchored in the middle of the river and watch the ongoing snows bury the old civilisation. The ruins the wraths have created are laid to rest and we travel onwards. We are Anne, Kate, Bear, Natalie, Ben and Brown. We are the first family of the quiet new world.

Chapter 24

17th June 2021
10 months, 13 days after

It hasn't snowed for a week, so we finally leave the comfort of our latest boat and find a black Land Rover Discovery that starts up. We try four cars before the Land Rover starts. Natalie thinks that the diesel is starting to spoil and that we won't be able to rely on engines for much longer. It's news to me that diesel even can go off. We decide to swap the yacht for a sailing boat for the next leg of the journey, wind power should be good for a few more years yet. But that's a job for tomorrow. Today is a special day and not just because the skies are finally clear. Today is a holy day.

The Land Rover makes light work of the slushy snow on the roads. It's the first time I've been on dry land for over a month and my inner ear is in revolt at the notion that the entire world doesn't gently pitch and roll. I steal two car seats from a partially buried Renault and spend nearly an hour working out how to safely strap them into the Land Rover. The seats are a brand called Easy-Fix, clearly named by someone who had an advanced sense of irony. By the time we're ready to get on the road, I'm exhausted and a bit shaky. Natalie asks if I want to do this another day. I've been feeling stronger since I finished the last round of chemotherapy, but I know that the thought of starting another is lurking in Natalie's mind.

"It might start snowing again, I don't want the girls to do this in snow," I say, even though all I want to do is sleep. I've been promising myself this since we carried Anne and Kate onto the barge on the Manchester Ship Canal. I've been promising Natalie this for more than two years. I've been promising myself this for over a decade. I'm not letting cancer, or anything, spoil this.

Natalie looks at me carefully. I know she doesn't buy my bullshit, but she nods, and I carefully load the sleeping girls into the seats and strap them in while Natalie watches the streets around us, her favourite Heckler and Koch assault rifle cradled in her arms. Once they're in, Natalie passes me the weapon which I store in the footwell. Natalie gets behind the wheel and we slither across the streets of Paris. Bedraggled wraths with long hair obscuring their faces look up as we drive past, and a few times Natalie has to knock them over as she navigates us around and eventually out of the city.

We follow signs and after about 40 minutes of heading south, we pull into a vast car park, which is still rammed with vehicles and buses from the day of the change. We cruise past them and enter a fast pass lane which takes us up to the famous gates. I ask Natalie to slow down so I can savour the moment. There are wraths around us, which takes the shine off slightly but I open the window and breathe in the air. It smells like spring. Both the girls are still asleep and I don't want to wake them, but I whisper excitedly to them anyway.

"Look girls, Disneyland."

"I NEED A HUG!" Bear chimes in.

I honestly don't know why we keep replacing the batteries on that fucking thing, but the girls seem to like it almost as much as Brown. Today it's Anne that has it clenched in her pudgy fingers.

"Look Brown, Disneyland!"

Sitting in my lap, Brown lifts her head to see out of the window. There's a sign like a ribbon over the green gates. In the middle is an oval portrait of Sleeping Beauty's castle. Beyond it, I can see the real thing, glittering in the sun. It's a moment I've anticipated nearly all my life. I briefly try and think back to my former life and count the number of tourists I must have sent to Disneylands across the world. It's a moment I never thought would arrive.

"Tu ne peux pas conduire ici, putain!" a wrath in a Winnie The Pooh costume shouts. I don't speak much French, but I don't think he's happy.

"You finished having your moment, or do you want me to run him over?" Natalie asks.

"I will not let you run over Winnie The Pooh," I reply, and try and savour the moment again, but it's not the same. "Okay, I've soaked up all the magic, let's go."

Natalie guns the engine and the gates in front of us split apart like they were cardboard. We take our time and drive around the park as much as possible in a place that wasn't designed for four wheels. We speed down Main Street U.S.A. and bounce wraths over the bonnet. I squeal and insist that Natalie pull up outside a gift shop. I kill the wraths inside and quickly fill the boot with mouse ears, Disney jumpers, pyjamas and armfuls of billowing, sparkly princess dresses of various sizes. The girls may not appreciate it now, but you have to think of birthdays to come. People say that it's expensive at Disneyland, but I really didn't find that at all.

We drive under the skeletons of rides that once drew crowds of people to the park in the time of humans. They already look like relics of a lost civilisation. Finally, we pull up in front of Sleeping Beauty's castle. It's quieter on the approach we've found, and the girls are starting to rouse from their monster sleep. They'll need feeding soon. We can head to a vantage point and I'll stand guard while Nat feeds them. Brown could do with a wee anyway.

"Nat?"

"Ben?"

"I got you something," I say and hold out my hand.

"You stole me something? Ben, that's so sweet."

"I dreamed of doing this years ago," I say and open my hand and a ring drops from my hand into hers. She picks it up and inspects it. She smiles and my heart flip-flops.

"Ben, you had a free choice of anything from that store and you managed to find the nadir of all jewellery."

"I knew you'd like it! Wait – is the nadir the up or the down?"

"The down."

"Oh." She holds the ring up, and the diamonds on Minnie's ears catch the light and sparkle. She stretches out her fingers and tries to slide it onto her thumb. It barely goes past the tip.

"Try a different finger," I suggest. She takes a deep breath and sighs in a resigned way. She sinks the ring over the third finger of her left hand. It jams on the knuckle.

"I can fix that," I say. "I'll just need to know the size of your ring finger."

"Are you doing this because I'm the last woman on earth?" she asks.

"I'm giving you this because you're the only woman on Earth I love. Aside from the girls. And Brown. I embrace the matriarchy. Let's not talk about Bear."

"Okay, ask me."

"Natalie Cross, will you marry me?"

"In sickness and in health?"

"One of those is more likely than the other," I admit.

"Till death do us part?" she asks.

"Till death do us part," I agree. "I love you Natalie, I always will."

"You promise we can still go to Monaco?"

"This changes nothing, I just need you to know."

"What if I go again?"

"Then I'll go with you."

Natalie looks in the rear-view and sees a wrath shambling towards us. She flicks the car into reverse and takes us over him. She spins the steering wheel and starts to drive us back towards the entrance. We can see the park laid out before us. Paris lies beyond it and our boat lies in the river beyond that.

Tomorrow we will travel through Paris on the Seine and pick our way to the Canal du Loing and head south. We will continue towards Monaco. We go there in the hope that the girls' fathers are still alive. We know that they won't be, but we have to go all the same. We will hope that the snow stays away, and that warmth continues to return to the world. I will stay alive for as long as I can and help the girls grow, while trying to keep the cancer at bay. I will do everything I can to protect my dog and her Bear, and to see her live a rich and full life. I will do all of this by the side of Natalie, who now wears the diamond-studded Minnie Mouse ring on a silver chain around her neck. She still hasn't said yes.

Tonight, we will drink a Romanee-Conti from 1945, a bottle of wine so expensive that in the time before the change its sale would have created global headlines. Natalie will mix her glass with Diet Coke. I will dunk custard creams in mine. We will read and play chess and take turns to go to the girls when they cry. Brown will fall asleep on Natalie's feet and Natalie will claim that this means she is exempt from going to the girls. I will go to the girls.

Later, when Natalie is asleep, I will stand on the top deck of the yacht and I will drunkenly stare at the unfamiliar stars above my head. I will look for the patterns that I can recognise in the stars and I will trust that there is a pattern here too. I don't know if it matters if it's a pattern that's been created for us, or one that we find for ourselves. It's finding the pattern that counts. I will cuddle the beautiful dog curled on my lap, then I will put my headphones on and press play. I will listen as the Vengaboys tell me that happiness is just around the corner.

THE END

My sincere thanks...

Erica and James Ashbrook

Steve Barraclough

Emily Babb

Katie Deakin

Carl Doherty

Chris Draper

Jodie Eckford

Pete Edwards

Caroline Elkins

Kevin Few

Caroline Firth

Angela Froggatt

Andrew Gallon

Alan Green

Jo Harris

Ann and Chris Harrison

David Hoffman

Emma Jones

Pippa Lambert

Sarah Latham

Wolfgang McFarlane

Craig Morris

Katie Mouat

James and Ruth Pierpoint

Tom Reeves

Joe Roe

Emma Shanahan

Frank Shanahan

Harry Shanahan

Matilda Shanahan

Quinn Shanahan

Clare and Chris Sheard

Elle Smith

Alison Wright

Yolander Yeo

My abject apology to the people I have forgotten.

Several names in this book were kindly donated by people from the I Will Literarily Kill You volunteer list. These are real people who have offered to let me use their name in books, because I find thinking of character names tedious. If you would like to join this list then sign up for free at www.iwillliterarilykillyou.com

A playlist of the music featured in this book can be found at www.helloshan.co.uk

If you are concerned about cancer or toxoplasmosis then more information about both conditions can be found at www.nhs.uk

Printed in Great Britain
by Amazon